Books should be returned or renewed by the
last date stamped above

Awarded for excellence
to Arts & Libraries

*is exciting but soon the challenges begin as they experience a strange
force working against the academy.*

The Colour Code Series
Will be available from
Pick-a-WooWoo Publishers

In reading order

The Red Ray
The Orange Ray
The Yellow Ray
The Green Ray
The Blue Ray
The Indigo Ray
The Violet Ray

Pamela Blake-Wilson

The
COLOUR CODE
—— Book two ——
The Orange Ray

Cover and Interior Illustrations by
Aaron Pocock

Edited by Sarah Evans

An imprint of Pick-a-WooWoo Publishers

Cast of Characters

Dan O'Sullivan (Cello)

Is a main character. He is 13-and-a-half, Irish, tall with strong dark curly hair and blue eyes of great intensity. Dan seems older than his years, maybe because others always seem to look to him for help. He is friendly, thoughtful and clever, but not in an academic way. His

interests are more to do with space, flying, climbing, the environment and the planet.

His mother died when he was young so his father, who is also his teacher and best friend, brought him up. His father gives him an insight into the values of life and encourages him to always look beyond what he sees. Dan is comfortable within himself but has missed his mother deeply. He doesn't talk about this too much but is not sure of himself with girls.

He was attracted to the website because he wanted to find out more about other planets and their influence upon earth.

Daisy Ferguson (Violin)

Is also a main character. She is tall and slim with curly, thick red hair and light green eyes. She is 12-and-a-half and the twin to Jonathan. She is sensitive and has the gift of being able to see

auras around people and nature. She grew up thinking this was normal, but when she went to school she found out that none of her friends could do the same thing. Since then she hasn't mentioned it because she knows that they would laugh at her.

Daisy's parents encourage her to talk about it to them, and suggest she paint what she sees. Her mother is a midwife who has told her that babies first see light and colour around their parents. Some continue to see, as she did, but most children forget it when they grow older. Her father, a landscape gardener, tells her about the rhythms and cycles of nature. When she asked him why certain flowers and colours appear at certain times of year, he couldn't give her the answer but said that there must be an energetic reason behind it. This fascinates Daisy and connects with her many questions as to why everything has colours around it. Her father suggested that her brother, a wizard on the computer, could find a website that might help.

This is a problem because Jonathan thinks Daisy has a screw loose and doesn't want to have anything to do with her loopy ideas, but Daisy is very persistent and persuasive.

Winna Sanderson (Flute)

Is from Brixton but her family is originally from Jamaica. She is tough and aggressive with a soft centre. She wants to study, but many of her friends just want to get out of school. She has wonderful plaited hair all over her head, gorgeous brown eyes and skin. She is clever and wants to be someone who makes a difference. Her aim is to study hard so that she can train as a doctor and work in Third World countries. Her father returned to Jamaica because he couldn't find work in this country. Winna misses him and so does her mum. Life is hard for the family. There is little money. Winna wants to help her mum, who works all hours as a nurse and is always tired. Winna has sworn to study and become qualified. She is feisty.

Jonathan Ferguson (Trumpet)

Jonathan is Daisy's twin. They are physically very similar, but Jonathan has brown eyes like his father. He is very clever, and wants to be a biologist and naturalist. He always wants to know "why" and is not content until he understands. He loves sport and is never still. He has a nervous energy and can be impatient, but on the other hand he can be extremely patient if a subject interests him. He has a love/hate relationship with his sister. They both love nature and share the same belief system as their parents. They come from a caring background and talk a lot as a family. Friends are always welcome.

Although he used to see energy around people as a little child, Jonathan would rather forget, feeling that he would never live it down with his friends. But secretly he often thinks about it when he studies the origins of life.

Hiromi Magashini (Oboe)

Hiromi is from Japan but her family lives in London. Her father works at the Japanese embassy and her mother teaches at an English school. Hiromi is also at the same school but wants to study dancing as a career. She is 12 years old, small and delicate in build. She has loose black hair with a plait around the crown to hold it in place. Her face is oval, with brown almond eyes that seemed to be filled with light. Her mouth is small, her nose slightly flattened. She is shy, courteous, graceful in all her movements, quiet and highly sensitive. She studies ballet and modern dance with a private teacher. When she is 16 she will enter a special academy for dance. Her place is already assured.

Aloysius Neweba (Clarinet)

Is a big, larger than life boy of 13. His family come from the Bahamas but now live in Liverpool. They have a strong religious background and live in a community that is open and friendly. Most of his family sing and play an instrument. His father is a teacher and

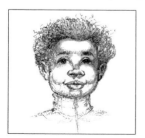

preaches at the local church. His mum helps out at a nursery school All his family sing and play anything from spiritual to jazz. They have friends of all races and all cultures. Aloysius can play many instruments. He has a very relaxed attitude to life and is generally accepted by everyone. His real passion is music and, with his natural spiritual belief, he wants to enjoy all that he does.

Marc Latham (Drums)

Marc is the opposite of Aloysius. He is afraid of life because of his upbringing. He was an orphan who was pushed around from one foster home to another. School is the only place that interests him. He has a capacity for mathematics far beyond his years. Most children find him strange and detached. He is a natural subject for bullying, and he almost expects it. He doesn't really care as long as he can be top in his subject. His teachers find him clever but difficult. No one talks to him, not even his foster parents. They also find him difficult. Marc is seeking a way out of the family, school and the place he lives. He wants to go to university and free himself from everyone.

Other Characters

University of Light

Calidus   (Lord of the Light)

Lo   (Light Server)

Shakita   (Lady of the Orange Ray)

Academy

Professor Carlos Sanandez
                    (Director of Academy of 'La Reunion)

Collette du Bois   (Second-in-command)

Yannish Kablinski   (Musical Director)

Francesca Domingo   (Art Director)

Hamish McTavish   (Art Director)

Frank & Veronica Antoine   (Dance Directors)

Students

Jovan Kurepo   (Violin)

Chelsea Twine   (Violin)

Felippe Tonisoni   (French Horn)

Louis Capello   (Bassoon)

Yoshi Atari   (Cello)

Eli Beke   (Trombone)

Massoud   (Cello)

Janeck Vassily   (Violin)

Kyan Khan   (Clarinet)

Ishmael   (Tuba)

Ariel   (Oboe)

Hannah Zimmerman   (Harp)

Other

Josefina   (Housekeeper)

Isobel Arnez   (Receptionist)

National Library of Australia Cataloguing-in-Publication entry

Author: Blake-Wilson, Pamela.

Title: The orange ray / Pamela Blake-Wilson; illustrated
by Aaron Pocock; edited by Sarah Evans

Edition: 1st ed.

ISBN: 9780980652062 (pbk.)

Series: Blake-Wilson, Pamela. Colour code; 2.

Other Authors/Contributors:
Pocock, Aaron Lee.
Evans, Sarah.

Dewey Number: A823.4

Publishing Details
Published in Australia
Pick-a-WooWoo Pty Ltd
Pick-a-WooWoo Publishers web address is
http://www.pickawoowoo.com

Printed - APOL Australasia Pty Ltd (Australian & NZ)
Printed – Lightning Source US/UK/Europe

Graphic Design - LKS Designs (www.lksdesigns.co.uk)

Contents

 *Chapter 1*

The Orange Ray

Daisy felt it first. Her sixth sense told her something was going to happen. It was an uneasy feeling, lasting for days. She thought it must be something to do with school. Being the end of term, there was the added pressure of approaching exams with the constant need to study and the feeling of never having enough time. So she brushed it aside and applied herself to her school work with greater determination.

Watching Jonathan eating his breakfast, Daisy noticed he appeared totally unconcerned. He took life in a much more relaxed way. Why can't I be more like him? she sighed.

The dreams came next. Strange flashes of travelling at lightning speeds that left her breathless and exhilarated. Images of golden curtains, gently swaying. She saw herself hovering above coloured marble floors that sparkled and shone as she moved. Faces drifting in and out – faces she couldn't quite grasp. They weren't clear enough but she knew what it meant. It was Calidus contacting her from the University of Light. It must be time for the Orange Ray.

Daisy was thrilled and shocked, unsure of her feelings. He'd told them he would be in touch at the right time, but this wasn't the right time for her or Jonathan.

'So, what's up?' asked her twin, noticing her concerned face as he stuffed cereal into his mouth.

'Calidus,' she whispered. 'He's been contacting me in my dreams.'

'Oh, that.' He smiled coolly. 'I know.'

'What do mean? How do you know?' Daisy hissed at him.

'Well, you're not the only one to get the hot blog, my dear sister.'

'I didn't think I was,' she replied irritably, but feeling rather hurt. 'So how's he been in touch with you, then?'

'Oh, you know, the usual way, in dreams and images,' he replied casually, biting into a piece of toast with added relish at her growing impatience.

'You are irritating, Jonathan. Why didn't you tell me?'

'To see your response when you found out,' He smirked.

'Well, thanks a lot. I hope you think it's worth it,' she growled, but quietly so her mother wouldn't hear.

'Oh, it's definitely worth it!'

'But what are we going to do, Jonno? We can't go now, with our exams coming up.'

'I suppose not, but if we live in a different time state of consciousness, as Calidus told us, it probably won't matter, will it?' He reasoned.

'You mean that we can be there and here at the same time?' she replied thoughtfully.

'Yeah, why not? No one here knew we were missing last time, did they? It was as though our time with the Cheyenne never existed for anyone else, except us.'

'What shall we do, then?' she asked him. He seemed so sure of himself.

'Calidus knows everything about us, doesn't he? So he must know we're taking exams, right?'

'You'd think he would wait until we had finished them, wouldn't you?'

'Not necessarily,' Jonathan explained, 'because we'll still operate here as usual, won't we? Being there won't affect our normal lives here in the slightest, so we can beam out there anytime. I think it's rather neat.' He grinned at her worried face. 'Actually, I'm surprised you're so bothered.'

'You're right of course, Jonno. I guess there's part of me that worries about what's happening here. I do trust him to do the right thing, though. The same thing must be happening to the others - Dan and Marc and the girls. Should we text them?'

'Yeah, why not?' he agreed with enthusiasm.

They both lived a double life. The 'normal' existence at home with their parents and friends, and the life they kept secret from them - the University of Light in space. Both Daisy and Jonathan felt something had changed since they had returned from their time with the Cheyenne. The twins already knew the importance of family life, because their parents had taught them, but not so consciously or as dramatically as their immediate life with the Indians.

Also, Daisy knew her relationship with Jonathan had deepened because they had faced dangers as well as wonderful discoveries together. She would never forget how great Jonathan had been when she had gone missing. He was devastated at the thought something had happened to her. She knew now that he would always be there for her, and she for him. This is what the Red Ray made them aware of - how people act or react within its power. She and the group had never really thought about it before, because they just didn't know that energy could work for or against them according to how it is used. This was the first part of the influence of what Calidus called the 'Code' or inner qualities; how they affect people's daily lives without them realising it.

They had experienced what it was like to be close to the earth in the same way as the Cheyenne did, for their very existence depended upon it, as well as the sun and the seasons.

The twins had been aware of the earth before but in a more casual way, because there was so much more going on in their lives - more technology, ease of transport, the media. Everything was faster and expectations were taken for granted. Their father would take them out into the countryside to experience nature, where Daisy would draw and paint everything that she saw within it; but nature seemed less important to them in the twenty-first century than it was for the Indians in the nineteenth century. The Indians knew the importance of living in the moment, of how to listen and feel the currents within the earth. They focused on what had to be done each day in order to eat and survive.

Daisy's group had to learn how to work together as a team, with the Indians and for themselves, though for some it took time and tears before they could trust each other. They'd learnt how to apply strength and willpower when things got tough. How to be positive when dangerous situations occurred and when fear filled them. Then they became aware of the negative side of the Red Ray energy, when the disruptive influences of their feelings created an imbalance, when anger, resentment and jealousy twisted their emotions, separating the group, threatening their whole project.

Daisy shuddered when she thought about it. They had all learnt from each experience and she, for one, felt the better for it.

 *Chapter 2*

Call for Action

Messages flew between Jonathan, Dan, Aloysius and Marc with immediate response, whilst Daisy text Hiromi and Winna telling them to be ready for action. The last thing Calidus told them was that they would know when to enter the colour code website again. The time was now.

There was the constant anxiety about their exams and the studying that must be done but, as Jonathan coolly pointed out, it was a question of trust. Daisy couldn't help but laugh at him, with his wise philosophical comments, when last time he'd been so furious with her. It was he who hadn't trusted her when she asked him to help her find the meaning of 'colour' on the internet in the Red Ray. He'd thought she was stupid. That's why she'd had to take action when the www.thecolourcode.com website came up. When she'd clicked on the site, they'd both been transported to the University of Light. At the time he was angry at being taken against his will, but later he'd thanked her.

'Wow, that's a turnaround!' she now giggled.

'No big deal.' He shrugged. 'So, when do we all synchronize?'

'How about 4.30pm after school?' she offered nervously.

'Got it!' Jonathan text Dan, Marc and Aloysius. '4.30 is lift-off time.' Daisy repeated the same to Hiromi and Winna.

Hiromi and Winna text back excitedly, saying they had also received messages and images in their dreams so they were ready and waiting for lift-off too.

'We're committed now. It'll be great to see the others.' Daisy said.

Neither Daisy nor Jonathan could concentrate on school that day. It was just a matter of getting through each lesson. Mr Donaldson, Jonathan's math's teacher, barked at him several times to pay attention.

'You! Boy! You may think you are above the rest of us in mathematics, so it will come as a shock to you to know that you are grovelling at the bottom.'

The class erupted with delight. Mr Donaldson was a thin, waspish kind of man who spat like a snake when he spoke, so they called him 'Sniper'.

'Sorry, Sir,' Jonathan apologised, though not really meaning it.

'Don't let it happen again,' Sniper snapped.

Daisy found it also almost unbearable. Part of her was desperate to do as much as she could before she was 'called away', while the other part simply couldn't concentrate on anything, even chats with her friends. Normally she would be right in there, loving all the chit-chat, but not today. She wasn't interested in the latest gossip about this girl or the new boy on the scene. Her mind was with Calidus and what their new adventure could possibly be. He'd told them they would enjoy this one with the Orange Ray.

'Hey, Daisy, is anyone at home?' said her best friend, Lucille, shaking her. 'I've been talking to you for ages and you don't seem a bit interested.'

'Sorry, Luce, I'm miles away. Probably because of the exams,' she apologised lamely.

'Well, as long as I'm not boring you,' Lucille said sarcastically.

'Of course not. Go on, tell me again,' said Daisy, this time paying attention. As she was listening, Daisy couldn't help wondering if Jonathan was having the same problems.

Agonisingly, the day dragged on and somehow the twins managed to appear as normal as possible until, thankfully, the bell rang at the end of the school day. Usually, leaving was a lengthy procedure, stopping on the way home to chat, but not this time. With a quick 'goodbye' to open-mouthed friends, they both dived for the exit from different directions. Fortunately they lived within walking distance.

Daisy imagined this must be happening to the others in their own schools and laughed as she ran. It was going to be brilliant to see them all again - soon, very soon. She didn't wait for Jonathan. He'd probably be waiting for her at home.

 *Chapter 3*

Together Again

Sure enough, there he was, leaning against the door as if he'd been there for hours.

'Thought you'd never get here,' he remarked dryly. Sticking out her tongue, she pushed him aside and opened the front door.

This time there was no delay. It was almost 4.30pm. They knew what they had to do. They went straight up to Jonathan's bedroom and turned on the computer. Their breathing came faster, their hearts pounding. After a few moments Jonathan was on line. He typed in www.thecolourcode - then waited, fingers poised and looked at Daisy. Daisy checked her watch. The second hand of her watch was slowly ticking towards 4.30pm. They both counted back from ten seconds, nine, eight, seven, six, five, four, three, two, one. Jonathan pressed 'enter' and grabbed hold of Daisy's hand.

The blast of dazzling light and wind came through the computer the same as last time but now, instead of being frightened and unprepared, they soared like two birds magnetically drawn into the thermals of space. After the first initial blast, when they almost lost consciousness, they found themselves safe inside the lightship. There was a stillness, even though they were travelling at the speed of light. This time they stayed awake.

The lightship was round, like a large circular ball, and comfortable with two reclining chairs into which they were both strapped securely. There were no pilots. The ship steered itself automatically and, although there was no sense of actual speed, the children were able to see dazzling, luminous images as they hurtled through space.

They felt the blazing heat of the sun as they sped by. They gasped at huge swarms of star clusters, immense in size with spiralling arms rotating like beautiful cosmic dancers. As they flew by, the children were in total awe at the sheer size and glittering display of countless stars that formed the Milky Way. Then higher, further, they whirled into outer space, beyond the solar system, until they reached a place of tranquillity.

Slowly the light ship began to descend, moving towards a flashing beacon of light that seemed to be drawing them in. Silently the lightship approached the enormous circle of coloured stained-glass which opened and parted for the ship to glide through to the landing stage. There to meet them was Lo, waving as they climbed down the steps.

'Welcome to you, Daisy and Jonathan. I am so pleased to see you again!'

Daisy threw her arms round his neck. Lo looked exactly the same as she remembered. A gentle man, dressed in a light blue robe. His hair white and fluffy, his blue eyes twinkling with pleasure to see them again...

'It's great to be back, Lo. I've missed you.'

Jonathan shook his hand a little shyly. 'Hi, Lo, I'm happy to see you, too.'

Lo smiled and led the way to their rooms, which had remained exactly the same as last time. Jonathan felt relieved somehow, as though they had regular bookings at this prestigious hotel.

'Are the others here?' he asked.

'Most of them, but we're still waiting for Dan and Aloysius. Would you like to join them? They're having a little refreshment.'

'Thanks, Lo. I think we know where to go.' Jonathan grinned.

'Of course.' Lo smiled.

They ran down the corridors, across the Halls of Dancing Lights and into the Golden Room where Winna and Marc were feasting on delicious foods.

'Hi, you two!' said Winna, stuffing her mouth. 'I thought you'd be here already.'

'Came as fast as we could.' Jonathan yawned nonchalantly. 'Traffic was awful.'

Winna exploded with laughter. 'Sure!'

'Hi, Marc.' Daisy smiled, giving him a hug. 'How's things?'

Marc looked different, taller and a bit wider she thought, and altogether more confident.

'I'm good,' he said grinning at her. 'Glad to be back here.'

'You've got it,' agreed Winna. 'By the way, did you know that we have a new tutor?'

'Has Calidus told you?' Jonathan asked.

'Not exactly,' she replied a little defensively. 'Well actually,' she whispered, seeing Hiromi coming over to them. 'I overheard him talking to Lo in the corridor.' Jonathan gave her a quizzical look.

'Hi, Hiromi,' Daisy said going over to meet her. 'Thanks for your text and everything. It's really great to see you. How've you been?'

'Just fine, Daisy. I'm so pleased to see you, too. Isn't it great to be back?' she said happily.

'Okay,' said Winna irritated, raising her voice. 'So no one's interested in what I was going to say!'

'What's up?' boomed out the rich voice of Aloysius coming up to join them. 'Hi, bud!' He slapped Jonathan's raised hand and then Marc's, then hugged the girls. 'What's new, Winna, my girl?'

'All I was trying to say was that we're having a new tutor.'

'I suppose there will be a new one for each Ray, won't there?' Aloysius said unimpressed. Jonathan smiled wickedly to himself.

'Well, of course,' replied Winna, shrugging her shoulders, 'but did you know it's a woman?'

'Orange is my colour.' Aloysius smiled, looking down at this tracksuit. 'Having a woman tutor will be neat.' He laughed. 'Hi, Dan. Great to see you, bro.'

Dan strolled in, his blue eyes twinkling with pleasure at seeing his friends again. 'Well, if it isn't the Colour Code Gang,' he said in his soft Irish lilt. 'How's everything? Did you see the star formations?' He rolled his eyes in disbelief. 'Boy, that was something. Do you realise how lucky we are to see all this amazing stuff? No one except astronauts has ever seen what we've seen.'

'You're right, it was fantastic and we are lucky,' replied Marc. 'I wonder if space is on the programme at any time?'

'Certainly it is, my friends.' Calidus suddenly appeared before them. 'When you move into the lighter rays you will discover the miracles of space and how stars are born, but for now I am happy to welcome you all back into the University of Light.'

He led the way to the Halls of Learning and, without a word, each one went to their own chair at the round glass table. Calidus looked at them individually for a few moments and nodded his head, smiling. Daisy thought he looked exactly the same in his white robe, cascading hair and startling deep blue eyes. He was as before, dependable and unfathomable. She wondered what he saw when he observed them. She hoped he would see the inner changes within each of them since the Red Ray. He made no comment but remained in silence for some time.

'Now, my friends, your next role in discovering the inner workings of the Colour Code is one of great interest. You have learnt what it is like to build a strong foundation upon the earth and within yourselves. The next Ray is built upon creativity and relationships. First, you have the red of the earth and now the orange, with all its wonderful warmth, abundance and richness.'

As Calidus began talking, the room began to change from the golden rays of light reflected in the room to deeper tones of orange. The children sighed with pleasure as each one breathed in its radiance, saw it moving and filling the space like a beautiful soft cloud, enveloping them in a blanket of warmth. They felt relaxed within its energy, yet it didn't make them feel sleepy; instead they fell full of life and energised. They could almost taste its colour as a soft fruit.

'I'm glad it's my Ray.' Beamed Aloysius, smoothing his orange clothes with pleasure.

Just like last time, each one was given a different colour ray to wear. Winna wore red, Aloysius orange, Jonathan yellow, Dan green, Marc blue, Hiromi indigo and Daisy violet.

'You're lucky, Al,' Winna retorted. 'Red was much tougher for me.'

'Indeed,' agreed Calidus, 'but you found your power, Winna.'

'Hopefully,' she said quietly, 'but I nearly lost all my friends.'

'It is often in the losing that we find what is important,' he replied gently. 'Colour is energy,' he continued, 'that everyone in the world responds to, would you not agree? Whether we're rich or poor, whatever culture we live within. We are all attracted to it like bees to flowers. Can you think of anything else that we all respond to?'

'Sound,' Aloysius said immediately. 'Everyone loves music of some kind.'

Calidus nodded his head. 'That is correct. Music has a similar effect. We all love music. It is like a passport between all countries. Music creates unity and harmonic relationships between people.' He watched as they began to realise that it was true.

'What about sport?' Dan asked. 'Sport certainly brings all countries together too.' They all laughed.

'That is so, Dan. Sport is another way to bring people together, but on a more physical level. Colour and sound work in a more subtle way, working within the energy fields and the environment. You will be working with both these vibrations together in this adventure. The energy of orange inspires creativity through the senses - how you respond through your eyes, ears, touch and taste.'

There was such a feeling of delight within the Halls of Learning. Daisy squeezed Hiromi's hand. This adventure was going to be great, she just knew it.

'Now,' continued Calidus, 'I have a new tutor for you to meet, and another one who you will work with later.' Winna nudged Daisy and gave her an 'I told you so' look.

'You missed the other one,' Daisy mouthed back.

Chapter 4

Shakita

Calidus lifted his hand. 'I would like you to meet the Lady Shakita of the Orange Ray.'

A vision of floating veils of every possible hue of orange drifted before them. The paler colours shimmered in the light and were barely visible. Streams of coloured materials, made of something very fine, like cobwebs or butterfly wings, seemed to hang in the air then came to rest around them. Daisy touched one as it fell beside her. It felt like sparkling dust and moved as if in slow motion. She watched her friends with mouths open, eyes wide with disbelief. Then, slowly, a figure emerged through the veils. It was Shakita.

Daisy saw her aura first, which radiated around her like the morning sun. She glided silently towards them. Her dress, in brilliant shades of orange, was of a material like tulle, and hung in layers, one upon another. The light shades of soft apricot and peach glowed around her shoulders and bodice, which was studded with gems and crystals. Panels of darker orange floated around her as she moved. On her feet she wore golden crystal sandals, delicate and fine. Her toenails were painted in glittering burnt sienna, as were her fingernails.

She was tall and slender. Her face had a Mediterranean olive glow with high cheek bones and red lips. Her amber eyes shone like jewels. They were large and expressive. Her nose was a little long. The most startling thing about her was her amazing hair. It stood out from her head in a flaming mass of bright orange waves. She smiled at their gaping faces and sat down next to Calidus. She exuded magnetism and warmth. She smelt of aromatic scents - vanilla, rose and sandalwood.

'I am happy to meet you.' She spoke in soft low velvety tones.

Daisy and Hiromi just gazed at her. They had never seen such a beautiful woman. No film star or model came close to this vision before them. Dan stuttered that they were all delighted to meet her. Aloysius just beamed with appreciation and pleasure.

Shakita looked at each one in turn with interest. 'Calidus has told me how brave you all were and how well you worked together as a group. I know how hard the Red Ray is. This time we have enrolled you in the Academy of Music, Colour and Dance. Here you will meet many young people who want to study the Arts.'

'Where is this academy?' Marc enquired. 'Is it up here, or on earth?'

'It is in a special place on earth,' she replied, smiling. 'In the mountains of Sierra de Guadalupe, Central Spain, and it has a wonderful reputation.'

Winna held up her hand. 'Will we be different to the other students?'

'In one way, yes, because you have been sent by us, but no one else will know. On the other hand, you and all the other students will be working for the same results - to learn about colour, movement and music. It will unite you all in an understanding and appreciation of the Arts and each other.'

'Not dancing!' Spat out Marc. 'I'm not going to dance like a fairy!'

Jonathan and Dan nodded in total agreement. There was no way they were going to prance around the floor. Calidus laughed heartily.

'No one will make you do anything you don't want to do,' he said reassuringly. 'The idea is the experience.'

'You will meet many students from other cultures and countries,' continued Shakita, 'and the wonderful tutor called Yannish Kablinski who will teach you all about the magic of music. It is his ambition to bring all countries together in harmony, through an understanding and appreciation of beauty and peace. It was his idea, with Professor Sanandez, the founder of the academy, to call it La Reunion.'

'That sounds terrific,' Marc said, shifting in his chair, 'but I don't play an instrument.'

'Nor me, except to sing a bit,' Winna added. 'So what do we do?'

'Have you ever wanted to play an instrument?' Shakita smiled encouragingly at them. 'If you close your eyes and saw yourself playing an instrument, whatever it might be, what would you choose?'

Without hesitation, Marc said, 'Drums and xylophone.' At this they all collapsed in giggles. There was no way any of them could have guessed that shy Marc would choose drums. Marc looked at their disbelieving faces and shrugged.

'Why not? It would be great. I'll make such a noise and get my own back on all those who have pushed me around. They'll be so jealous,' he finished with a flourish.

'I play the violin a little.' Daisy almost apologised. 'It's not great, I'm just learning.'

'What about you, Jonathan?' asked Shakita.

'I tinker a bit with the trumpet at school,' he said, 'and I quite fancy the guitar. I like both instruments.'

'Hmm', she murmured, 'they're very different. They suit both sides of your nature, one loud and one soft.' Jonathan made a face like a clown, first happy and then sad, to the delight of his friends.

'I play the oboe.' Hiromi offered softly. 'But not to an orchestra's standard.'

'That doesn't matter. Yannish will help all of you, even if you have never played an instrument before. What about you, Dan? What instrument do you see yourself playing?'

'My father taught me a little about the double bass. He told me that it holds the orchestra together.'

'That is the right instrument for you, Dan. Somehow you have that quality within you in your group.' Dan blushed red with embarrassment, but Daisy knew exactly what Shakita meant. He was the strong one in their group, that's why he antagonised Little Wolf, the Chief's younger son in the Red Ray.

'That just leaves you, Winna,' Shakita said quietly.

'The piano's good, so I could accompany Jonathan, Al and Marc in jazz sessions,' she laughed, delighted with herself.

'You've got it, girl!' Aloysius slapped her right hand. 'Together we'll make wicked music.'

'Like Jonathan, you may like to choose another instrument. The piano is more of a solo instrument. Think again, Winna.'

'Okay, the flute is good and perhaps the piano for fun,' she replied, grinning at Aloysius.

'So you see, it's not so bad is it?' Shakita smiled. 'Each one of you has chosen an instrument which you like. As you leave here you will be able to play well enough to be in the youth orchestra, so please do not worry.'

Calidus continued on from Shakita. 'The Orange Ray is an expansive healing energy which works with relationships and communication. We want you to be a part of an idea which will bring together all nations. The world needs fresh ideas from young minds to make this work. There are some wonderful people who hold this dream to unite people together and it is our wish to help support this beautiful concept.

"Yannish is one of these special people who work for the good of man. He is a Light Server who has chosen to spend his life on earth serving this cause. Professor Carlos Fernandez is the Director of the academy, and his second-in-command is a lovely lady called Collette du Bois. She will be looking after all of the students, so feel free to go to her if you need support.

"On a cautionary note, whenever there is a good idea which is intended to help the world, there is often opposition from those who wish to prevent this concept spreading. Their desire is to create turmoil and separate nations. Light attracts the dark and negative forces and will do everything in their power to wreck Yannish's work, so be aware. And stick closely together. Do not tell anyone why you are there. Are you ready for this adventure, my friends?'

The teenagers looked at each other in turn, excited but nervous. This time they wouldn't be going as novices. They had learnt last time that, to achieve the most from their experience, they must stick together as one force. They realised that the levels of expectations had risen. Calidus and Shakita believed in the group's strength and inner resources to succeed in this venture. They would be behind them, without interfering with their mission. As one, Daisy, Jonathan, Aloysius, Marc, Hiromi and Winna raised their hands in acceptance.

'Last time Many Lives and Silvan came with us. Will we have someone to turn to for support?' Daisy asked.

'I will be there, but not in my present form,' replied Shakita. 'I will make myself known when the time is right. Yannish is also there for you, but be discreet. It is better the other students don't know this.'

'You are more experienced this time,' explained Calidus, 'and must use this wisdom to guide you. Shakita will reveal herself if necessary. She is there to keep the balance of the Orange Ray. You go with our blessings and trust that you will not only enjoy this mission but will make a difference to those who wish to help your kind. Are you ready?'

'We're on our way,' said Daisy.

Chapter 5

Sierra de Guadalupe, Spain

Volarus and Kassan, the two pilots of the spaceship, were waiting for them at the airstrip, beaming with delight to welcome the teenagers once again. It was great to feel they would be in safe hands and Daisy was comforted by the sight of them. She felt that Jonathan would be also. She wondered if they would accompany them on all the other Ray adventures, and inwardly knew they would.

The teenagers were going on another mission but this time it would be different. They were all wiser, hopefully, and trusted each other more than last time. The friendships she had formed with the other four in the group were becoming the most important relationships she'd ever had, except for Jonathan and her parents. It was a strange feeling that they all shared this secret part of themselves.

The spaceship was just the same as last time. Sleek and fast with seats facing each other. The pilots to the front, flicked switches and spoke rapidly together as the machine powered up.

Shakita came with them, as Manus had done before. It seemed a little strange without the huge surge of the red force emanating from him filling the ship. This time, Shakita emanated a warm peaceful vibration, making them all feel relaxed and comfortable. She was magnetic but not all-consuming as Manus. She told them a little about the place they were going to in Spain.

'The academy itself was built in the countryside in a beautiful area called Extremadura. You will be staying close to the Sierra de

Guadalupe. Below the mountainous range lays a haven of forests, meadows and rivers,' she said. 'It will be very warm at this time of year. There are also many wonderful birds and some glorious butterflies that you won't see anywhere else. The academy lies within this area.'

Aloysius grinned at Jonathan. 'Right up your street, bro.'

'Sounds good.' Winna smiled at Daisy. 'A bit of sun is exactly what I need.'

'The energy there is special,' Shakita continued. 'This is why Professor Carlos Fernandez built the academy there. It is quiet and in tune with nature. The buildings are both modern and old in design.'

'Can you tell us about Professor Fernandez and Yannish Kablinski?' asked Dan.

'Professor Sanandez is a renowned Spanish composer. For the last few years he has been involved in helping young people from disadvantaged backgrounds, to give them a chance to play an instrument. Many of them have developed into fine musicians and now travel the world. Yannish Kablinski is a pianist and conductor. He was so inspired by the Professor's work that he wanted to extend it to countries at war with each other, offering them a chance to play in an orchestra. It is the most ambitious plan ever and one to which they are totally dedicated.'

'That's brilliant,' said Aloysius. 'I was lucky, because my dad taught me until he could find a teacher.'

'This academy also teaches dance and art, doesn't it?' enquired Hiromi. 'I want to do everything, don't you, Daisy?'

'You bet!' Daisy nodded her head vigorously, pulling her tongue out at her brother.

'On your own,' Marc muttered. 'It's going to be bad enough trying to keep up with drumming with a famous conductor without prancing about like a girl.' He rolled his eyes in disgust to Jonathan. Jonathan snorted in agreement, ignoring his sister.

'You may be surprised,' said Shakita, laughing at their derisive faces. 'It isn't a ballet school. It's more to do with freestyle, even rock and rap dancing.'

'Really!' Aloysius eyes lit up with interest.

'It's not my scene,' replied Marc stubbornly. 'But no offence, Al,' he added quickly. Aloysius was great and Marc really liked his casual humour. There was no way he wanted to upset him.

'It's cool, man,' replied Aloysius, gently cuffing his hair.

All the time they were talking they hadn't noticed they were fast approaching the earth. Below them were soaring peaks, some still covered with snow even though it was mid-May. There was a network of winding roads crisscrossing the range. Daisy saw an area of large forests and green meadows spread out beneath with a few little villages dotted along a river. Volarus decided to set the spaceship down close to one of the forests, out of view.

'Now, if you follow the winding path south, close to the river, beyond the villages, you will see before you some large white buildings set in a square,' instructed Volarus. 'There is a gateway with a bell. Pull it and someone will come to welcome you. You are expected.'

'Right, just follow the river until we see the academy. Got it,' Dan repeated, stretching himself.

'Good luck.' Volarus and Kassan shook their hands in turn. 'We will be here when the time is right.'

'Enjoy yourselves, my friends,' Shakita told them. 'Remember, as soon as you pick up your instruments you will be able to play, so please do not worry. Yannish is incredible and you will be achieving something so special with him. You go with our blessings.'

'Okay, guys, here we go again,' Daisy said with a laugh. 'Let's get on our way. Dan, you lead.'

'Righty-o, Miss Daisy.' Dan strode out with a last wave to the beautiful Shakita.

Shakita watched the group as they walked together beside the river, hearts high and singing as they went, until she could no longer see them.

'Come,' she said to the pilots, 'we must go quickly before anyone sees us.'

***

It was mid-afternoon and the sun was warm and relaxing. The meadows were covered with a carpet of colour. The smell was intoxicating. Spring flowers filled the landscape so it was easy to stop and admire each variety. Some they had never seen before. Flittering above them were beautiful butterflies darting here and there, displaying their dazzling wings. The desire to stay was strong for the girls, and for Jonathan in particular, who loved all aspects of botany and wild life.

'Come on, Jonno,' Dan called. 'We can come back later. But now we have to press on.'

Daisy knew Dan was right and drew her brother back onto the path. Jonathan followed, grumbling as he caught up with the others. As they passed through the villages, several people, with weather-beaten faces and straw hats pulled down to shade them from the sun, stared at them with interest.

'Buenas tardes,' called Aloysius, smiling as he passed.

'Buenas tardes,' replied a woman politely.

'What's that you said?' asked Marc, turning to Al with surprise.

'Oh, just saying good afternoon to the natives,' he grinned cheekily.

'Well, get you!' Winna laughed at him. 'You've been holding out on us. What else do you know?'

'Hello, goodbye - that sort of thing. Nothing much,' he apologised.

'Better than us, Al,' replied Daisy with respect.

They passed terraces with white cherry blossom and orchards of olive trees and continued walking along the dry dusty roads. It was quiet and no one came in sight.

'Hey, what's that ahead?' said Hiromi. 'That is some large building. Is it the academy?'

'Looks like it. It's huge. This is where I am beginning to feel nervous,' said Marc, and clutched Daisy's arm.

'Hey, come on, Superguy,' she replied encouragingly. 'Remember how you led the way into the Cheyenne camp, all fired up with the Red energy?' Marc had been very frightened at the thought of meeting the Cheyenne tribe in their last adventure with the Red Ray. Daisy had helped him by encouraging him to breathe in its energy. It was an injection of strength and courage. Afterwards, he had led the way, confident and strong.

'Well.' He looked sheepishly at her. 'I guess I can do it again.'

'Course you can,' chorused Hiromi and Winna together.

It was an enormous place, rather like a palace, set in an area surrounded by trees and exotic plants. The walls were high with motifs around the top. Peering through the wrought iron gates, they saw high arched colonnades running along each side of the buildings with long corridors behind them as a protection from the sun. The roofs of each building were tiled. A fountain lay in the middle, water spouting playfully into the basin below.

'Wow!' Winna whistled. 'This is some place.'

'Is that the bell?' said Marc, pointing to a long chain.

'I guess.' Daisy gave it one long pull and the sound echoed around the building.

***

A dark-haired woman appeared almost as soon as the bell had rung.

'Holo encantado, children.'

Jonathan winced. 'Hardly,' he muttered, irritated.

'She's just saying she's pleased to meet you,' Aloysius translated.

'It's not the molt de gust bit,' grumbled Jonathan. 'It's the children bit.'

'I guess she thinks that all young people are kids,' said Daisy.

As they walked through the gates they entered a courtyard of warm, sun-baked cobbled bricks set in a diagonal form. The fountain, set on a stone platform, was situated in the middle like a glistening jewel. Around the thick white walls Daisy saw swathes of jasmine and vivid pink flowers that looked like Bougainvillea hanging down, with lavender reaching up to meet it. Rosemary and thyme grew in enormous terracotta pots beneath, creating a fresh, herby, sweet smell.

Looking up, they saw a low building. Shutters framed each window. Below were beautifully carved frescoes, each one displaying special designs from the area - wild flowers, animals and birds. Daisy had never seen anything so lovely and peaceful.

'Com, com theese way,' the woman said, hustling them along the corridor to the main building.

Chapter 6

La Reunion

Josefina, the Spanish woman, led them down the cool corridors, through an arched doorway and into a large reception area. The floors were tiled in a geometric design in bright orange and blue, with oblong pieces of scarlet and turquoise cleverly interwoven. The main feature was a huge fireplace hewn out of rock. Logs were burning, even though it was mid-May, but it was welcoming for the students.

A large wooden table was placed in the centre upon which was set a long oblong vase full of flowers that spilled onto its polished surface. Easy chairs and coloured cushions were placed randomly around the room. On the walls were hung brightly coloured collages, some woven from local designers, and some paintings in brilliant reds, oranges, yellows and purples from past students they were told later. A desk was placed in one corner which was the reception area for students coming to register. This is where Josefina led them, handing the group over to a young, dark-haired girl who politely shook their hands in turn.

'I am Isobel and I welcome you to our academy.' She spoke in perfect English. 'Josefina will take you to your rooms. You will share together. The ladies will be in one room and the gentlemen in another.' She smiled at their obvious relief. 'Supper will be served at 6.00pm in the Dining Hall where Professor Sanandez will greet you. If there is anything you need, please feel free to ask me.'

Josefina took them through several corridors, eyeing them fiercely as if they could be criminals.

'Theese is privit – the Professor's room - prohibido el paso. These eese Dr Yannish's room. Theese eese Mademoiselle Collette's room. Theese - all privit - ninguna entrada - all personal.'

'Okay, we get the idea,' Jonathan said, eyeing her back. Josefina grunted as she walked. Through the windows, Daisy could see that they had now crossed over to another building lying adjacent to the main one. She guessed that this must be the main residential area. It looked as though they were built in two squares - separate but joined together by the colonnades and corridors.

Finally, Josefina stopped, opening the door to the girls' rooms with a flourish of her hand.

'You com,' she told the boys sternly, marching on without looking to see if the boys were following.

'See you later,' called Dan, laughing at the astonished girls.

'Six o'clock in the dining room,' shouted Daisy at the fast disappearing figures. 'By the way, where is it? Oh, never mind, we'll find it.'

Their room was large with three beds in it, with spaces in between for a small table each. It was a light, airy room, with white arched walls and windows with coloured rugs upon the floor. At the foot of each bed lay an opened case with all the clothes they would need. Winna shrieked with delight. With all that had been going on, the thought of packing cases had completely gone out of their heads.

'I bet Lo just flicked his fingers,' Hiromi giggled.

They all checked their cases to find all their best T-shirts, trousers and dresses were there, as if their own mothers had packed for them.

'Brilliant.' Daisy smiled. 'I think I shall definitely adopt Lo.'

***

'Come on, let's explore,' said Winna. 'We don't have to meet the boys until six.'

They went back the way they had come to check out the rooms that Josefina had hurried past, avoiding the private rooms of the Professor and other members of the academy. Just before the reception, an archway led into the dining room. It was big enough to seat at least a hundred to a hundred and fifty people. Long wooden tables with straight-backed chairs lay in six long rows. Behind the tables were beautiful stained-glass windows in the most stunning kaleidoscope of colours in concentric designs.

'Wow!' Daisy exclaimed. 'It reminds me of the University of Light. I wonder who did it?'

Isobel came to meet them. 'I am sorry. I should have given you this plan of the academy. It is very big and confusing to a newcomer. This part is residential and the rest belongs to the academy. You may enter each section as you wish. Nothing is locked. We have an open attitude here.' So saying, she backed away smiling.

'Thanks, Isobel,' replied Daisy with equal politeness.

'Tell that to Josefina.' Winna laughed good-heartedly. 'Oh well, I guess she belongs to the old school who don't trust newcomers or young people. Poor old bird!'

The girls went out of the main entrance and followed the colonnade around the square. It was easy to see now how the buildings were laid out. There was a large pebbled square courtyard in between the main reception and residential area and the studios. Walking across, they entered the first one which was obviously the Music Studio.

It was an enormous room. The walls were painted a vibrant orange, while the ceiling was a light yellow. It was very imposing and rather frightening to the girls who had, until now, only been in an audience listening to an orchestra. There were about seventy chairs facing them with music stands in front of each chair. A platform for the conductor stood facing the orchestra.

Winna gulped. 'We must be bonkers coming here. All these students are musicians. We're definitely not! I think Calidus has gone too far this time. They'll know in five seconds that we're rubbish!'

'We've got to trust Calidus.' Hiromi reasoned. 'He's a Light Server. If he doesn't know what he's doing, who does?'

'It's scary all right.' Daisy agreed. 'But we've got to believe that as soon as we pick up our instruments we'll know what to do. Shakita promised us that.' She stopped suddenly, hand on mouth. 'We weren't given any to bring with us!' She looked at the others with horror. 'What on earth are we going to do? Don't musicians bring their own instruments?' Her voice faded into a whisper.

'Maybe we could visualise them and they would appear, like the boys did with the penknives?' Winna suggested hopefully.

'Look, there's loads round here,' said Hiromi, pointing brightly to different cases lying by the side of several chairs. There was also a cupboard with a glass front through which they could clearly see instruments lying on velvet. 'See? We're going to be all right.'

'Who's going to be all right?' sounded a voice with a guttural accent behind them. 'Is there a problem?'

The girls turned round to find a boy of about sixteen years standing just behind them. He was tall and thin with dark straight hair and very dark eyes. In their distress, they hadn't heard anyone coming into the room. How much had he heard?

'No problem.' Daisy laughed uneasily. 'We left our instruments in the hands of a carrier. We were just saying wouldn't it be awful if they got lost - but they're all right.' She finished quickly, looking at the others. They both nodded their heads in agreement.

'Indeed, it would be a problem if something happened to your carrier - no instruments, no music.' He smiled thinly. 'I would never be without my violin,' he said arrogantly. 'For I trust no one. What do you play?'

'Oboe,' Hiromi replied first, quietly.

'And you?' He looked at Winna. For one moment she hesitated. Daisy stood next to her stiffly, hoping she wouldn't forget.

Winna looked him directly in his eyes. 'Why, the magic flute of course.' She smiled.

'Of course.' He smiled too. 'And you?' He directed his gaze towards Daisy.

'The same as you,' she replied.

'Not the same as me, my friend. I am gifted and will most likely be chosen as the leader of the string section.'

'Good for you,' said Daisy dryly. 'Come on, girls, let's get some fresh air.'

'Pompous ass!' Daisy exploded outside. 'Yuk. Not the same as me,' she mimicked in low tones. 'I am so gifted. He gives me the creeps.' Then she added, thoughtfully, 'He's probably right, though. I hope he didn't hear anything.'

'Hmm, maybe. We'll have to keep away from him and warn the boys,' said Winna.

'It's all right for you,' Daisy said bitterly. 'He'll be right in my face if we're in the same section.'

'Come on, Daisy, let's look at the next building,' said Hiromi, grasping her hand. 'There must be an Art Studio.' As they walked across the beautiful green gardens they saw many other students. Some were just arriving, while many others were walking around, exploring the premises.

'Hi, there,' called a girl with pale blonde pigtails. 'Have you been here long? Meet my friend, Felippe Tonisoni, from Italy, of course.' She giggled. 'I am Chelsea Twine, from the States. We shared a taxi. Wow, you have wicked hair!' She ogled at Daisy. 'Is it real?'

'All mine.' Daisy laughed, beginning to feel better. 'We're happy to meet you. These are my friends - Winna Sanderson and Hiromi Magashini. I'm Daisy Ferguson and we're from England.' They all shook hands, delighted to make friends.

'What are you studying?' asked Felippe, looking at Hiromi with interest.

'Music mostly,' she said. 'And hopefully some dancing.'

'Me, too. I play the French horn. They say Yannish is a legend and we want to study with him.' They all nodded with enthusiasm.

The smells of oil paint hit them as they opened the door. Easels of different heights filled the room. There were trestles of pots of paint laid out neatly, boxes of pencils, rubbers, crayons and a variety of flowers, ornaments and sculptures in natural fibres, paint brushes of every size and type and stacks of paper ready for use. Daisy sighed with pleasure. The room had a feeling of activity and purpose.

The last section was the Dance Studio with long mirrors fixed along each wall. A piano stood in one corner with modern CD equipment and speakers. Leading out from the studio, they discovered a magical room which housed costumes hanging on rail after rail. They weren't traditional ballet dresses, but modern designs. There were flouncy skirts in bright glaring colours, tight hipped jeans, jewelled waistcoats, boleros and some more classic costumes in soft dreamy materials for boys and girls. Every kind of design and fashion was represented from all over the world. They hung there, waiting in expectation for someone to bring them to life. Shelves carried hats, shoes, feather boas, in fact everything that a dancer would need. It was like entering a fashion emporium.

Daisy, Winna, Hiromi and their new friend Chelsea were in heaven. Felippe quickly moved on, totally disinterested. With glee the girls tried on all the costumes. Daisy found a red Spanish dress and shawl. Then she rummaged in a basket and found a fan. Clicking her heels and flicking her fan open, she fell upon the others with shrieks of laughter. Chelsea seized upon a dreamy dress in light blue tulle and drifted around with a feather boa slung round her shoulders like a movie star, eyes half shut to make her look more mysterious. Winna dressed herself in a matador's costume, hat and high-heeled shoes. She snapped her heels together shouting 'Ole!'

Hiromi found a beautiful robe with floating panels that moved elegantly around her.

'You look like Shakita,' said Daisy, marvelling.

They tried on one costume after the other, becoming more excited with each one. They found rolls of coloured material ready to be made up when needed. Shoes of every size and shape were neatly stacked. Leotards, too, were piled carefully in boxes.

A bell suddenly rang out signalling that supper was ready. Quickly, in a panic, the girls hung the clothes back where they had found them.

'Be careful,' shouted Winna. 'We mustn't tear them.' They scrambled over each other in an effort to replace everything back neatly.

'Where did you get this?' Daisy asked Hiromi, clutching a headdress.

Hiromi scanned the shelves. 'Over there on the top shelf.'

'Right, we've done it,' laughed Chelsea. 'That was so fabulous.'

They closed the door and made their way towards the reception area, when Daisy suddenly gasped, grabbing Winna's arm.

'You've still got the shoes on, Winna! You go ahead,' she told Chelsea, 'I'll wait for her.'

'Okay.' Chelsea smiled. 'See ya.'

'Come on.' Daisy giggled at the thought of someone seeing Winna in her matador's high-heeled shoes.

'Probably no one would notice.' Winna grinned. 'Anyway, I like being taller than you. I am meant to be the Red Ray, remember.'

Chapter 7

The Team

Students appeared from every direction, hurrying towards the reception entrance. Daisy, Winna and Hiromi caught up with the others after several minutes. Daisy craned her head to see if she could find Jonathan and the boys, but there were too many people jostling and pushing.

'Let's wait,' Winna said exasperated. 'There's no way I'm going to fight my way through this lot.'

It was a relief to sit quietly on a bench, watching and listening to so many different languages as each student passed by. It was exciting to be among so many cultures.

'Hey. Look whose coming.' Hiromi nudged Daisy. Peering up into the sun, Daisy suddenly saw the boys. She sighed with relief.

'Waiting for us?' Jonathan smirked.

'As if,' she said.

Most of the seats were taken except for a few on the very last table nearest the door. 'This will do,' said Jonathan, sitting down. The others joined him.

The noise was deafening as everyone talked excitedly at the same time. Above it all, Chelsea suddenly stood on her chair at the middle table and bellowed out to Daisy.

'Daisy! Come over here next to me!' Daisy stood up and waved back.

'It's all right, Chelsea. I'm with the rest of my group. See you after supper.'

'Okay, make sure you do now,' Chelsea shouted back, then continued chattering with her friends. Jonathan looked at her with interest, as did Dan to Daisy's annoyance.

Food appeared from all directions to feed the hungry students. It was warm, delicious and plenty. There were pizzas of every possible kind to delight their palettes, paella, vegetables, fritters and rice. To finish there were strawberries, peaches and mangoes with ice cream.

'Hello,' said a curly, fair-haired boy sitting opposite Jonathan. 'I am Louis Capello from France and I am here to study music.' He held out his hand.

Jonathan, delighted to find a new friend, introduced himself and the group. Other students, encouraged by this friendly gesture, joined in too.

'I am Yoshi Atari from Japan.' Yoshi introduced himself to Hiromi with a little bow. 'I am a cellist, but am also interested in dancing.'

'Me, too,' laughed Hiromi. 'I am living in England at the moment, to study dance, although I do love the oboe.'

'Hi, I am Eli Beke from the Sudan. I'm studying art and music – in fact everything.' He laughed at Aloysius. Eli was tall and thin. He was a Rastafarian with long dreadlocks falling down over his shoulders.

'Me, too, man.' Al clasped his hand as though he had found a long lost brother.

So it went on, each one in turn introducing themselves, each from another country, but all there to study together at the academy. There was a wonderful sense of excitement and curiosity in the air as the students met each other for the first time.

Daisy glanced across the tables and spotted the dark-haired boy who'd come into the music studio. He was talking earnestly to a girl next to him. As Daisy looked up, he met her eyes momentarily, then quickly looked down and continued talking to the girl. Daisy felt irritated and a little disturbed. She hoped they wouldn't have to sit next to each other in the orchestra.

A bell was rung loudly, requesting everyone to be silent. A beautiful blonde woman stood up.

'My friends, I hope you have enjoyed your meal.' Everyone nodded and stamped their feet on the floor in appreciation.

'Merci beaucoup, mes amis. Now, I would like to introduce you to our Director, Professor Carlos Sanandez.'

Professor Sanandez came forward. He was a tall man with grey curly hair, a large nose and light brown eyes that twinkled as he shook hands with Mademoiselle Collette Du Bois. He was dressed simply in red trousers and a light green shirt, open at the neck. On his feet he wore sandals. He stood quietly, looking at all of the students, before speaking.

'It is wonderful to see so many countries being represented here. I welcome you all. Our philosophy here is to try to bring all people together and to share the qualities that we all have.' He paused, watching their eager faces. 'Communication and relationships are the most important components in life. In some ways we are losing touch with this human factor because of the growth of our wonderful technology.' He smiled. 'Don't get me wrong. I love technology too. Where would we be without our computers and mobiles?'

Everyone laughed.

'There are many ways of communicating,' he continued in his rich warm voice. 'But the most wonderful and inspirational way is with creativity and beauty - music, art and dance. It attracts the very essence within our souls and has nothing to do with the unpleasant events that happen in our world. Everyone here is equal. It has long been my wish to invite countries together here to see what can be achieved. To hear how we can all play music together in harmony. To create the most wonderful art together and dance together. Nothing else matters. We will perhaps inspire others to do the same. Some of you may have prejudices working with other people with different religions and politics. I say to you now, put this behind you and look beyond your judgements and criticisms. If you cannot, you do not belong here. If you can, your soul will sing.'

The students looked at him with interest, some with caution and some unbelieving that such an ambition was achievable.

'These are our tutors who will guide you. First, Yannish Kablinski, who is our Musical Director.'

Yannish strolled up to Carlos, standing quietly by him. He was as tall as the Professor with black wavy hair swept back from his pale forehead. He bowed to the students. There was an extraordinary feeling of tension and electricity about him. Aloysius looked at him with fascination, as though he had met his master. He nudged Daisy who nodded in silent agreement. Yannish sat down.

'Next, Senora Francesca Domingo and Hamish McTavish, your Art Teachers,' said Carlos, continuing in his introductions.

Francesca Domingo was small and dark with scarlet streaks in her hair. Her dark eyes flashed as she moved. Her nose was pierced. She wore a scarlet dress with a yellow sash around her waist and several coloured bangles on each arm. Hamish was a large, red-faced rock of a man with a paunch which obviously didn't bother him. His eyes were pale blue and his fair hair stuck up on end. His hands were huge-looking, more like a farmer's than an artist's. He was from the Highlands of Scotland. Both of them smiled greetings to the students.

Daisy thought they looked an odd pairing, and yet they both seemed to fit together in a nice, eccentric kind of way.

'Frank and Veronica Antoine are your Dance instructors.' Carlos finished.

Frank was from New Orleans, United States of America and Veronica, his wife, was from London. He was black, she was white. He was thin, wiry with neatly plaited hair over the crown of his head. He looked like a beautiful smooth panther, quick to action. She was tiny, with short, spiky, purple hair and green eyes. She wore an orange tunic and tights in contrast to her hair. Both of them waved their welcome.

'Hi gang,' said Frank beaming.

'They're brilliant,' murmured Hiromi.

'This is going to be interesting,' Jonathan whispered to Daisy.

'Great!' she hissed back. 'We haven't even got our instruments yet. Some of these guys are real pros.'

Jonathan shook his head in mock disbelief. 'You heard what Shakita said. We've nothing to worry about.'

Daisy sighed, looking across at the dark boy and remembering his arrogance.

'You're right, Jonno. Bring it on.'

Collette du Bois rose, tapping her knife on the table for silence.

'Mes amis,' she said, smiling. 'Please to feel free to wander round the gardens and enjoy yourselves. Tomorrow morning you go to your studio to begin your lessons. Yes? But please be respectful for those who wish to retire early. So, Bon Nuit.'

All the students shouted 'good night' as they rose to their feet. Chelsea bounded over to Daisy, her friends close behind.

'This has gotta be a relation or something,' she exclaimed, seizing Jonathan from behind. 'He's cute.'

Jonathan looked both startled and pleased to be singled out by this fabulous girl who didn't seem to care what anyone thought of her. He gave her his best laid back leer.

'Yes, I am.' He smiled. 'I'm Daisy's twin, but older by a few seconds.'

Chelsea shrieked with delight then looked at Aloysius, Dan and Marc standing close to him. 'You all together?' She pointed to them. 'You look like a group of friends who've known each other for some time.'

'Yes,' said Daisy, stepping in to introduce them. 'We're old friends who like the same things.'

'That's so cool.' Chelsea moved a piece of chewing gum around her mouth as she observed them closely. 'Do you mind if I tag along?'

'No problem.' Jonathan laughed. 'The more the merrier.'

Students began to group together according to their country and culture, more comfortable with their own familiar language. Some remained alone, feeling excluded and uncertain as to why they had come. Others were just reluctant to join in, instead seeking solitude in nature or returning to their own room. For many this was the first time they had ventured out of their own country and they felt unequipped to deal with so many worldly people.

Finally, La Reunion became silent as each retired to their rooms, excited, fearful and hopeful as to what the next day would bring.

The Colour Code

 *Chapter 8*

Yannish

Upon waking the following morning, Daisy felt a sense of dread even though Jonathan had cheerfully told her everything would be all right. Winna and Hiromi said little, sensing each other's anxiety.

'We can't be like this, dreading the moment,' Daisy said. 'What's the point of going through the Red Ray if we don't put it into action when we need to?'

'Absolutely.' Winna agreed. 'Didn't we suffer enough last time until the penny dropped?' She gripped Daisy's hand, remembering the struggle she'd had with Daisy. 'You too, Hiromi, you had a difficult time as well.'

All three girls clasped each other's hands.

'This is how it is,' Daisy told them firmly. 'We breathe in strength and the power of the Red Ray, then Orange, so that we will be good musicians.'

'You bet!' They enthused as they made their way to the music studio.

Daisy spotted Chelsea elbowing her way through the chairs to the string section, clutching a violin case. Brilliant, she thought, she can sit next to me.

Marc made his way over to the drums and percussion area as bravely as he could. He was terrified, not looking left or right. He was feeling very sick. Close behind came Jonathan with Chelsea's Italian friend, who was carrying his French horn.

'One moment, please,' Yannish called to Jonathan. 'This is yours, I believe.'

Yannish handed him a musical instrument case. Shock and relief flooded through Jonathan's face as he took his instrument.

'Thanks very much. I think I left it somewhere...' he said lamely.

'No problem.' Yannish smiled. 'Oh, and tell your friends we also have their instruments waiting here safely, as arranged.'

'Brilliant!' cried Jonathan. 'I knew it would be all right - I mean, I knew they would be here.' He coughed nervously.

'Of course, all is in hand and you will play beautifully.' Yannish waved his hand over the instruments, then moved on to talk to other students.

'Daisy, Hiromi, here,' he shouted across the room. 'Get Winna and Al.'

Pushing her way through, Daisy glanced back to see if she could find Dan, then saw him plucking the strings of his double bass. She thought he looked a natural.

'I wonder if Calidus heard me when I said we should visualise our instruments,' said Winna, giggling and holding her flute in her hands. 'All I have to do now is play the thing!'

'When you have settled yourselves into your sections,' ordered Yannish. 'We will begin.'

Daisy and Chelsea sat next to each other. The dark-haired boy who Daisy had met earlier sat closest to the stand from where Yannish would conduct. Daisy looked back at Hiromi and Winna, who winked in sympathy.

With a scraping of chairs being pulled back or forward and a readjustment of musical stands, everyone became quiet.

'Settle down, my young friends. I would like each of you to play the first few bars of the music in front of you. Then I can judge how you play and the best place for you to sit. Does that suit you?' he asked, smiling at their nervous faces.

'Great.' Winna snarled, her eyes beginning to show panic. 'This is where I get booted out.'

'You'll be all right, Winna. Hold on and think orange,' said Hiromi soothingly.

'Very well. We will begin with the string section. Please to start, Jovan.'

Jovan Kurepo was the dark, arrogant boy. He smiled smugly to be chosen first to play, as if it were his God-given right. Tucking his violin under his chin, he played the music before him with a flourish and confidence, sure of his talent.

Yannish stopped him. 'Thank you, Jovan. Enough.'

Jovan stopped in mid-bar, cross that he was prevented from finishing.

'Now, my young American friend, you will take up the next phrase,' Yannish said, looking at Chelsea.

With a wide grin, Chelsea took up her bow. Daisy thought she played beautifully.

'Very good.' Yannish stopped her and then pointed to Daisy. 'Next.'

Nervously, Daisy took her violin in her left hand, bow in the right and followed on from Chelsea. She imagined the colour of orange flowing through her. She couldn't believe how easy it was, not only to play but to read the music as well. Reading music had always been a bit of a problem at school and here she was, reading the written notes like a pro!

'Next,' he said, one after the other. Daisy saw one of the Russian boys take up his violin, then a dark boy from Poland with his viola, until the violin and viola section was complete. Next it was the turn of the cellos and double bass. Daisy recognised the Japanese boy, Yoshi Atari, who played his cello like a dream. After him came Massoud. He was a quiet, rather withdrawn boy. Dan's turn came next. Daisy thought he showed great authority. She was proud of him, beaming her pleasure when he finished.

'Thank you. Now we will hear our friend Marc on the timpani. Give me a roll of drums.'

Marc's hands sweated as he adjusted his feet. His breathing was laboured, his face red. He wanted to be sick, but somehow he managed to grasp the drum sticks. In his mind, he tried to think of Manus, the Red Ray, then Shakita with the expansive Orange Ray. Please help me, he whispered inwardly.

He felt as if he was moving in a dream. Each moment and movement seemed to be in slow motion. He adjusted his grip on the drum sticks and began. It was though he knew exactly what to do. How to use the pedals and how to operate each of the five drums placed around him. He finished with a flourish, waving his stick in the air, red-faced, triumphant. Everyone erupted. It was a great performance.

'You'll do.' Yannish laughed.

Jonathan's turn came next. He felt much more confident now,

especially after Marc's debut. He handled it with ease, like a professional. Daisy clapped her hands in delight.

'Good.' Yannish nodded.

Louis Capello came next with his bassoon, then Eli Beke with his trombone. Daisy knew her friends had been great and everything was going fabulously well. There was only Winna on her flute and Hiromi with her oboe. She felt Hiromi would be fine. She was already a student but Winna, like Marc, had never played an instrument before. But Winna was such a gutsy girl, she knew she would be all right.

Hiromi's playing was delicate and lovely. Winna's turn came next. She took the flute in her fingers and placed it lightly between her lips as if she had been playing in an orchestra for years. Daisy breathed a sigh of thanks and relief. There was no doubt both Calidus and Shakita were with them.

Aloysius played his saxophone, which Yannish listened to with interest.

'Do you play the clarinet?' he asked.

'Sure thing,' replied Al, switching easily.

'That' is what I need in this orchestra.' He then turned to Janeck Vassily, one of the Russian boys.

'You will be the leader of the string section. Felippe Tonisoni, you will be the leader with your French horn in the brass and woodwind section for now.

'This is not what I expected!' exploded Jovan from the violin section. 'I should be the leader player. I am the only one here capable of taking this role.' His face was pale, his eyes blazing with fury.

Yannish said quietly. 'You are a good violinist, Jovan, there is no doubt about that. But Janeck Vassily has a better ear.'

'You are mistaken. I am above average.'

Yannish looked at him coolly. 'I sometimes make mistakes, but never in music. This is my decision. Deal with it.'

Jovan glared at him. He felt humiliated. To be told he wasn't good enough in front of everyone was an insult to his pride. Daisy and the other students watched with embarrassed fascination. Part of her felt sympathy, while the other part felt delighted because he was so pompous. She switched from one emotion to the other as they all waited, wondering what was going to happen next.

'You have my testimonials,' Jovan said through clenched teeth. 'My teachers all recommend my gift. How can you ignore that?'

'Well, young man, I have no wish to disappoint or hurt you – or, indeed, disagree with your illustrious teachers, but here I make the decisions. You do have talent and will be of great assistance within the bulk of the violins. Here we work as a team and you have to learn to be a team worker. At the moment you want to be singled out and that is not how we work in this orchestra.'

Sparks of rage flew from Jovan's eyes and something close to tears.

'Now, I would suggest that you calm down and look at the reasons why you wanted to come here.' With these last words, Yannish brought his attention back to the students.

'It is time we had a break. Be back here in one hour.' He strode out of the studio without looking back.

Daisy leaned over to Jovan. 'Try not to be too upset. All it means is that you sit with us.'

'Leave me alone,' he snarled. 'You don't know what it is like to be snubbed after knowing I was the best here.'

Daisy gasped at his arrogance and at his self-belief. 'Why aren't you a soloist then, instead of having to play with idiots like us?'

At this point, the girl who was sitting next to him at last night's evening meal came up to him, nudging Daisy out of the way.

'Come, Jovan,' she said quietly. 'Come with me. You are not needed,' she told Daisy, placing her arm firmly around Jovan's shoulders. 'You are not in his class.'

'Right, thanks.' Daisy laughed. 'I suppose I'm not.'

'Thank heavens,' Chelsea said. 'Really! What a plonker.'

'Which one?' Daisy asked.

'Both.' Chelsea smiled wickedly. 'Hang on,' she called after Felippe. 'Wait for me - see ya!' she mouthed to Daisy and was gone. Really, she was the funniest girl Daisy had ever met. One moment she was all over her and the next she was off to do more interesting things.

Aloysius, Dan and Marc joined up with the girls. Jonathan was exhilarated with their performances and shocked at how easy it was.

'This flute thing is really nice.' Winna chuckled. 'How did it sound to you?'

'Fantastic!' they all said. 'It was as though you were a professional.'

'Mmm.' She beamed, basking in their comments. 'Maybe I will continue when we get home. You were wicked, Marc and Jonno,' she told them generously.

'So was everyone else,' said Marc. 'Well, I guess we're here to stay.'

'What did Yannish mean, to be the leader of different sections?'

Daisy asked. 'I didn't get it.'

'Well, apparently there are so called leaders in the different groups of an orchestra - woodwind, brass, strings and percussion,' explained Aloysius. 'It's a bit like a hierarchy, like school with prefects. These leaders or prefects are all responsible for their group. Your section, Daisy, is divided up into two groups, with the first violin who is Janeck and a second violin, who Yannish will probably choose later. Maybe he'll choose you.'

'I hope not!'

'Anyway, it's a bit complicated,' he said.

'What about Jovan?' Daisy added. 'It's going to be tough with him fuming only a few chairs away.'

'Stay away from him,' said Dan warningly. 'Calidus told us there would be disruptions, so we'd better be on our guard.'

'Got it.' Daisy agreed. 'We stick closely together.'

 *Chapter 9*

Learning to Listen

One hour later the students assembled back in the music studio. The lights had been dimmed so there was only a soft orange glow from the lights above. It was a beautiful room. Daisy realised that although the stage was flat, where the orchestra and conductor played, the main part of the floor was raised in tiers, housing seats for the audience. None of them had noticed this before.

Yannish laughed at their obvious surprise. 'Take your seats and listen.'

The students sat facing Yannish, as if they were the audience. They sat enshrouded in subdued light, whilst he stood before them with the light streaming down upon him.

He had great authority and ease of manner as he addressed them. He was a romantic figure, dressed simply in cream trousers and a yellow silk shirt. His face was alive with the passion of his subject. His eyes glowed with enthusiasm.

'Sound is one of our senses.' He began. 'We have to learn to open ourselves to auditory effects of sound. There are many sounds which we love and those which we dislike.'

'Like your nagging voice,' whispered Jonathan, pulling a face at Daisy. Daisy pinched him back.

'What sounds do you enjoy?' Yannish asked the students.

'Pop music,' shouted one. 'Rock,' said another.

'Classical too,' Ariel added.

'Call to prayers,' one said bravely and some of the others smirked.

'Sounds of nature,' shouted Daisy. 'I love bird song and the buzz of summer.'

'Rap,' said Aloysius, laughing. 'And jazz.' Many agreed, whooping their applause.

'What don't you like?' asked Yannish.

'Nagging women,' Marc said, sighing deeply, to everyone's delight.

'See.' Jonathan grinned at Daisy.

'Whining girls,' scoffed Louis.

'Bully boys,' shouted Winna as she glared at Louis.

'I hate it when people shout and swear,' said Hiromi. 'Everyone swears all the time now.'

'Grow up. Learn the language, girl,' one of the boys told her. 'Be one of the crowd.'

'Why?' Hiromi stared at him.

'Actually, I agree with her. Why should she accept it, just because you like it?' Yoshi Atari argued.

'I hate the noise of guns, bombs and women screaming.' Kyan Khan from Palestine spoke quietly from the back of the studio.

The room became hushed. The atmosphere changed from one of light banter to one of frightening reality. Kyan's words were spoken in a matter of fact of tone but had the most profound effect on everyone. No one spoke. Many students from the West were shocked. Others from the Middle East were taken back into their own memory of violence. Those from neighbouring countries glared at him in opposition. Yannish quietly moved to stand in front of him.

'You are right, Kyan. These are the worst noises any human being could ever hear.' He paused to allow the students to come back into balance.

He reached over and took Daisy's violin in his right hand and quietly began to play a beautiful piece of music to calm his students. Gradually a sense of acceptance and stillness returned to the room. Feeling that the moment of grief had passed, he gave the instrument back to Daisy and continued.

'We now know what pleases us and what offends us. That is good. Now, close your eyes. Be still and listen.' After a moment's silence, he spoke softly. 'When we close our eyes, our ears open. The more we listen, the more we hear. As one sense lessens, another expands.'

It was an interesting experiment which calmed some of the students, making them more responsive. Some of the more volatile and outspoken ones found it difficult to be still for long. They were used to constant chatter and background noise. Others found the exercise silly and a waste of time. Several, who had been brought up in violence and terror, cherished the peace and safety, like Kyan Khan and Ishmael from Israel. Both sat on opposite sides of the room, avoiding all contact with each other. All experienced stillness according to their upbringing and experience of life.

Slowly, other sounds could be detected. Daisy could hear the gentle rustle of leaves on the trees; the continuous sound of chirping grasshoppers; bulls mooing contentedly in the far off plains; the twittering of birds as they went about their business; the squeal of animals caught off guard before they could escape to safety; the soft movement of the air as it expanded in the heat of the afternoon sun; bees humming happily as they moved from flower to flower, gathering in nectar.

She heard the sound of scythes thrashing as they cut through grasses, horses snorting as they galloped freely in wide open spaces. There was a sense of a rhythm and cycles within nature and regeneration giving, perhaps for the first time, a sense of continuity and order to those who listened, soothing their nerves. Breathing became easier, deeper even, though some students were not aware of the effect of quietly relaxing. Yannish waited until there was a deeper peace within the studio, then quietly brought them back. Some of the more aggressive students were embarrassed to be seen as stupid and weak. Yannish understood their struggle.

'Sound is more to do with listening. We may hear many noises and sounds but we don't always actually listen. We may hear someone speak and be engaged in conversation with friends, but do we listen? We are so used to hearing background noises in shops and restaurants, of mobile phones, etc, that we have got into the habit of not listening. Noises become mental irritants so most of us block them out, especially those that are frightening to our sensitivity. We try to erase them or else we eventually become immune to them to escape the forced volume. Noise can actually hurt your ears.

'When we really want to listen to something special we have to apply ourselves much more. Music is a way of opening our senses to a higher level of receptivity. It fills our bodies and delights out senses. We are told that the ear is the most intelligent organ in the body. Aristotle, the great Greek philosopher, said that the eyes are the organs of temptation and the ears are the organs of instruction.'

The students sat poised on their seats, concentrating on all he told them. No one had talked about sound in this way before. Most of them had never even thought about the subject.

Yannish continued, as though he was talking to himself, but his eyes held everyone's attention. 'The ear helps us to remember and to accumulate knowledge, which helps both the performer and the listener.'

Aloysius knew exactly what Yannish was talking about. He felt his words in his heart. He looked across at Daisy and smiled. Daisy looked back at him with understanding.

'Now, my friends,' said Yannish. 'We have experienced enough for today. This afternoon you may enjoy the further pleasure of art. I will meet you again tomorrow morning. Until then, I thank you for your company.' He bowed deeply with great grace and left.

Daisy wanted to escape with Winna and Hiromi to their room to discuss the day's events. She didn't feel like talking to Chelsea or anyone else.

'Come on, Hiromi, let's go now.' Hiromi nodded in agreement.

Silently, the Colour Code Gang followed, feeling the need to talk among themselves. After the door closed, Marc was the first to speak.

'That was some day!' he blurted out.

'It was fantastic,' Aloysius said with admiration. 'Yannish is a genius. He talked about listening in a way I knew but could never put into words. But he's right, we don't really listen, do we?'

'My foster parents certainly don't,' replied Marc dryly. 'They're so busy shouting at each other and me that nobody hears anything anyway. We might just as well be saying carrots! Nobody would even know. It's a madhouse.'

'We all listened when Kyan brought up the subject of guns and tanks,' Hiromi said. 'It was awful. It made me want to cry.'

'Me, too,' Daisy said seriously. 'I can't imagine what it's like to live like that. It must be horrible.' She looked at Jonathan. He nodded, not saying anything.

'It must be dreadful sitting next to someone who's responsible for your parents being killed or your house being bombed,' Marc said, round-eyed.

'These students aren't responsible,' replied Daisy, shocked at his remark. 'That's a stupid thing to say, Marc.'

'He's got a point,' Winna agreed. 'I wouldn't want to sit next to someone from a country who killed my family.'

'Daisy said that these students aren't responsible and they're not. You can't blame the kids, Winna. You're as bad as them,' Jonathan said hotly.

Winna was beginning to get very aggressive now. 'Well, you two may be the exception, but imagine having to play with someone you hate.' She glowered at him.

Jonathan stood up shaking his head, exasperated. 'You're nuts.'

'No, I'm not, bozo. How can you or any of us know how it feels to sit next to your enemy? I wouldn't want to,' she finished flatly

'That's not fair. It's not their fault that their countries are at war. It's their parents and the government.'

'I know that. You're not telling me anything I don't know. All I'm saying is that it's tough, that's all.' She shrugged her shoulders.

'Hang on a bit.' Dan intervened. 'Most countries represented here have probably attacked each other at some time, anyway. If we get our knickers in a twist about it how are we going to help Yannish to bring them together?'

Daisy beamed at him, relieved he had brought sense and calmness to the group.

'Just saying, that's all.' Winna sniffed. 'Okay, I get a little heated sometimes.' She squeezed out a little smile as an apology. 'Sorry, guys. I guess I'm still feeling the effects of the Red Ray.'

'Yeah, you're right,' agreed Marc 'It was brilliant today. I still can't believe I actually played the drums! If that's the effect of orange, bring it on.'

 *Chapter 10*

Jovan Challenges

D aisy was excited to be going to the Art room. So was Aloysius and Hiromi, but Jonathan and Marc dragged their feet.

'Why do I have to go?' Jonathan complained. 'You're the one who loves art. Marc and I could do something else. We could practise playing our instruments.' Marc nodded in agreement, excited by the prospect.

'We did promise Shakita we would support the academy,' said Daisy. 'And if we back out, others will too.'

'Why should they?' asked Winna 'It's not compulsory, is it? Nobody has to do everything.'

'So why are we here?' Daisy looked at them all. 'We promised Calidus and Shakita we would work as a team.'

'But we're not glued together,' growled Jonathan.

'Daisy is right though, Jonno,' Dan said thoughtfully. 'Art isn't exactly my first choice either, but we agreed to keep our eyes open and stick together.'

Jonathan and Marc both sighed deeply, exchanging exasperated looks at having to always obey Daisy, otherwise known as the Initiator. Calidus had told them in their first adventure in the Red Ray that Daisy had initiated the Colour Code through the website, where the gang had all met in the University of Light. That meant, energetically, she was the first one to bring them all together. They had come to accept this, but now and again it irritated Jonathan.

This was one of those times.

Daisy hated being cast in this role, but she knew somehow it made sense. Together the seven of them created a dynamic whole. Seven was a spiritual number and the seven colour rays of the spectrum, which each one represented, completed the energy through which the qualities of the Colour Code worked.

'Come on, Jonno. Please, I can't do this without you and Marc,' she begged him, anxiety written all over her face.'

Jonathan gave in reluctantly, grimacing at Marc. 'Oh, all right.'

'Does this mean we have to do dancing as well?' Marc asked in sudden horror.

'Let's deal with that when we get to it,' said Dan, laughing. 'Come on you two, you might even enjoy it.'

In the Art Studio, they found most of the students were already there. Daisy saw Jovan and his girlfriend talking to some of the Middle Eastern group, grumbling away about something.

Francesca Domingo and Hamish McTavish were busily clearing a long trestle table, handing pots of paint to anyone willing to place them along the length of the table. Francesca smiled a radiant, wide smile to all of the students. The boys couldn't do enough for her because she looked like Tinkerbell from Peter Pan. Her personality sparkled. She wore yellow baggy trousers with braces to hold them up, and they had patches of dried coloured paint all over them. Her green T-shirt blended beautifully well with the scarlet streaks in her hair and green hair band. A large loop earring hung from one ear. Jonathan quickened his pace, now anxious to help her, with Marc coming fast behind. Hiromi poked Daisy, giggling behind the boys' backs.

'I don't think we'll have any more problems, do you?'

Daisy grinned, showing her approval.

Hamish McTavish was a large man in stature but gentle by nature. He was known as the Gentle Giant. The difference between them was such a contrast. Francesca was dynamic, flittering from one place to the next, bringing excitement and inspiration to those she taught, whilst Hamish brought stability and encouragement to those who were struggling to find a way to express themselves.

Thanking the students for helping her, she asked them to sit down. She spoke in English with a pretty Spanish accent.

'Hamish and I welcome you to our Art Studio,' she smiled. 'Do you like our academy?'

Most of the students nodded in agreement. Jovan remained silent. Oh well, thought Daisy. What's new!

'Professor Sanandez has told you about our philosophy in this special academy.' There was an enthusiastic response. 'La Reunion is a place where we encourage all people to come together. It is an oasis from the conflicts of the world - where we can share beauty and harmony together. This is where the human spirit shines. Yes?'

The students smiled in agreement. She was bewitching in her eagerness. Hamish stood at her side, quietly surveying the students.

'Painting is a way of expanding your sense of appreciation of beauty and can improve your ability to respond to all forms of art, music being one of them,' she said. 'As Yannish always says, the more we respond to beauty and open our senses, the finer each sense deepens. This helps us to experience more at a deeper level.'

'Are you saying that if I paint, I will become a better musician?' Jovan asked slowly, looking with sarcasm at those around him.

'What's he up to now?' gasped Hiromi, shuffling uncomfortably in her seat.

'It can help,' Francesca replied. 'Does that surprise you? Painting is another form of expression.'

Jovan stood up, exercising his role of authority and challenge. 'So you're saying that if I don't paint, I can't be a good enough musician?' He laughed scornfully. 'Now I see where I went wrong! So if I'd learnt to paint, I would have been chosen as the first violinist.' There were howls of laughter.

At this point Hamish came in. 'Why are you here if you don't want to be?'

'I have worked so hard all my life to be a musician,' replied Jovan. 'Since I have been here I have been insulted and not taken seriously. First, I was told by the Great Yannish I am not good enough, and now you are telling me I should learn to paint!'

Francesca and Hamish looked at each other sadly.

'No one is making you take part in our Art Studio. It is a free choice. We offer art as a way of relaxation after working so hard in the orchestra, as well as discovering beauty in another form. Do you all feel the same?'

'Well, some of us have studied very hard, it is true,' Ariel from Iraq told her. 'It does sound a bit frivolous to say painting or dancing will improve our music. We haven't had time for such nonsense.' Jovan nodded emphatically, delighted he had found some allies.

'Hang on,' Aloysius joined in. 'Music is my first choice, of course, but it doesn't mean to say I can't enjoy other skills. I want to do everything offered here.' Francesca smiled her thanks. Hamish remained silent.

'What's your bee?' Eli said, looking at Jovan. 'Someone stole your light, man?'

Daisy clapped her hands in absolute glee. 'You're right, Eli. It's about time you grew up,' she said to Jovan. 'You've been complaining ever since you got here.'

'Hear hear,' echoed Jonathan. 'Get a grip, Jovan.'

Hamish put up his hands. 'Steady, girls and boys. Those of you who want to stay, we welcome you. If anyone wants to go, that's all right too, but Jovan do give it a try. You never know, you might even enjoy it. Now Francesca, tell our friends what we are going to do.'

'Okay,' she said, glad to begin at last. 'It doesn't matter if you've painted before or not. We are going to paint a huge mural across the whole of this wall,' she pointed to a long white wall across the length of the studio. 'You can use whatever colours you like and paint whatever pictures you want, as long as it works within the theme of La Reunion. We don't have to be artists to enjoy ourselves, but the act of coming together will create a masterpiece.'

'Brilliant!' cried Daisy. 'What will you paint, Hiromi?'

'Something from Japan and my family,' Hiromi replied happily. 'What about you?'

'Perhaps something from nature,' Daisy said thoughtfully.

'Okay, we're here,' said Jonathan to Marc. 'What do you think?'

'What about the Cheyenne?' Marc offered brightly. There was nothing in his own life that had inspired him enough, but their adventures with Soaring Eagle were exciting.

'Maybe I'll do something about mountain climbing or flying,' Dan mused.

'I'll paint my saxophone and maybe my playing with Tatanka,' laughed Aloysius. Tatanka was a special Cheyenne musician who Aloysius had met in the Red Ray. He would never forget him and sometimes, when he listened to Yannish, he felt something stir within him, as though he knew him.

Winna told them that, since she wanted to become a doctor, she was going to paint something to do with treating people and helping to make them better.

'That's a brilliant idea, Winna,' Daisy said.

'Thank you everyone,' Francesca told them all. 'We will begin in harmony the day after tomorrow.' She stopped in front of Jovan. 'Please stay. You have such a passion for music. I would love to see how you use it in art.' She touched his hand lightly and moved on. He grunted but said nothing.

 *Chapter 11*

Servant

Far away from the bustle of students two people spoke in muffled voices, not wanting to be overheard.

'So, what have you to report?' a female voice asked.

A young male voice replied, 'The students have only been here for two days, Oleander.'

'Don't call me that,' she hissed.

'Sorry,' he mumbled nervously.

'We have to move quickly.'

'I know, but there are already signs of division within the Middle Eastern countries and…'

'I know that already, you fool.' She smacked him hard on the head. 'That's why we're here.'

'Yeah, I know.' He added hastily. 'But already I have stirred up bad feelings between them.' He looked at her from under his eyelashes, hoping to regain her favour.

'Well! What else?' She glared at him, exasperated.

'It's beginning to work, but it will take a little time.'

'Come here, you miserable worm. Don't you realise Yannish has an idea to save the world, and there is nothing as irritating as a man with a good idea. It will take all my cunning to destroy his plans.'

'We have another opening which is promising.' The boy began. 'There is one called Jovan who was very angry when he wasn't chosen to lead the string section. I know we can make use of him.

He hates Yannish. He tried to upset the Art class too. Lot's of the others agreed with him that it was a stupid idea to paint. The Art teacher thinks we would be...'

'I'm not interested in what anyone thinks,' she spat at him, grabbing his hair. 'I have to answer to a greater authority and we don't have the luxury of time or stupid theories from someone who doesn't matter.' Her cold blue eyes drilled into his.

He dreaded this look, for he knew she had no mercy. He had worked for her for four years now. Coming from a background of poverty and violence in Afghanistan, she had suddenly arrived like an angel, offering him the opportunity to escape and make something of himself as a musician.

She paid for his training and gave a sum of money to his mother, telling her she would fulfil her dreams for him. How could his mother refuse such an offer? She already had three other mouths to feed. Soon after he had finished his training, he discovered there was a bigger price to pay. His freedom. His life. She owned his very soul. If he didn't obey her, she would kill him horribly. Sometimes she would taunt him with terrifying descriptions of what she would do to him, with a malevolent light gleaming in her eyes until he whimpered with fear. He knew she would enjoy every moment of it; then she would laugh, lightly cuffing his head, saying he was her good boy and that one day she would free him.

She called him her Servant. This became his name. 'Come here, Servant.' Servant ran immediately to her to do her will. He had nightmares about her but, as much as he feared her, he knew she worked for a greater, more sinister power that wished to create evil in the world, and was far more influential than any existing divisions between countries, cultures and religions. This force used any negative energy to separate goodwill or dreams to unify nations.

'Go now,' she said abruptly. 'I will see you in two days and you'd better have some good news for me.' She moved away as silently as a ghost.

Servant sighed, relieved she was gone, but dreading what he had to achieve to find his freedom. Deep inside, he knew there was no way out. He would never be free.

 *Chapter 12*

The Edge of Uncertainty

The following morning the students were to meet at the music studio. Today was going to be a momentous day when Yannish would take them through their first musical score.

For most of the students it was normal to read a score and be part of an orchestra, but for the Colour Code Gang the prospect was terrifying. Even though they knew they would be looked after, the very notion of actually playing a classical piece of music seemed unbelievable. Although Daisy and Jonathan grew up with classical music, which their parents loved, it wasn't their own musical choice. Jonathan liked rock and pop whilst Daisy loved ballet and pop music. Hiromi, being a dancer, had more knowledge of established music. Aloysius loved all kinds of music, especially jazz because he could create his own themes, but he still loved traditional music because of its structure. Winna liked contemporary music, mostly pop. She had no inkling of classical style.

Dan grew up listening to all kinds of music, from folk to classical music, mostly because of his dad. They went to concerts together. Through attending these, Dan decided to learn the double bass. Marc had never played an instrument, or even listened to music seriously, but in his dreams he imagined himself as a famous drummer in a band with long hair and dark shades. Now his dream was going to be realised, though not quite in the way he imagined! Calidus had a weird sense of humour, he thought to himself. But hey, don't knock it!

Daisy wanted to talk to Dan before anyone came into the studio. She had the ability to see colours around people and plants, which was the reason why she and Jonathan had found the website in the first place in the Red Ray. Her gift gave her an added sensitivity so that, even though she may not always be able to see the auric energy around people, she could sense a disturbance around them. They sat together amidst the double basses. He was like a sounding board for her. He listened.

'Have you felt anything strange?' she asked him.

'I'm not sure,' he answered. 'But I think I know what you mean. Tell me what you feel.'

'I'm not sure exactly,' she said quietly. 'It's as if something is about to happen. Probably wrong,' she smiled. 'Perhaps I'm picking up Jovan's stuff. He's so weird and aggressive. Do you think he's up to something, Dan? Or is he just paranoid and feels nobody likes him?'

'Well, I don't think he really cares if he's liked or not as long as he's the cleverest,' Dan said. 'By the way, I thought you were brilliant when you told him to grow up. I nearly fell off my chair. I hope he doesn't hold that against you.'

'As if I care!' She sniffed.

'Somehow I don't think he's smart enough to cause real problems for Yannish,' Dan said thoughtfully. 'Yannish would soon deal with him, but someone else might make use of him. I tell you what, Daisy, let's just keep our ears and eyes open.'

'Thanks, Dan, I feel so much better just talking about it.' Daisy got up and joined Chelsea who had just come in.

'Wow!' she smirked.' Look at you!'

'What d'you mean?' asked Daisy, not really wanting to listen to Chelsea.

'You've got something going on with Dan, haven't you?' she giggled.

'I have not!'

'You have. Look at your face!' Daisy's face went scarlet with embarrassment. 'Mind you.' Chelsea teased. 'I don't blame you - he's so cute with those gorgeous blue eyes and that Irish accent.'

'For heaven's sake, Chelsea, shut up. What about you and Felippe Tonisoni, the gorgeous Italian?'

'Well, he's cute too and so is your brother.'

'He thinks you're stunning.' Daisy was beginning to feel calmer now. Her face had resumed its normal colour.

'Oh, really?' Chelsea smiled with interest, tossing her hair back.

Their attention was suddenly brought back to the present when Yannish tapped his baton on his music stand. Everyone waited for the maestro to speak, their musical instruments poised for action.

'Good morning, my young friends. Today we are going to play the first movement of Mozart's Symphony No 40.' He raised his baton, fixing them with his dark eyes. 'We try the first bar.' He lifted his baton and everyone began to play.

Daisy gulped. This can't be real, she thought.

'Stop!' he said. 'You are too slow. We start again.'

And so it went on, bar by bar until the musicians played to Yannish's satisfaction.

'Next bar,' he continued.

Each individual conductor has his own special way of communicating with his orchestra. The music has to be taken apart and then the conductor and his players work as partners to put it back together again, so that both understand the piece they are creating. For Yannish, it was a natural process. He pushed his young students more and more with passion and intensity until they could fulfil the potential he knew they held within them.

It was extremely hard work. He was generous in his praise and humorous, making them laugh when they found it difficult. The Colour Code Gang had to get used to the way Yannish used his hands and what he wanted to convey with them. Usually the hands of the conductor communicate what he wants from the orchestra. It took time to get to know him and what he wanted to achieve. Eye contact was crucial and before very long all of them became used to his individual style.

They played all day with breaks in between. They repeated a phrase over and over to get it right. For the first time, Daisy began to understand why people loved music so much. It was a team effort where each one played his or her part to create a whole.

'This is enough now,' said Yannish, his eyes shining. 'You have worked very well and I am so proud of all of you. Now you may rest and enjoy your food. Early to bed, I think. I see you tomorrow'. He bowed once again, leaving them dazed but happy.

Each one put away their instruments without saying much. Food was what they needed now, and sleep.

The evening air was sweet and soft as they walked towards the dining room. The smell of the flowers and shrubs was intoxicating.

'That was brilliant,' said Aloysius sighing, savouring the pleasure of the music as it echoed in his mind.

'Awesome.' Marc agreed.

Daisy nodded. 'My fingers feel quite tingly.' Noticing Chelsea's questioning look, she added quickly, 'They're always like that before we really get going.'

'Yeah,' Jonathan said, trying to help his twin. 'My mouth takes a bit to warm up too.'

Daisy shot him a look of thanks.

'I need to eat,' he said,. 'Beat you, Chelsea?' He began running towards the dining room.

'You will not,' she shouted, bursting into a sprint. 'I'm a two hundred metre champion.'

'Well, I'm a one hundred metre, so there!'

Daisy followed the others. She felt relieved Jonathan had spirited Chelsea away. Now she didn't have to guard her tongue. It had been a struggle to learn this with the Red Ray, but somehow this was different. Although the Orange Ray was more relaxed it also had its dangers, because they could become too relaxed and mention something that would alert anyone to their true identities. They had to be just a bunch of students who wanted to learn music. As yet, none of them knew if anyone was against Yannish's plan or not, but Daisy felt uncertain. They had to be vigilant.

Aloysius beamed as he caught up with them. 'That was some wicked piece of music.

This is my friend, Louis Capello. He plays the bassoon.'

'Hi, Louis,' said Daisy and grinned. 'You've met the Master musician, then!'

'He is very talented, I think,' Louis said seriously, looking at Al with admiration. 'I would like to hear him play the saxophone.'

'You will,' Winna said. 'We're gonna play some wicked jazz, right, Al?'

'You bet, Winna, my girl. Perhaps Louis can join us?'

'That would be so cool.' Louis smiled at them.

 *Chapter 13*

The Terror Begins

Servant sensed her first, like a huge shadow over his soul. A feeling of dread descended, as though his life was being squeezed out of his body. With reluctance he left the dining room, his food unfinished. He had no appetite now.

Most of the other students talked animatedly about the day's happenings with shrieks of laughter. There was the beginning of a shared understanding and some tentative friendships; just a beginning of an appreciation of others' cultures and differing points of view. For the first time there was genuine interest and communication, but it would take time.

He turned quickly to check no one was looking - the English girl with red hair noticed his quick withdrawal. She smiled and quickly carried on with her conversation with the blonde girl beside her. Servant clicked his tongue in irritation. She had spoken to him before about music and how he had got there. He didn't want anyone to know him or even remember him. It could be dangerous for him to be involved with anyone.

Secretly he admired Yannish and his musical ideal. His talent was inspirational in drawing out the best in his students, but Servant couldn't afford to think about this too much. He had a job to do. How it would affect his music later, he didn't know.

He spent his time with those who were dissatisfied. First Jovan. He was easy, being so arrogant and full of his own self-importance.

All he had to do was encourage his hatred of Yannish. Poison his mind with little remarks like, 'It's easy to see you are more talented than Janeck.'

Servant soothed his ego. He then spent more time with Jovan's constant companion, complimenting her on her playing and support of Jovan. As he stoked their resentment, he turned his attention to some of the more aggressive students, saying just enough, but not too much.

He was punctual for his meeting with Oleander. She was waiting for him with a cold smile on her face.

'You forgot to mention the English group,' she said softly, ready to strike.

'The English group?' he repeated innocently.

'Yes, the English group, you dolt,' she hissed at him. 'There are seven, are there not?'

'I believe so, my Lady,' he whispered, mesmerised by the cruelty in her eyes.

'These people have a different energy and another reason for being here. You should have told me, you miserable little toad.'

'What do you mean?' Servant asked, terrified he had missed something important.

'You neglected to tell me they were connected to Yannish.'

'They're not,' he spluttered. 'They're just a bunch of students from England who aren't particularly good students - well, maybe the black one is.'

'Have you asked yourself why they are here, numbskull?'

'I don't know why.' He shrugged, his legs now beginning to tremble with fear.

'They are here, you fool, to help Yannish and Professor Sanandez with their plan to bring countries together.'

'How do you know?'

'I know, idiot, because it is my job to find out.' With a hiss Oleander grabbed his throat with both her hands, pressing as hard as she could, her sharp nails tearing his skin. Her strength was formidable.

Servant found himself beginning to lose consciousness, relieved in some ways that, in dying, she could never use him again. Then she suddenly let him go, pushing him to one side so that he dropped like a stone, gasping and struggling for breath. She kicked him brutally several times where he lay.

'Now listen and listen good, you idiot. Find out everything you can about them. Why they are here. Remember,' she said soothingly, caressing his hair. 'One bite from me will poison you and you will die in agony.' So saying, she stepped over him and disappeared.

He lay there, clutching his throat, sobbing his heart out. Whatever he tried to do to please her, it was never enough.

'Hello,' a voice called. 'Is anyone there?'

Servant tried to sit up, frightened he may have been overheard. Daisy suddenly appeared in front of him.

'Hey, Massoud.' She bent down, concerned. 'What's happened to your neck? Who attacked you?'

'No one,' he spluttered.

She stared at him in horror, seeing a red jagged mark round his neck. 'So what's this?' She pointed to his throat. 'Is this my imagination? Come on, Massoud, I knew something was wrong when you suddenly left the dining room.'

'It's none of your business,' he croaked with difficulty. 'Stay out of it.'

'Sorry,' said Daisy, backing off. 'I was concerned, that's all.'

Massoud staggered up, straightening his clothes. 'Thanks, Daisy, but it really is all right. I just had a fight with a man. I think he was trying to steal money or something. Probably a villager or gardener...'

'You're kidding me? In that case we should tell Professor Sanandez or Collette du Bois.'

Massoud put out a restraining hand. 'Please, Daisy. Tell no one, I beg you. No one must know. It was nothing.'

Daisy stared at his face, shocked at his look of terror. Clearly he had been viscously attacked, then she realised there was more to this than he was letting on.

'It's all right, Massoud. I won't tell anyone, but please let me help you.'

'I'm fine, really,' he gasped. 'It was probably a case of mistaken identity.'

'Did he take anything?' she asked, not believing him.

'No, I don't think so,' he answered, a little calmer now. 'I think you must have interrupted him. You won't tell anyone, will you?'

'Okay,' she said, 'but I and my friends are here if you need us.'

He looked at her strangely. Perhaps Oleander was right. Maybe the British group did have another agenda in being here.

'I have to go.' He looked around nervously. Clutching his side he began to move away. 'Thank you for helping me.'

Daisy nodded, thinking there was something very wrong going

on. She felt disturbed and knew she must warn the others. If only Shakita was here.

***

She went quickly to her room. They were all there. Winna was lying on her bed as if she had just woken up. Hiromi sat on the edge of hers, making room for Dan and Aloysius. Jonathan and Marc lounged on Daisy's bed.

'So! Where've you been?' her brother questioned her irritably. 'We've been waiting for ages. You just shot off without a word.'

Daisy sat down facing them. 'Sorry. But there's something going on. I felt it this morning.' She paused, looking at Dan. 'Now I know for sure.'

'Well, what is going on?' her twin demanded.

Daisy explained what had happened after she'd abruptly left the dining room in mid-conversation with Winna and Chelsea.

'To be honest, I really hadn't noticed him,' Hiromi murmured.

'Well, that's because you were ogling Yoshi Atari,' said Marc, giggling. 'But I do see what you mean. Massoud isn't someone who stands out somehow.' He pushed his glasses back up his nose, thinking he used to be like that. But since hooking up with the Colour Code Gang, his life had changed completely. Now the shy, intellectual Marc was a wizard on the drums and brave too. He smiled inwardly, loving his new identity.

'I've only spoken to him a few times,' Dan said. 'He's a good musician, but a bit nervy.'

'I've seen him with Jovan,' Hiromi told them. 'He seemed pretty pally with him, which surprised me. Not quite his scene I'd have thought.'

'Perhaps he was sorry for him when Yannish bawled him out,' Winna suggested, smirking a little.

'Where does he come from?' Dan asked. They all looked at him, uncertain.

'Afghanistan or Iran, I think,' Winna replied.

'So,' Dan began, looking at them all. 'What have we got?'

'Didn't you see anything to give us a clue?' Marc asked Daisy.

'Something, but it could have been my imagination,' she answered. They all focused their eyes upon her with growing fascination.

'Well?' Jonathan pushed her.

'Hang on. I'm trying to remember to get it right.' She closed her eyes. 'There was an awful smell. First it was sweet, then really horrible, like rotten eggs or something like your gym shoes, Jonno.' She giggled, trying to release the tension in the room.

'Thanks a bunch,' he snorted.

'Anything else?' Hiromi asked.

'I know this sounds soppy, but I felt frightened. Something made a terrible mark on his neck, as though it was trying to kill him, and I know he was kicked because he kept holding his side.'

'Was it a wild animal?' Marc stared at her, his eyes as round as saucers.

'Animals don't kick or make marks like that. And the mark on his throat was like someone was trying to throttle him.' They gasped in horror.

'Did you hear anything? Anyone talking before you got to him?' Jonathon asked.

'No, only him gasping for breath. He couldn't move. He begged me not to tell anyone. He was so frightened. In fact, he was terrified.'

'So what do we do now?' Winna asked, looking at them all in turn, then back to Daisy.

'Nothing,' she said firmly. 'We pretend that we don't know he's being threatened, but we keep our eyes and ears open.'

'You don't think it's someone in the orchestra, do you?' Marc whispered.

'Could be,' Daisy replied. 'But they'd have to be awfully strong. Maybe it was more than one person. I did tell him he could talk to us and that we wouldn't tell anyone.'

They nodded in agreement.

'Do you think Calidus knows what's going on? Or Shakita?' Daisy asked them.

'I guess so,' replied Jonathan. 'Do you think it's anything to do with Yannish?'

Daisy shrugged her shoulders, perplexed. 'I shouldn't think so. But whatever happens, we'd better keep quiet and watch Massoud.'

'Hey, Marc,' said Jonathan. 'You're good at detective work. You should be our main investigator. You were awesome at finding out what the Cheyenne needed.'

Marc's chest filled out with pride. 'All right,' he said. 'If you really think so. Massoud won't know I'm there.' He blinked, already on the case.

 *Chapter 14*

Rap, Hip Hop and the Tea Party

Yannish told the students to spend the day having fun. 'Move your bodies,' he said. 'We love to sing and dance. We have a passion for music. You, too.' He spoke directly to Aloysius. 'I am thinking about using you to play a little solo at our end of term concert.'

Al gaped at him. He couldn't believe what Yannish had just said.

'I have surprised you, I think.' Yannish chuckled. 'Do not worry, there is plenty of time. We will talk about it later.' He waved his hand elegantly, shooing them all away. 'Go now. Frank and Ronnie Antoine are waiting for you in the Dance studio.'

Aloysius was speechless. He couldn't wait to tell the others. As he walked out of the door he nearly bumped into Collette du Bois.

'Hello.' She greeted him. 'How are you all settling in?'

'Everything is wonderful.' Aloysius beamed at her. 'We are so enjoying it and Yannish is marvellous. What an opportunity to work with him.'

She smiled prettily. 'He is a genius. We all know how lucky we are to have him here. Where are your friends?' she asked.

'Around, I guess. We're never far away from each other.'

'That is so nice,' she purred. 'I tell you what, why don't you all come for tea today after your dance class? We can have such fun. I will make you a special tea for my British guests and you can tell me all your news.' She laughed at his delighted face.

'Thank you, Mademoiselle du Bois. We'd love to come.'

'Please call me Collette and a tout a l'heure.'

He hurried to the Dance studio to tell the others first about tea with the gorgeous Collette and then about his solo part.

Frank and Veronica (Ronnie) Antoine were stretching their muscles to the punchy sound of Snoop Dogg. Around them students squatted down wherever they could, clapping to the music and joining in the song. Frank was so light on his feet. He could twist his body into any shape and uncurl it as gracefully as a cat. Ronnie danced beside him, shadowing his movements. They moved together in perfect synchronization.

The students whistled, taking up the beat of one of the most famous Rappers of all time. Frank signalled for them to join in and immediately the floor was swarming with swinging students, each dancing in his or her own style, all trying to out do each other. Daisy, Jonathan and Marc held back whilst Aloysius, Dan, Winna and Hiromi plunged into the middle, gyrating with the others.

'Okay, guys,' Frank said, slowing down and grinning at their enthusiasm. 'Glad you like to rap.' Shouts of approval echoed round the room.

'As you know, my name is Frank Antoine and this is my wife Ronnie. We are here at this academy because we want to be. We believe in Professor Sanandez's philosophy and want to work with students from all over the world. My own life,' he explained. 'Began in New Orleans where we lived in poverty, but our culture of music was so strong it allowed me to survive. I was rescued by a Rap singer called 50 Cent Facts–Friday, who helped me to study at a school in New York for Theatre and Performing Arts. He told me he also had grown up in poverty with violence and drugs where gang crime is high. Since then he has tried to help others. Now I feel the same and, together with Ronnie, we try to reach many people who have similar problems.'

'My life was not so dramatic or as colourful as Frank's.' Ronnie smiled. 'Sure, it was a tough life growing up in the East End of London, but I won a scholarship to go to an academy in the West End. Frank came in as an instructor and that was it.' She grinned at the students cheekily. 'After that we teamed up together, travelling all over the world. What we want to do here is to give you the opportunity to move your bodies and express yourselves in any way you choose. Of course, there are certain rules and structures in choreography as to how we move, but you will find that it excels your movement rather than restricts it. There may be some of you who have not yet tried to dance, but Rap and Hip Hop are the most fun and you will surprise yourselves how quickly you learn.'

Jonathan and Marc looked at each other with dismay. Daisy wanted to try but, like Jonathan, she felt rather stupid. She was used to flowing movements and some of these steps were jerky and complicated.

Ronnie smiled at her. 'Don't worry, lovey, it's not so bad,' she said in her broad cockney accent.

Dan came over to Marc. 'You have nothing to fear, Marc. If you can play the drums like a pro, you can certainly dance Rap.'

Marc laughed in spite of himself. Aloysius clapped him on the shoulder.

'No sweat, man, you're a natural.'

Marc's pale, worried face began to lighten. 'Oh, do you really think so? I will give it a try. Will you help me?' he asked.

'You've got it, bro.' Al grinned encouragingly.

'The thing to remember,' Ronnie told the students. 'Is that before you even dance, listen to the song. The beat will start to take you over. Then begin with a few steps. Try and act out the movements of the lyric. All those who haven't rapped before, come with me.'

She led them to another part of the studio. There were about twenty people in total, much to Daisy's relief. Ronnie put a different CD on.

'Now listen. Really get the words and rhythm. Don't try to do anything too ambitious.' She began to move her arms from side to side in a swaying motion. She strutted across the room as though going for a brisk walk. 'Really relaxed,' she showed them. 'Now, quicken up the pace.' She rotated her hips, bent her arms. 'Hey, take it easy, mister,' she called out to one of the students. 'There's plenty of time.'

Jonathan and Marc's bodies gradually began to thaw, responding to the music.

'Everyone's a natural dancer,' she said, encouraging them.' Look at children. Good,' she told Daisy. 'Stick with it. Now, open your hips and stretch those legs. We are dancing Hip Hop now so be real cool. Have fun.'

Within a short while, they all began to enjoy themselves, introducing new steps naturally and forgetting their inhibitions.

'This is great,' Jonno told Daisy as he waved his hands in the air.
'Isn't it?' She giggled.

They looked over at Marc who was attempting some complicated movements, diving to the floor and kicking up his legs. His face was flushed. His breath came in gasps as he twisted his hips.

'Steady on, fella!' Ronnie laughed. 'Don't do yourself an injury! Okay, guys, that's enough. Well done.'

They stopped, exhausted but proud of their efforts. Frankie stepped forward.

'This is the deal. We'll have two groups, not because of excellence but more to do with space. This studio will take thirty people comfortably. I'll take the first group and Ronnie will take the next.' He paused, looking at all the students. 'I believe that Yannish told you there was going to be a concert at the end of August, when we finish.' They nodded. 'Yannish will present the orchestra and we will give a demonstration of dancing. It will be hard work, but hopefully you will find it rewarding and fun. You will also have completed your mural from the Art Department.'

'Did you notice that Jovan was there?' Hiromi asked Daisy after the lesson.

'I thought I saw him, but we went to another part of the studio so I wasn't sure. What was he like?' she asked curiously.

'Not bad,' she acquiesced. 'Better than I thought. Once he relaxed he was quite good, but he's a bit of a poser.'

'What's new?' Daisy sighed.

***

With a quick tidy-up, Al knocked on her door. The door swung open and there was Collette.

'Entre, mes amis,' she said, her eyes sparkling with pleasure to see them.

She beckoned them into a beautifully spacious room. On the white walls hung paintings from a French painter, Camille Pissarro, and two Spanish painters, Picasso and Dali. Daisy knew of Picasso but didn't know the others, but she thought they were interesting.

Two sofas sat opposite each other with two armchairs at each end, mirroring the sofas. They were covered in an off-white material with silken cushions in bronze, ochre and burgundy. Persian rugs adorned the stone floor. A grand piano stood at the other end of the room, close to the French windows. On the stand, sheet music lay open. Next to the piano stood a long table made from local wood. It was light-grained, like cedar. On the top, Daisy noticed a huge bowl of flowers. The room was elegant and rich in colour. It was a room that belonged to someone with exquisite taste.

'You must be tired after so much…activity.' She wrinkled her nose with distaste. Exercise was abhorrent to her. 'I have some delicious pastries for you, mes enfants.'

They quickly took off their shoes and sat down. 'Such thoughtfulness,' she murmured.

Daisy, Hiromi and Winna sat on one sofa and Dan, Jonathan and Marc sat on the one opposite them. Aloysius sat in the chair opposite Collette.

'This is nice, isn't it? We have cold drinks instead of English tea,' she told them. 'It is too hot.' She dabbed her brow. They nodded their heads gratefully. 'Now, tell me all about yourselves.'

'Well, there's not much to tell,' Daisy began. 'We're here to play music with Yannish.'

'Oh, indeed.' Collette clapped her hands. 'The Maestro. He is so wonderful, is he not?'

'He's a genius,' said Aloysius and warmed to the subject. 'He makes us work hard but everyone wants to.'

'Not everyone,' interrupted Winna. 'Some of them still have issues.'

'Still some?' Collette asked with round eyes. 'I thought these race and political problems had been resolved?'

'It's beginning to get better,' Dan hesitated. 'But there are still those who find it hard to relate to people from certain countries.'

Collette nodded in sympathy. 'Of course it is, très difficile, n'est-ce pas? It is early days. Now tell me, Aloysius, you have been chosen to play solo - yes!'

'Yes.' He grinned. 'I couldn't believe it when Yannish asked me. It's brilliant.'

'And what about - Jovan. Is that his name?' She paused. 'Has he also been chosen?'

'We're not sure,' Daisy answered. 'He's a bit arrogant, so Yannish may choose someone else.'

'Like you?' Collette smiled.

'I don't think so!'

They tucked into the wonderful pastries of chocolate, almond and orange, enjoying every mouthful. Everything was delicious.

'Tell me about yourselves,' Collette asked again. 'You are a strong group and everyone likes you. Did you know each other before you came here?'

'No,' said Daisy.

'Yes - a little,' Jonathan began at the same time.

Collette looked at them with interest. Daisy glared at her brother. Jonathan stared back at her, embarrassed.

'We met at the airport,' Dan explained easily, 'so I suppose it feels as though we've known each other for ages.'

'I know what you mean.' Collette nodded. 'You are sympathique.'

Daisy relaxed, relieved Dan had smoothed over a dangerous moment.

They talked of many things and Collette told them she had been a concert pianist and had played all over the world. 'Now I want to give something back to all those who have helped me in the past. I believe in this concept of La Reunion.'

'It's brilliant,' Hiromi said enthusiastically. 'That's why we're all here.'

'Not because of your music?' asked Collette.

'Of course, that comes first,' Hiromi added hastily. 'But Yannish's philosophy is important too.'

'Exactly,' Collette agreed.

Aloysius stood up. 'Is it possible to play your piano, Madame de Bois?'

'Call me Collette, and yes I would be delighted if you would play my piano.' She smiled, waving him prettily forward.

He sat down and began to play the music already on the stand. It was a nocturne by Chopin which he played beautifully. Then he made a quick change into jazz, delighting them all.

'Bravo!' cried Collette.

Time flew by as he improvised, one piece after another, until the bell for supper rang out loudly.

'We'd better go, Collette. Thank you for a fantastic time,' he said. 'We all enjoyed it.'

They all shook her hand, thanking her in turn. 'You must drop in again. I am usually here at this time of the day if you have any problems,' she said, looking deeply into Jonathan's eyes. 'Or we can just have fun.'

Chapter 15

The Colour Code Gang go into Action

Supper that night was animated with more communication than ever before. Students were mixing more and feeling more comfortable. It was like a turning point for them. There were those who began to find common interests rather than ones that divided them.

In time, they also talked more openly about their problems and their confusion over the lack of knowledge. Very little information was allowed to leak out of each country, so speculations were often false and exaggerated. Sometimes, Professor Sanandez and Yannish would join the students and encourage them to talk and question those who they believed were their enemies. Often there were heated discussions. Some stormed out, but Carlos Sanandez always encouraged dialogue, gently intervening when needed.

Daisy decided it was time the Colour Code Gang took more action with the Israelis, Iraqis, Syrians and all Middle Eastern friends, to give support instead of keeping to themselves.

'It's time we really supported this project,' she said.

Daisy was sure Yannish had heard her, but he continued talking.

'Do you think we'd be exposing ourselves by being openly supportive?' whispered Winna.

'Probably,' said Daisy. 'But we've got to start using the Orange Ray to help bring people together, haven't we? Isn't that what we're meant to do?'

'Exactly,' Dan whispered back. 'That way we can keep an eye on Massoud.'

'Well, he wasn't at the dancing studio,' Marc remarked. 'I don't know where he was because we were all involved, but I shall keep my eyes on him tonight. He's here now, sitting next to Jovan's girlfriend.'

'So he is.' Daisy mused. 'I wonder what's going on. Come on, let's circulate. I think it would be a good idea if we all split up individually and try to be friendly with the others. Who do you want to take on, Dan?' she asked.

'I think I'll try Jovan and Massoud, if that's all right with you, Marc? It won't interfere with your detective work? He plays the cello and is close to me in the orchestra, so it might work.'

'Good for you,' said Daisy. 'Go for it, you might just get somewhere with the genius as well. What about you, my brilliant brother? Who will you attach yourself to?'

'Ariel can be a bit testy. He's sitting next to some of the guys from Syria. It should be fine,' he said confidently.

'I'll saunter over to chat with Louis Capello and Kyan Khan and some of the guys around him,' Aloysius told her. 'Eli Beke is there too. Should be cool.'

Hiromi looked for her friend Yoshi Atari. He grinned at her to come over. He was talking with the Polish group. One of the girls from Israel had joined them too. Hiromi waved back, making her way over.

'Winna, who do you fancy?'

Winna looked around. She saw Hannah Zimmerman, who played the harp, talking to Felippe Tonisoni.

'They'll be good,' she said. 'Make Chelsea jealous.' She moved towards them, smiling in welcome.

Daisy placed herself between Ismail and an Israeli girl. They smiled at her, making room. She couldn't help grinning as she saw Jonathan join Ariel. Chelsea was chatting animatedly to them. No wonder Jonathan chose them, so he'd be close to the girl of his dreams. Chelsea, in her usual flamboyant way, was arguing a point with Ariel. Ariel began to get heated, telling her she had no idea what she was talking about.

'Oh, yes I do,' she argued back. 'My dad's a congressman.'

'So your dad's a congressman, is he?' Laughed Ariel. 'My dad is dead, along with my mother and two sisters. You know nothing, you people in the West.'

'I'm sorry,' replied Chelsea, horrified at Ariel's reaction, realising she gone too far. 'I didn't know.'

'We all have much to learn and understand,' said Professor Sanandez, raising his hand to quieten the room. 'Conversations like this show us that accusations do not help the healing process. Listening to each other does. This is where acceptance and under-standing is born. You young people want new ways of dealing with these issues to bring peace and communication to the world, don't you? Let's begin by sharing our love of music.' His voice was quiet but held great authority.

Jonathan whispered to Ariel, then to Chelsea, who looked shocked at her indiscretion. She looked at Ariel in desperation. Jonathan spoke quietly, reassuring her. Yannish looked at them with approval.

None of this went unnoticed by Massoud.

He observed the way the British group had spread themselves out between all the students, or rather those who had problems. Oleander was right. There was something going on between them. And with Yannish, too. He would have something to tell her. He felt relieved, especially after last time when she was so violent. He shuddered.

Marc was the only one who wanted to be free to move around and not be attached to anyone. In this way he felt he could see more clearly what was going on. As with the Red Ray, no one really saw him. He had that quality of faceless uniformity and so could drift invisibly wherever he chose.

He noticed Massoud had a strange look on his face as he looked at Jonathan. Then Massoud quickly spoke to Jovan's girlfriend, who laughed. Jovan asked what was said and she told him, behind her hand. Jovan nodded his head, ruffling her hair. He saw Dan trying to engage them in conversation. Jovan turned round to answer with a quick smirk at Ariel.

Altogether too smug, thought Marc. He wondered what Massoud had said. He'd have to keep his eyes on all of them. He thought Dan would have a hard time with the three of them.

Maybe Dan could get Massoud by himself...

 *Chapter 16*

An Important Decision Is Made

When they got back to the girls' room, they saw Josefina in the corridor. Aloysius nodded and smiled politely to her.

'Anything you want?' she asked them, her dark eyes searching his face.

'No, no Josefina, but muchas gracias all the same,' he said.

'Bien hecho.' She smiled and moved on.

'What did she say?' Daisy was curious.

'She said well done. Isn't that odd?'

'Yeah, it is a bit.'

'Probably the language,' said Aloysius. 'She doesn't really understand English.'

'She's weird if you ask me,' muttered Jonathan.

'You're only saying that because she called us children when we first got here,' said Winna, laughing. 'Perhaps she thinks we've grown up now!'

'Whatever,' said Jonathan with a snort.

Back in the safety of their room, they revised the evening.

'Well, we've really put ourselves out now for someone to see out intentions,' said Winna, looking gravely at the others.

'Not really,' said Daisy. 'Why shouldn't we circulate a little? As Jonno said, we're not glued together. We're looking at things from our point of view, but actually no one is in the least interested in what we do.'

'Yannish is interested,' Dan said. 'He knows exactly what's going on - and remember, he's the one who gave us our instruments.'

'Yeah, but he can't say anything or treat us differently from anyone else can he?' Winna reminded him.

'Of course not, but he knows why we're here.'

'I watched Massoud tonight after Chelsea did her grand performance with Ariel,' Marc told them. 'He looked strange somehow. He also watched you, Jonathan. I think he's gathering information.' Marc continued on in his detective role. 'I'm going to follow him – from a distance,' he added, seeing the concern in Daisy's eyes.

'You'd better let us know where you are,' she warned him. Whoever attacked him is probably still around. I wish Shakita was here,' she said with a groan.

'Maybe she is,' said Jonathan. 'She might have been here all the time. Probably in disguise so no one knows who she is.'

'Perhaps she's Collette?' offered Aloysius. 'She seems very caring.'

'Maybe,' Daisy said thoughtfully. 'But we can't ask her in case she's not, because then we'd really have blown our cover.'

'You're right.' Dan agreed. 'And you fancy her Al, so you would really like her to be Shakita. Right?' he laughed.

'My secret's out, man,' Al grinned. 'She's a doll.'

'She's great. But as Daisy says, we must be careful not to give ourselves away,' Hiromi said seriously. 'By the way, she was quite insistent about asking if we knew each other before we came here. Did you notice?'

'I think that was just good manners. She was just interested in all of us,' Al insisted. 'And I would love to see her again.'

'I bet,' Winna said dryly, rolling her eyes.

'I've just had a thought. Tell me what you think about it.' Daisy leaned forward in a conspiratorial way. 'We're on our own, right? There's no one here to help us, at least that we know of anyway.'

'Except Yannish,' offered Jonathan.

'Yeah, but we can't ask him, Jonno. We're here to help him, so we must work in the background.'

Jonathan nodded his head in agreement. 'So what are you suggesting?'

'Well, we're working with the Orange Ray, right?' They all agreed. 'Suppose we all meet here every morning before sessions begin, to concentrate on the Orange Ray? Really breathe in the energy and ask Calidus and Shakita to help us support Yannish in his plan to bring everyone together.' She looked at them expectantly.

'You mean, like sort of praying?' Marc asked, blinking nervously behind his glasses.

'I guess so,' Daisy replied, hesitating. 'I mean, we do it at school in assembly, don't we?'

'Yeah, but we don't really mean it,' Winna said and giggled. 'It's just something we do, isn't it?'

'This situation is a bit different from school, Winna. We're on a mission, aren't we? Calidus told us to stick together, so don't you think it could make a difference? Remember we're on our own. We have to make our own rules.'

'Okay, sounds good,' Jonathan agreed. 'It can't hurt, can it, Marc?' Marc looked at him, uncertain. The idea of praying was the last thought in his mind.

'I think it's a great idea,' Hiromi said enthusiastically.

'So do I,' said Dan. 'Plus we're already circulating, so it must strengthen that.'

'Great,' said Daisy, relieved to get them on her side. She hadn't really thought about it before. It'd just came into her mind as they were talking. She felt pleased there were no arguments. 'Thanks, guys. We're the unbeatable Colour Code Gang.'

'All for one and one for all!' said Winna.

They all looked at each other feeling strength, a unity, a coming together - rather like La Reunion.

The Colour Code

 *Chapter 17*

First Strike

Early the following morning, Daisy and the Colour Code Gang began with their new regime of linking together with the Orange Ray. First, Daisy decided to wear a purple T-shirt to go over her jeans.

'I mean business,' she told Winna and Hiromi, hands on hips.

'Okay,' said Winna, rummaging in her case for her red top. 'You've got it. I'll join you.' She pulled her shirt over her head, admiring herself in the mirror. She stood before Daisy. 'Like it, Oh Initiator of the Violet Ray?'

'Fantastic!' said her friend, smiling.

'What about you, Hiromi?' Winna teased. 'What's the beautiful Japanese blossom going to wear?'

'I think dark blue, as I am indigo.' She fluttered her eyes, joining in the game. 'I am dark and mysterious and very dangerous,' she said, looking at them through slit eyes.

The boys joined them for their morning session, eyeing them silently. Sitting quietly, they closed their eyes, not because they had to but because it seemed the most natural thing. They held each other's hands as a token of connecting with Calidus and Shakita. A warm glow flooded through them, bringing a sense of peace and purpose.

Inwardly, each one asked for strength and the ability to support the project of La Reunion. Daisy thought of Massoud and asked that he be protected. She thought of Yannish and Professor Sanandez too, and then she asked that she and her friends receive protection from a force they couldn't see but knew was there. She didn't ask for anything for herself, only the group as a whole.

Renewed, they opened their eyes, surprised at the effects that such a connection had upon them.

'It's a bit like when we breathed in the Red Ray before going into the Cheyenne camp,' Marc said in awe, looking at Daisy. 'I could move a mountain.' He pounded his chest.

'Good on you,' said Dan, laughing. 'But you're right. I feel great too.'

'Yep,' agreed Jonathan. 'Let's get to it.'

The morning was going to be tough again, as they would be working on the next movement of the symphony. Yannish made them repeat each bar until he was satisfied. It was beginning to sound much better. As each student began to relax within the orchestra, they felt a new understanding of what he needed from them as they began to come together as a team.

They filed in and took up their places, chattering to their neighbours, before taking up their instruments. Chelsea appeared in a black mini skirt and a shimmering silver top. Long earrings swung as she moved her head. Her blonde hair was tied in a pony tail.

'Hi Daisy. Can you forgive me for last night?' her big round eyes pleaded.

'There's nothing to forgive, Chels. You just shot your mouth off.'

'Yeah, I know. Me and my big mouth!' she groaned as she chewed gum. 'Jonathan was brilliant. He just took over and calmed us both down. He really is something else.' She rolled her eyes. Daisy smiled, proud of her twin.

Jovan sat down heavily next to her and opened his violin case.

'Good morning,' he said to both of them.

'Good morning,' they both echoed, hardly believing their ears. Could this be the bad-tempered Jovan who'd disrupted the whole orchestra? They looked at each other, eyebrows raised. Hiromi and Winna looked amused.

Yannish walked in briskly, waving his baton in welcome.

'Did you enjoy the dancing?' They all stamped their feet in response. Some whistled their delight. 'I told you that you would like it,' he said, laughing. 'Now, all you have to do is have fun with painting - eh!'

There was some mumblings from a few. Jovan remained silent, impassive.

'Take a challenge, my young friends. Now to work,' he said

briskly. 'We will begin from the beginning then we will try the next movement.'

Everyone took up their instruments. It was curious that the Colour Code Gang didn't question their ability to play anymore. They knew they would be alright. Confidence was strong.

The music started with a good attack. Jonathan raised his trumpet to his lips, drew in his breath, and then screamed. Out of the mouthpiece hundreds of spiders erupted. The music stopped. Everyone turned to look at him aghast. He dropped his instrument to the floor, clutching his mouth. He looked terrified. Spiders ran all over him, in his mouth, up his nose, his eyes, in his hair. His whole body was covered with little red spiders. He spat, waving his arms about like someone demented, screaming again and again under the vicious attack.

Yannish and Daisy ran to him. Eli Beke and Felippe, who were close by, started to stamp on the spiders that were crawling everywhere. Yannish reached him, encircling him in his arms, lifting him over the heads of the students and laying him on the ground.

'Get rid of them!' Jonathan screamed, his eyes tight shut. Daisy leant over him, brushing his hair with her fingers, wiping his face which was now beginning to swell. With a tissue she wiped the inside of his mouth and nose.

'Please Calidus, help him,' she whispered.

Yannish picked him up and carried him out of the studio to the sick bay, calling for the resident nurse. Jonathan was whimpering with fear and pain. His body was shaking with shock.

'We have to take his clothes off and bathe him in cool water,' Yannish told Daisy. He tore at his trousers, socks and shoes. Daisy pulled off his T-shirt.

A nurse came in, hurried after by Professor Sanandez. Immediately she went into action. She gave Jonathan an injection to counteract the allergic reaction of the bites. Then she ran a cool bath, pouring in medication to soothe Jonathan's poor body.

'You can go now,' she told Carlos Sanandez and Yannish. 'I will look after him. Thanks to you he will be all right now. You may stay with your brother,' she said gently to Daisy.

Yannish nodded, touching Daisy's hand. 'I will find out what happened.'

The nurse, with Daisy's help, lifted Jonathan and wrapped him in gauze. His face was badly swollen. His body was not so bad.

His clothes had protected him to some extent, but his hands were terribly sore. The nurse spread a light lotion over the worst areas and gave him another injection to help him sleep.

'Can I stay until he sleeps?' asked Daisy.

'Of course,' said the nurse, sympathetic. 'It must have been a terrible shock.'

Daisy nodded, the tears running down her face. Her body shook with reaction. Her mind raced as to how it was possible for such a thing to happen. She relayed the scene in her mind from the moment he first screamed. There were hundreds of spiders, not just a few. The place was covered with them, but they didn't attack anyone else around him. Why not? They made a beeline for Jonathan as though they had been instructed. Where did they come from? She hadn't even seen a single spider in the area. These were like a swarm of bees or wasps attacking when disturbed. Her father had told her how dangerous they could be. Did spiders do the same? And how did they get into his trumpet?

She shivered suddenly, very scared. Chelsea had told her how brilliant Jonathan had been in calming her and Ariel. She wondered if it could possibly have been Jovan. Marc had seen them joking with Ariel. Perhaps that was why Jovan had been so polite, because he knew what was going to happen!

Daisy gasped at the enormity of her thoughts. She sobbed with grief and fear and total confusion. Then her thoughts turned to Massoud and the strange things around him. He was terrified that anyone knew that he had been attacked. Could it all be about Yannish and La Reunion?

Daisy was so tired with thoughts chasing round and round in her head that, thankfully, her head dropped onto Jonathan's bed and she fell into a deep sleep.

Chapter 18

Facing the Enemy

Yannish returned to the studio to find complete disarray within the orchestra. Some of the students saw the spider event as a bad omen and were arguing amongst themselves, gesticulating at each other. Others sat horrified, unable to do anything. They quickly checked their own instruments in case a spider epidemic would occur.

Dan and Marc helped the three boys closest to Jonathan to clear away the mess of dead spiders. There were still hundreds of them crawling around but now they were passive, having achieved their aim. Winna rushed out to find an insect deterrent from the main house and Hiromi found brushes and pans to get rid of the insects. Chairs were pulled back to give greater room to clear up the devastation. Yannish noted the atmosphere in the room. There was shock and disbelief, and an underlying feeling of unease. Strangely enough, Jovan was actively helping Winna to spray the insects.

Marc looked at Winna, who winked in response.

'Come on, guys,' said Yannish encouragingly. 'This was an unfortunate accident and we must move on, but first we clear up our studio, yes!'

'How's Jonathan?' Dan asked Yannish. Marc, Winna and Hiromi came closer to hear the news.

'He's asleep now, but he'll be all right in the morning,' he replied casually, not wanting to upset the group anymore than was necessary. 'Hey, you're doing a great job,' he said, congratulating the workers.

'Thank you very much. It is important we don't let this episode disturb us too much. Spiders can be like a bee swarm when it's hot, and a cosy place like a trumpet must be like heaven to them.' He laughed outwardly to ease the tension. 'It is no more than that, I assure you.'

It took some time to clear away the debris. Jovan sprayed the remaining spiders. Winna and the boys brushed the remains into sacks, which were then taken into the garden and placed in bins. Yannish made a mental note to burn them.

'We are two musicians short for the moment, so now we play even better. Carlos, my friend, you will play like a maestro.' Carlos Domingo was the second trumpeter sitting next to Jonathan. He picked up his trumpet with a broad smile. 'And Jovan, you will give all your inspiration in place of Daisy.' Jovan nodded his head solemnly.

'Let us resume our symphony, ladies and gentlemen.'

The music began slowly, reluctantly at first, but Yannish understood the degree of fear and distaste that the spider incident had created, especially among those with strong religious backgrounds. Anything unusual or macabre could cause a stampede. Superstitions were strong.

As he conducted, remaining calm for his musicians, he felt an underlying concern that some negative force was working against him through his students. He felt angry and sad at the same time. He knew the Colour Code Gang had been sent by Calidus. He had been very careful not to attract their attention in any way but now, after this incident, he would have to alert them. Shakita was in place but was not ready to show her hand. He made up his mind he would speak to them this evening, before bedtime.

Some hours later, Daisy woke up refreshed from her sleep. She was surprised to find herself lying across Jonathan's bed with a blanket over her. The nurse must have come in to check he was all right. Jonathan looked a little better. His face and hands were still swollen but he appeared more peaceful. Daisy prayed the horror of the attack wouldn't cause a lasting problem. She sighed deeply as the nurse came in.

The nurse was Canadian. 'How's our patient doing?'

She checked all his vital statistics then turned her attention to Daisy. 'Now, young lady, your brother is doing fine, so why don't you join your friends for lunch? I will watch over him. Professor Sanandez has instructed me not to let anyone in except you and Dr Kablinski.'

'That's a relief.' Daisy sighed again. 'I will go. The others must be worried about Jonathan. I don't understand it...' Her voice faulted.

'Try not to worry too much, my dear,' soothed the nurse. 'I have never heard of spiders here in such huge numbers, but things do happen. I will get the gardener to check outside. Maybe they nest like bees?'

'They made Jonathan's trumpet their nest,' Daisy said bitterly, turning towards the door. 'Thank you so much for looking after my brother. We fight sometimes, but we're always there for each other.'

'I know,' the nurse said sympathetically. 'Now, off you go.'

Daisy returned to the music studio just as the students were filing out for lunch. Everyone crowded around her, asking how Jonathan was.

'He's okay,' she said. 'He's asleep now. The nurse said he would be better tomorrow.'

Dan placed an arm around her shoulder. 'Come on, Daisy, let's go to lunch.' Hiromi, Chelsea and Winna followed. Chelsea was crying.

'He's all right, Chels, don't worry,' said Daisy. 'Jonathan's tough. A little thing like this won't stop him.' She wiped Chelsea's tears away. Chelsea was a good friend. A little kooky sometimes, but she was okay.

'You're sure?' Chelsea pleaded, crying afresh.

'Sure,' replied Daisy, sounding more confident than she felt.

Marc came up later. He'd been doing a little detective work which he would tell them about later.

Yannish stopped Daisy before they reached to the dining room. He asked how Jonathan was, and then quietly spoke directly to her.

'I will see you later.'

'Come to our room,' Daisy offered.

'I will be there at ten o'clock tonight,' he replied, then quickly walked away.

***

Lunch was a quiet affair. For Daisy, it was good to be with her friends. This time they all stayed together rather than taking up their new roles with the other students. Even Marc abandoned his detective guise to be with Daisy. His friendship with Jonathan had grown through their last adventure with the Red Ray and now they were like brothers. He kept a watchful eye, just the same. Massoud was there, listening to the chat nearby and adding a few words now and again. He seemed calm.

'It's painting after lunch.' Dan reminded Daisy. Daisy's eyes widened.

'I can't come,' she said firmly. 'I have to go back to Jonno.'

'Come on, Dais, the nurse told you he wouldn't wake up for hours.' Hiromi looked at her tense face.

'She's right,' said Dan, touching her arm lightly. 'Let's do some wicked art with the most bizarre colours, and then you can check on Jonno after. He might be coming round by then.' He gave her a lopsided grin. She suddenly laughed and relaxed.

'Okay, Dan, I'll come.'

Aloysius and Winna, watching her attentively, whooped with delight when she decided to go with them.

'We'll get through this,' Winna whispered in her ear.

As they got up to leave, Jovan came over. 'I am sorry for your brother,' he said curtly. Daisy looked closely at him, wondering if he really meant it. Whatever, she thought, sighing. 'Thanks, Jovan.'

He paused and moved on.

'Wonders will never cease,' said Hiromi, giggling. 'Maybe the beast has changed into a lamb!'

 *Chapter 19*

After Effects and Questions

F rancesca and Hamish had already heard about the grizzly happenings with Jonathan. Although they didn't actually mention the fact, Daisy knew because of their caring attention. They welcomed all the students. Jovan was among them, to their delight and surprise.

Some of the students had drawn sketches which they hoped to re-create. Others waited anxiously for the attention of one of the teachers, unsure how to begin.

Daisy and Hiromi hovered over the many pots of paint, trying to decide what colours to choose. Hiromi chose a golden yellow as the background. Daisy went for different shades of green. Marc was irritated. His mate Jonathan wasn't there and he felt lethargic, without any inspiration. Aloysius made a beeline for the orange. Whatever he painted, it would have to be warm and vibrant. He grinned at Winna, who was contemplating the red tin. Dan began to sketch a horse with Hamish looking on.

'Nice choice,' Hamish said, smiling. 'But spread yourself out a bit. There's plenty of room, man.'

'Right you are.' Dan rubbed it out and started a much larger drawing, then added another. Hamish patted his shoulder.

'That's the idea. Don't be afraid. Be bold.'

'What's up, Marc? Can't you find a topic?' Francesca asked.

He grinned weakly. 'I'm just not in the mood for it,' he apologised, shrugging his shoulders. 'Usually Jonathan and I work together. He's the creative one. I just do what he says.'

'Do you want to be excused today, Marc?' Francesca gently asked him.

'Yes, please, Francesca. I will be here next time, I promise, but somehow my mind is on other things.'

'No problem. Off you go.'

Marc whispered to Daisy, who nodded her head in return and left the studio. One of the reasons why he didn't want to be there was to find out where Massoud was. He just caught sight of him through the window, making his way towards the main gates. There was no time to lose. Marc's nose was twitching to find the scent...

The rest of the afternoon was fun. There was no sense of restriction as to what they could paint as long as it was about the La Reunion theme. The music helped to create a mood of joie de vivre and light heartedness. The students shouted and sang to their pop favourites. They danced as they painted, adding paint to each other's work with shrieks of glee. Hamish and Francesca encouraged them to use their initiative and to express themselves naturally and many interesting ideas began to emerge in the mural.

Daisy forgot her sadness over Jonathan and became deeply engrossed in her work. Stepping back, she was satisfied, at least for the moment. Her face was covered with blotches of paint, as were her hands. Dan appeared pleased with himself too. He showed the beginnings of his painting of horses and wide open fields.

'That's good, Dan. It gives a feeling of horse freedom.'

'Yeah,' he said. 'That's what I wanted.'

'Let me see.' Chelsea pushed her way through. 'That's so brill,' she said, marvelling. 'Mine's rubbish!'

'Come on, Chels, let's see what you done.' Daisy edged her towards her painting. She looked at it, not knowing what to say. It was a complete mess.

'I don't know what to do,' said Chelsea, looking at her like a tragic drama queen. Daisy drew in her breath, thinking madly what she could do.

Hiromi looked over her shoulder. 'Paint over it,' she suggested. 'And start again.'

'Hi, bud,' shouted Chelsea to one of the boys. 'Want to join forces?' She gave him a brilliant smile. His face lit up at being asked by the gorgeous Chelsea, who everyone admired.

'Me?' he asked.

'Sure you. We'll make like a wicked painting together.' She giggled and, with a thankful nod to the girls, joined her new friend without a care in the world.

'Job done!' Hiromi smirked, slapping Daisy's hand. 'She's okay really, better than some of these straight-faced dorks.'

After Art, Daisy rushed over to see if Jonathan was awake. He was just beginning to surface. His red eyelids fluttered. He opened his eyes, not yet sure where he was and why he felt so rotten. He licked his still swollen lips. They felt foreign to him. Like rubber tires and not his lips at all. Then suddenly he remembered. Daisy saw the recognition in his eyes. He struggled.

'It's all right, Jonno. You're safe. This is the sick bay and I'm here.'

He looked at her with relief. 'What happened, Dais? Why?' 'I don't know,' she replied simply. 'Yannish is finding out. It must have been an awful accident and somehow the spiders got into your trumpet.'

'How could they?' he asked. A puzzled look came over his face. 'The mouth piece is too small for anything to get through or out.' He shivered. 'Maybe they got in some other way and the volume of them all pushed them out.' He was silent. The horror was still showing in his eyes. 'I just feel I never want to touch a trumpet again.' Tears ran down his face.

The nurse came in, smiling at them both. 'So the warrior's returned? How are you feeling, Jonathan?'

'I don't know,' he replied, close to tears again.

'Try not to worry. You're still suffering from shock. By tomorrow you'll feel a lot better and the swelling will have gone down.'

'What do I look like?' he asked Daisy.

'Like the Green Giant but red,' she teased, pulling a face. He managed a giggle.

'I'm going to clean you up again and give you a little something to help you sleep, all right?' The nurse gave him a drink with a straw for his swollen lips. 'He's in good hands,' she said to Daisy. 'Come back in the morning.'

Daisy reached over and kissed him lightly. 'Sleep well, Jonno. Everyone sends their love.'

The Colour Code

Chapter 20

Joining Forces

Later that night after supper, the Colour Code Gang returned to the girls' room minus Marc. They were anxious to see Yannish and were worried about Marc's absence.

'Where on earth is he?' Winna whispered as if the walls had ears. 'He's been away for hours.'

'I hope nothing's happened to him,' Al said. 'I told him not to do anything stupid. We don't know what we're dealing with.'

Daisy walked back and forth, listening to them, her imagination spinning out of control.

'Daisy, come and sit down.' Dan tried to calm her. 'Marc is one of those people who can move invisibly. He says he's faceless so no one sees him. He'll be fine and I don't think he'll take risks without one of us being there with him.'

'Yeah, I know that, Dan, but why's he so late?'

There was a knock at the door. Daisy opened it and was met by Yannish.

'How are you all?' he asked.

'Fine,' Daisy answered on their behalf.

Yannish nodded, looking at each one in turn. 'Where's Marc?'

'We're not sure,' she said looking at Dan. 'He likes to snoop around, but I'm sure he'll be here soon.'

Yannish sat down on one of the beds. 'I know why you are here.

Calidus informed me you were coming. That is why I have tried not to single any of you out. I am grateful for your help.' He smiled a beautiful, sweet smile. 'You have brought the Orange Ray in with you and already the effect is helping the students to come together.'

They looked at each other, amazed at what he had said. How on earth could that be? Yannish saw their astonished faces.

'Sometimes we do not know what we do, but it is within the intention and working together that brings results.'

'We believe in your work, Yannish,' Aloysius said. 'And it's a privilege to play in your orchestra.'

'You bet!' said Winna. Hiromi, Daisy and Dan slapped their hands together in agreement.

'Thank you,' he said modestly.

'What happened today?' asked Daisy.

His face became grave. 'There are energies working against us and this was the first demonstration to show us they mean business.'

'How did it happen?' Daisy persisted.

'There is no way that spiders could possibly have entered the trumpet. I checked it carefully. The mouthpiece is far too small,' Yannish said quietly.

'Could they have come through the other end, where the music comes out, and travelled up the tube part to the mouth piece?'

'That way many spiders would have suffocated. The bore of the instrument is too long and too thin. They would have never survived.' He finished, looking closely at Daisy. He didn't want to frighten her, or the others, but being sent by Calidus and Shakita must mean they were stronger than they knew.

'So what happened?' Dan urged him.

'I am sure it was some kind of Black Magic,' he said slowly, watching their reaction. They stared, mesmerised by his words.

'But why was Jonathan attacked?' Daisy asked. 'Was it random or was he the target?'

'I believe someone knows, or has guessed, you are here to help me. Yesterday, you all circulated amongst the students where there had been disagreements. It was noted.'

'But everyone mingles,' she protested.

'Your group is different. There are seven of you and there is - somehow - an aura around you. You get on with all the students.'

Daisy stared at the others. She knew for sure now she had not been mistaken in her feeling that things were not right.

'I think we knew,' she said slowly, looking at Dan. 'What do we do now?'

'We continue carefully. Check your instruments each day and make sure you don't leave them in the studio. Sorry, Dan, but I think it's best.' Dan's double bass was huge and difficult to move around. Dan nodded in agreement.

'No sweat,' he said.

'Stick together,' continued Yannish. 'If the other students come up to you, that's fine, but stay together. In that way you hold your power. If you separate you create more danger for yourselves.'

The door suddenly swung open and Marc almost fell in. His clothes were wet and muddy. He had scratches on his face and twigs in his hair. His face was pale and his glasses were missing. He gasped for breath, holding his sides.

'Phew, that was close,' he said, trying to smile. Then, suddenly seeing Yannish, he stopped.

'What's happened to you? Where have you been? We've been so worried about you, Marc.' Daisy got up to wrap a blanket around him.

'Sorry, Dais,' he said, shivering.

'Take your time, Marc,' Yannish said quietly.

Marc started slowly. 'Well, it all started when I saw Massoud's face after Jonathan blew his trumpet. He looked pleased, almost relieved. The next time I saw him was through the Art Studio window. He was leaving the academy, so I thought I should follow him.' He paused for a moment to make himself more comfortable. 'I followed him for ages at a distance. He never knew I was there. He went up the road, crossed the meadows and terraces and went down into the woods by the river. He nearly saw me once when he checked no one was looking, so I dived behind a tree. Then he almost disappeared. I couldn't find him anywhere. Then suddenly I heard him talking to someone.' They all leaned forward, not wanting to miss a word.

'I heard him telling someone about Jonathan and the spiders. He was laughing and so was the other person. It was a woman, I'm sure. The voice was light. Massoud told her how he poured the mixture she had given him down the trumpet and whispered the words she'd told him. She said, "Well done, my little servant. You did exactly right." I was so horrified I nearly gave myself away.' Marc shivered.

'She then told him she was stepping up the activity and it was his job to incite the students about superstitions and bad omens after what had happened and tell them more disasters would surely happen. She told him to frighten them. She whispered something to him but I couldn't quite hear, except I heard him say Oleander.

'Then I trod on a stick and they heard me so I had to run. I ran and ran, dodging around the trees and leaping over ditches, but they kept following me. Then I saw the river ahead so I quickly went in, keeping to the bank so they couldn't see me. I found a piece of bamboo. I remember seeing this in a film when a guy escaped his enemies by using it to breathe through under the water. It worked too,' he said triumphantly.

Daisy ruffled his hair. 'Wow, some story. You must never do that again, Marc. You could have got caught.'

'Yes.' Yannish agreed. 'You did a remarkably brave thing, Marc, but you put yourself in great danger. This is some evil force we're dealing with. You may not be so lucky next time.'

'The name Oleander is interesting,' Hiromi said. 'Do you know anyone by that name?'

Yannish thought for a moment. 'No,' he said. 'But there is a shrub called Oleander. We've have one here, by the fountain. We have one with red flowers, but you can get them in pink or white. The most important thing about them is that they are very poisonous. They are beautiful but deadly. Only a small amount is lethal.'

'What does that tell us about the woman talking to Massoud, then?' Winna asked, searching their faces.

'That she is deadly.' Yannish looked grave.

'Did you smell anything, Marc, or feel anything?' Daisy asked him.

'It's hard to say. There were so many smells from the trees and undergrowth, but there was something a bit like decaying matter, leaves or maybe a dead animal. I only noticed it when I began to run.'

'Why do you ask such a question?' Yannish turned to her.

Daisy repeated her story about how she found Massoud and the strange smell that lingered around him.

Yannish was silent for some time, thinking about all that was said. Finally he spoke to them. 'This is more serious than I realised. I don't want to place you in any danger. This is my responsibility.'

'Of course it is, but we're part of this now, by our own choice. Isn't that right?' Daisy asked, checking with the others.

'Yes, it is.' Dan spoke for the rest. They were in this together, to the end.

'We've had some experience of tough times,' Winna said. 'And we are all the stronger for it. That is why Calidus sent us on this project, so we're here to stay.'

'Well said.' Aloysius echoed.

Yannish bowed his head, truly touched by these brave young teenagers.

'I thank you deeply. We must pool our knowledge and meet when needed.'

'Where's Shakita?' Hiromi asked. 'Isn't it about time she appeared?'

'She is close by and is fully aware of everything. She will reveal herself soon, I think.'

'Hey, Marc,' said Daisy, searching his face. 'Where are your glasses?'

'I lost them either in the woods or in the river,' he moaned. 'How am I going to read the music?'

'We'll find some others,' Yannish told him. 'Now we must get you back to your room. I will arrange for some food to be sent to you. Goodnight, my friends and may the Light protect you.'

Walking back through the corridor, he saw Josefina. He asked her to find some food for Marc. She answered him in Spanish.

'Gracias, Josefina,' he said, bowing to her.

'Buenasa noches, Maestro,' she smiled, flashing the gold fillings in her teeth, of which she was very proud.

Chapter 21

Who is Oleander?

The Colour Code Gang met early in the morning to again make their link with the Orange Ray. Although they were not aware of it, the colour rays that each one represented added to their energy and power as a whole. Daisy, with a fine Violet Ray, created the purpose to succeed. Winna, with the Red Ray, provided the foundation and the driving physical force. Hiromi, with the Indigo, brought insight and perception. Marc, as the Blue Ray, was the seeker for truth. Dan with the harmonious Green Ray created balance and love. Aloysius was like the heat of the sun with the Orange Ray. He represented expansion and creativity. Jonathan, although he wasn't physically there, brought in clarity and wisdom as the Yellow Ray.

Calidus could see the wondrous spectrum of colours circulating around them like a beautiful rainbow. He was right to choose them. They were true and brave.

'Do you think the name Oleander is the real name of the woman you heard talking to Massoud, Marc?' Hiromi asked.

'I don't know,' Marc replied. 'I think it's probably a code name.'

'That means that she's probably someone here.' Hiromi held her breath as she searched Daisy's face. Daisy looked back, dismayed.

'So, who have we got?' she whispered.

'Francesca, Ronnie...' Winna began counting on her fingers.

'What about Isobel, the receptionist? We hardly see her. She'd have plenty of time to act against us,' said Daisy.

'I like her,' Dan replied.

'It doesn't really matter if you like her or not, Dan.' Daisy reasoned. 'They may all be nice to our face, but horrible inside.'

'Okay, so what about Collette?' He retaliated.

'No, she's fine,' argued Aloysius shaking his head. 'I am sure she's above this sort of thing. Look how she invited us to tea and everything.'

'Exactly,' replied Marc meaningfully.

'What do mean, exactly?' Aloysius challenged, irritated.

'We know how you fancy her, Al, but her being nice might be a cover to find out why we are here,' said Marc, eyeing him with a piercing look.

Aloysius was furious. 'It's not her, I know she's okay,' he said, raising his voice.

'Steady, Al.' Hiromi tried to calm him down. 'But she did ask a lot of questions.'

Aloysius glared her.

'We haven't even mentioned the old bird Josefina,' Winna said, smirking. 'She's weird and bad tempered.'

'She's too slow and too old,' Hiromi remarked, discounting her. 'But she does hang about the corridors a lot. She's just a nosy old bag.'

'Well, that's just the thing, isn't it?' Daisy snapped. 'We just don't know. I would be surprised if Oleander was either Ronnie or Francesca, but we don't know. There's no one to help us. We'll just have to be careful of all of them.'

'Okay, to sum it up,' said Dan. 'Oleander could be anyone here. Incidentally, she could be one of the students too?'

'Oh no, Dan. That is makes it impossible.' Daisy groaned.

'No, it doesn't, Dais,' Dan continued. 'We now know, thanks to Marc, that Massoud is the servant to a woman, which we didn't know before. So we'll have to be very careful of all the women here.'

'I don't think it's a student,' Marc said thoughtfully. 'Oleander had too much authority and he's frightened of her.'

Daisy nodded, remembering Massoud's face when she found him.

'I think you're right. So that narrows the field. I think we should talk to Yannish, but until then let's keep close and not accept any invitations,' she said markedly to Al.

'Thanks a bunch,' he replied bitterly. 'So what do I say when Collette asks me to play on her piano?'

'I don't know.' Daisy looked at him. 'Lie! I've got to go and see

Jonno…'

***

Daisy ran to the sick bay, taking in fresh clothes for Jonathan. He was up, hungrily tucking into breakfast.

'You look better,' she said, noticing that the swelling had gone down. His lips were back to normal, though a little scarred. His eyes were no longer puffy, but still slightly red around the rims. His nose was sore around his nostrils. The nurse had washed his hair so that the curls had sprung back to life. She checked his hands, seeing they were also much better. The scars would take time to heal, but his mood was bright. He waved to his sister.

'I need to get out of here.'

She laughed, giving him his clothes. The nurse came in to take his tray away.

'Well, doesn't he look better?' she asked. 'He can go now, but if you feel any adverse reaction, Jonathan, you come straight back. Right?'

'You've got it, Nursie,' Jonno replied cheekily.

***

All the students surrounded him, delighted to find that he was all right. 'It wasn't the same without you man,' Eli Beke said. Felippe, the French horn player, came to greet him and Ariel hugged him, saying how pleased they were he was better.

Aloysius, Marc and Dan waited for all the students to finish their greetings then, joined by the girls, embraced him. Jonathan noticed Marc looked a bit odd with scratches on his face.

'Been in a fight, Marco?' he giggled. 'You look worse than me!'

'Had a fight with a wild cat.' Marc smirked. 'It's cool. How are you feeling, Jonno?'

'Great, really. It's odd.' He lowered his voice so only his friends could hear. 'I thought I would feel much worse about the spiders, but I had this weird dream that Shakita came into the sick bay and talked to me. Whatever it was has done the trick. I feel fine. Imagine me dreaming about the beautiful Shakita. No wonder I feel better!'

'That is the most awesome thing I've ever heard!' Aloysius gaped at him.

Daisy and Hiromi looked at each other, remembering what

Yannish had said. Shakita knew exactly what was going on and, even though she wasn't ready to show herself, she had visited Jonno. Daisy breathed her thanks.

Professor Sanandez and all the tutors came in to the dining room to greet the students. As it was the weekend, the professor had decided it would be a good idea for all of them to visit the surrounding area and local towns. It was at the request of one of the students. He suggested it might be a good idea to clear away any shadow that the spider incident had left in their minds, particularly any unwanted superstitions.

Professor Sanandez thought this was a brilliant idea and agreed instantly. Some of them would love the idea, while others might prefer to do something different.

'Who would like to go on a trip today to see the countryside and visit some of the historic towns?' he asked. 'Tomorrow you can do whatever you want, practise your playing, dance or paint.' He smiled encouragingly.

About half of the students showed interest in visiting local towns. The others preferred to stay at the academy.

'Very well, I will order a coach to take you on a tour,' he told them.

Some of the students shouted their approval. It would be brilliant to escape and just have fun without being regimented. They loved the orchestra but it was hard work. Concentration was a priority.

Jonathan was relieved. There was no way he could play. His lips were still too raw. Two days would make all the difference in the healing process. The day out would also give them the opportunity to get to know each other in a relaxed way. Some of the staff wanted to join them. Francesca and Hamish from the art team came, with Frank and Ronnie from the dancing team.

Aloysius saw Josefina standing a little distance away. She beckoned to him to come. Leaving the others, he went over to her.

'Is everything alright?' he asked her in Spanish. From behind her back she produced a pair of spectacles.

'Theese for Marc. Me.' She pointed at herself. 'Encontraron en el bosque.' She placed her fingers on her lips and was gone.

Aloysius stared at her retreating figure before going off to find his friends. He kept the glasses in his pocket. The boys went back to their room to collect whatever they needed for the day. He gave Marc his glasses.

'Where did you find these, Al?'

'I didn't. Josefina gave them to me a few minutes ago.'

'But where did she find them?'

'She said she found them in the forest.' Al answered.

'Josefina found them? 'What! That old bird? How on earth could she have possibly found them amongst all that undergrowth? It's like a jungle in there and its miles away.' Marc stared at Aloysius.

'Oh, she can move all right and she is a native of this area. She's probably lived here all her life.'

Dan leaned over, looking at the glasses. 'Are you sure that these are yours, Marc?'

'Yeah, they're mine all right. I stuck a bit of plaster on one of the frames. This is fantastic. I never thought I'd ever see them again. What a relief. Now I'll be able to read the music. I must go and thank her. Where did she go?'

'Steady on, Marc. I don't think she wants anyone to know she found them. When she gave them to me, she put her finger on her lips to keep it a secret.'

'How weird.' Marc looked at Dan and Al. 'I suppose we must do as she says.'

As soon as he placed his glasses on, life became much more comfortable for him. His confidence returned. 'That's better,' he sighed. 'I felt lost without them.'

The boys rejoined the girls and headed outside to the waiting bus. There was an air of excitement as the students climbed aboard.

 *Chapter 22*

Time Out

Yannish chose to join the students. He felt if he were there, there would be less danger for the Colour Code Gang. However, he kept his distance, choosing to sit amongst the Russians and Italians.

Daisy and her friends stayed at the back of the bus. Chelsea sat next to Felippe Tonisoni, chatting happily. Seeing Jonathan, she excused herself to Felippe for a moment. She wanted to see how Jonathan was and to thank him for being the peacemaker when she'd argued with Ariel. She also thought he was cute, especially with his scars. She whispered her thanks, squeezed his knee and dashed back to her seat.

The driver was also a travel guide. He was able to tell them about all the interesting places around the area. Their first stop would be at Caceres, famous for its many historic monuments, including Roman foundations. The guide told them there was a long avenue called the Plaza Major which was the cultural centre of the town. There they would find dancing and singing and guitar playing as people sat outside the local cafés.

'That's more like it.' Aloysius grinned. Everyone agreed with a sigh of relief. They just wanted to hang out and see a bit of Spanish life.

Aloysius had brought his saxophone with him and softly began to play a little jazz. Ronnie, the dance tutor, began to sing in a deep throaty voice. Eli Beke banged on the frame of the seat in front of him to the beat of the music.

'This is wicked,' shouted Louis Capello. 'We have ourselves a jazz band.'

Aloysius quickly looked at Yannish. He didn't want to offend him.

'Go ahead, guys, this is excellent. Perhaps we can use it in our concert. You may practise tomorrow in your own free time, but now entertain us.'

Teachers and students tapped to the rhythm on whatever they could find.

Aloysius was in his element. Dan and Jonathan looked at him with admiration, longing to be part of it. Jonathan forgot his sore mouth and pretended to play his trumpet. Dan plucked his imaginary double bass and Marc beat his imaginary drums.

All the students joined in. Daisy watched as each one forgot their differences, shouting their appreciation of the music. She watched Ronnie, the dance tutor, enjoying every moment as she sang. She couldn't possibly be involved with Massoud, could she? she wondered to herself.

Massoud was there and he didn't seem the least frightened of her as far as she could see, unless she wore a disguise. Francesca and Hamish were having a marvellous time, too.

She turned her head to see Yannish looking at her. He smiled softly to show he understood her concern.

They reached Caceres unaware of the length of time. Their love of music made time pass quickly.

The town was large with huge Moorish walls. They were an ancient reminder of the time of the great Arab civilization of Spain with its beautiful art, music and scholarship. This was an old Renaissance town where art and literature had been revived and developed from the fourteenth to sixteenth centuries. In the old town, up a grand flight of stairs, stood the magnificent cathedral, the Concatedral de Santa Maria, built in Romanesque and early Gothic style in the fifteenth century. Another impressive church, the guide told them, was called Iglesia de Santiago which founded the first knightly order of Spain.

There was a buzz to the place. With the bus parked, they walked through the narrow cobbled streets to the main avenue, the Plaza Major. It was market day with sellers shouting their wares, bargaining and exchanging money. Fresh vegetables and fruits were for sale. Clothes, hats and coloured materials hung for all to see. Ceramic pots and plates lay on the ground as people passed by. Earthenware dishes were stacked in piles and boxes of flowers lay like a carpet of brilliant jewels.

Cafés were busy where people sat viewing the scene while they paused for light refreshment between shopping. Many of the students wanted to discover the delights of the market or just to move around by themselves. They agreed to meet the others at a later time. Francesca and Ronnie happily tagged along.

'Come,' Yannish said to the remainder as he directed them to a café where a young guitarist sat playing. He played softly, unaware of the people chatting among themselves. His interest was only for his music. Occasionally passersby dropped a few coins into his hat, which he acknowledged with a nod of his head.

Yannish sat down at a table close to the pavement, where they could be part of the activity of the town without being drawn in. All the students wanted to sit with Yannish. He was their inspiration, opening their minds to new ideas.

Some of them were still uncertain in their approach to those who were officially their enemies, but here, far away from fighting, destruction and the constant opinion of others, there was a growing curiosity about people of their own age and a sense of relief that, for now at least, the shadow of war was lifted and they could just be ordinary students. There was life apart from politics where they could just be themselves; young people who shared so much more and wanted a new way to live.

They chatted and laughed about anything and everything, with Hamish and Frank joining in their pleasure.

Daisy wished Shakita could see them. Perhaps she could,' she thought. Maybe Calidus was watching also? If this was so, perhaps Oleander was there too! She shivered slightly.

'Are you cold, Daisy?' Hiromi asked.

'Not really,' Daisy answered quietly. 'Just thinking. It all looks so great here, away from the academy, but Oleander may be here too, or she might be with the others at this very moment.'

Hiromi looked at her friend. 'Maybe, but I have a feeling she's more interested in where Yannish is and our group.'

'Maybe.' Daisy nodded. 'Have you seen Massoud?'

'Yes. He's sitting with the group on Yannish's table and seems to be enjoying himself.'

'Whatever he's doing for Oleander, it's because he's being forced to. Look at him now. He loves being part of the group.' Daisy watched him closely. 'Trouble is, she controls him so we mustn't be too sympathetic towards him. He's dangerous. He almost killed Jonno.'

Massoud looked up, sensing someone watching him. Their eyes met. He showed no fear as he looked directly at her. No sense of recognition that she knew part of his secret. His eyes were quite clear and determined, as though he was warning her there was more to come and that he would do whatever he was ordered to do.

Daisy sipped her drink. She'd got the message.

'Come on, Dais,' Jonathan teased his sister. 'Lighten up. Don't let them see we're bothered, whoever they are.'

Daisy suddenly realised he was right again. He always had this knack of making sense of problems, of being reasonable, while she always got so emotionally involved.

'You've got it, Jonno. We're the Colour Code Gang.' She laughed with relief, clinking her bottle of coke with his.

They stayed at the café, enjoying their freedom telling stories, teasing each other and sharing jokes, until the others came back with Ronnie and Francesca. Chelsea strolled towards them in her latest hat which was in a sombrero style, pulled low over her eyes, that gave her a mysterious look. She grinned at Yannish. He bowed and the other students howled with whoops of admiration.

'There she goes again,' Winna said, smirking.

'You're only jealous,' Jonathan said, joining in the cat calls for Chelsea. 'She's gorgeous.'

'I am not jealous,' argued Winna hotly. 'I just think she's a bit of an airhead.'

'Well, she is, but who cares when she looks like that!' he sighed.

'Anyway,' Winna said nastily. 'She's not interested in you. Felippe Tonisoni is her latest conquest.'

'True,' Jonathan sighed again. 'But she was concerned about my face, and she did squeeze my knee.'

Winna fell about laughing. 'Come on, Jonno. I fancy Eli Beke, but he's not interested in me either.'

Daisy linked her arm through Winna's. 'Chels is okay, really. I think she's a lot cleverer than she let's on.'

'Interesting,' Hiromi murmured, studying Daisy's face. 'I wonder if she could be...'

'No way!' Jonathan blazed at her.

'Well, we've got to consider everyone,' she replied calmly.

'No, Chelsea was with us painting when Marc followed Massoud.

And she was there at supper,' Daisy pointed out.

'You see.' Jonathan glared at Hiromi.

Whoa!' Hiromi put her hands up at the sudden attack. 'Just checking, that's all. My mistake.'

Yannish gathered all his students together to return to the bus and the academy.

The day had been great. They had all enjoyed hanging out together and being able to spend time with their tutors in a relaxed way. Ronnie had a gorgeous voice. She told them she had sung in night clubs as a student to earn a little money. Francesca had earned her extras for her training as an artist by painting houses, pet dogs and cats. Hamish made them laugh with his wicked humour about his life as a boy growing up in Scotland.

Frank didn't talk so much. His energy was more in movement so he listened to the others, content just to be there.

The ride home was even more rowdy than before. Everyone joined in with Aloysius's melodious playing. Ronnie, then Hamish, sang. Jovan joined in and so did Ishmael. In the end it was a free for all with all the students fooling about, wanting to be heard.

Marc watched Massoud, who remained in his seat next to Kyan Kahn. He looked puzzled, unsure, anxious - not as confident as he was in the café. He slunk back in his seat, unnerved by the evidence before his eyes that Yannish's plan to bring all the students together was beginning to work, despite all his efforts. He shuddered within himself. He would have to start all over again or Oleander would destroy him. He sighed visibly. Would it never end?

Marc signalled Daisy in his mind to look his way. She picked up his thought immediately amid the laughing and singing. Marc motioned to Massoud with a flicker of his eyes. Daisy saw a fear within Massoud she had seen before. She realised the pressure he must be under and knew they must prepare themselves for another attack.

 *Chapter 23*

Destructive Forces

They arrived back to chaos. Blinding acrid smoke filled the air like a dark ominous cloud, spewing out its lethal toxins. It looked like a war zone with fire engines and police cars stationed outside the main entrance of the academy. The reception area of the main building and dining room were guttered. Two fire engines had forced the entrance to get closer to the fire, knocking down the stone wall and iron gates. One hung on a single hinge, forced out of its socket. The other gate lay twisted on the ground.

A Police Inspector came to meet Yannish. He told him there had been an explosion and that some of the students and staff had been hurt as they ate lunch.

Yannish tried to suppress his growing panic as he attempted to push past the policeman.

'Where is Professor Sanandez?' he asked, dreading the answer.

'He's been injured, but not fatally,' replied the inspector. 'He is badly burned as he tried to rescue the students. One of your tutors, Mademoiselle du Bois, was also hurt but her injuries are less serious.'

'I must go to my friend.' Yannish demanded, pale faced but determined.

'He has been taken to the hospital at Trujillo, Senor, along with some of your students.'

'Why didn't someone phone me?' he shouted at the policeman. 'This is too much. We could have helped.' He was overwhelmed by feelings of shock and guilt. He had been enjoying himself while his friend had been fighting to save the lives of his students. He might even die.

'What about the staff?' he asked again.

'I am afraid we cannot find one of the older members.'

'Josefina?' asked Yannish. The Inspector looked down his list.

'Yes, Josefina, that is the name,' he said. 'And there is another woman called Isobel Arnez.'

'Isobel,' gasped Dan who was standing behind Yannish.

'Yes, we haven't been able to find her. There has been so much damage. It will take time, Senor.'

'Has anyone been killed?' Yannish forced the words out.

'Not as far as we know, Senor. There are two students who are seriously injured. A boy and one girl. They were close to the incendiary when it went off. They suffered bad cuts, burns and smoke inhalation. The ambulance has taken them to hospital, together with eight others to be checked over. I would suggest you take a roll-call, Doctor Kablinski, so we can see who is missing.'

Yannish nodded his head as though in a trance. 'I must go and see the rest of the students first to make sure they are all right.' He turned to the Inspector. 'How could this have happened?'

'I do not know, Doctor. It was no accident. We will know more later, from the Fire Chief. Meanwhile, your students are in the music room waiting for you. I have warned them not to attempt to go anywhere near the main building as it is unsafe and any wrong move might cause more damage.'

When Yannish opened the Music Room door, he was confronted by a sight of injured and frightened students. They were covered with the effects of black smoke. The smell was heavy in the air. Coughing and spluttering echoed round the room as they tried to clear their lungs. Many of them had been treated for bruises and lacerations from shards of glass and debris.

Sylvie, the nurse, was tending to them, cleaning their faces and ministering to their superficial wounds. None of them were too serious, thankfully. Most had torn clothes and scratched faces. All of them were deeply shocked. They were lucky to be alive.

Collette du Bois had come in to help when she'd heard the explosion. She had also been injured though not seriously. Her face and hands were cut. Her once impeccable blonde hair was black and straggled. Now she was doing her best to calm them. Seeing

Yannish, she almost cried with relief.

'I am so happy to see you, Maestro.'

'Why didn't you call me?' he asked her sharply, ignoring her dishevelled state.

Collette waved her hands in the air. 'Well, you know, everything happened so quickly. I must have been disoriented. There was so much to do. I went to help as soon as I could.'

He nodded then went to each student in turn, inquiring if they were all right. Some of the girls were sobbing. Daisy and Hiromi went to comfort them. Winna and the boys went to those who had been injured to give moral support.

'Let's visualise the Orange Ray around them,' Daisy whispered. 'I'm sure it will help. Remember how Yannish told us the effect it created the other night.'

'Yeah, good one, Dais.' Dan agreed. 'Let's put it into action.'

The other students from the bus followed to be with their new friends.

'What happened?' Yannish asked a student.

Yoshi Atari raised his head. 'I don't know. We were eating our lunch and chatting together. Fortunately, most of us sat at the far table by the kitchen, away from the entrance. Whatever it was exploded around two o'clock, when we were just about to leave. It came from the entrance nearest the reception. I said something to Hannah Zimmerman and Ariel as they got up from the table to go out and then it happened. The ambulance people said they could have been killed if they hadn't dived under the table in front of them.' He sobbed into his grimy hands.

'I see.' Yannish looked at his poor students, suffering from the terrible trauma of having seen their friends almost killed.

'Professor Sanandez came in and attempted to put out the fire. He tried his best to get us all out. I don't know where he is now,' Yoshi said, sighing.

'He was badly burned,' Yannish said. 'I am going to see him soon, and the others who were injured. Fortunately, Mademoiselle du Bois came to help you too. She will stay with you while I go to the hospital.'

'Of course,' Collette said. 'I will not leave our poor ones.'

'This was an accident.' Yannish told the students to calm their fears. But he knew it wasn't. 'It was a stupid accident and we will make sure you are cared for. The shock is great, I know. Wait here until I return and it is safe to go to your rooms.'

The students nodded at his instructions. They had little energy to do anything else except to lie or sit down.

Before Yannish left, he spoke to the Fire Chief and the Chief Inspector of Police. The fire crew had been sifting among the rubble in what was once the academy reception area and part of the dining room.

'It is too early to say much about the incident, Doctor, but we know there was an incendiary device which was intended to do as much damage as possible. We have cordoned off this area. The kitchens are all right and the private area for sleeping is clear. We will be here for several hours to make absolutely sure everything is safe.'

'Thank you, Chief,' replied Yannish. 'By the way, Chief Inspector, who called you?'

'I don't know,' the Chief replied. 'But it was only a few minutes after the explosion. In the meantime, we have interviewed all the students and staff as to their whereabouts, including gardeners and casual staff. As I mentioned, there are still two members of staff missing.'

'It was a Saturday, so I don't think the receptionist was there.'

'Even so, Doctor, we must check everyone's movements.'

'Thank you, Inspector. I would now like to go to the hospital.'

The Inspector told him he would still be there when Yannish returned to the academy.

With a heavy heart, Yannish went to find his car. He noticed the fountain had been demolished as a result of the fire engines forcing their way in. Several terracotta pots were also strewn about the ground. Their flowers were scattered around, discarded and forlorn, when once they had been so proud and beautiful. Was this an omen? he thought.

At the hospital, he was taken to Professor Sanandez's room. He found him unconscious; his head and face were swathed in bandages, as was most of his body.

Nurses were by his side adjusting drips in his arm. A doctor came in. He looked at Yannish gravely.

'He is a very brave man, Senor. He managed to get the two worst injured out before they were asphyxiated. He saved their lives. They have no broken bones but suffered cuts, burns and severe smoke inhalation. Others, too, are injured and we will keep our eye on them overnight.'

'Will he live?' Yannish looked at his friend.

'The next twenty-four hours are the most critical, but he is a strong man, so who knows?' said the doctor philosophically.

'How are the other students? May I see them?'

'Of course,' the doctor replied, opening the door. Come.' He gave further instructions to the nurse about checking the Professor's vital statistics before leaving.

In a separate room lay both Hannah Zimmermann and Ariel. They looked very frail. Ariel had suffered smoke inhalation and burns to his body. Hannah's right arm was badly cut as she had tried to shield her face. Her body had also been lacerated by flying glass, as the main windows of the dining room had burst in the explosion. It had been a painful ordeal for her as the nurses picked out fragments of glass and gently removed burnt clothing. She was sleeping with the relief of pain killers.

Ariel was awake. Breathing came in gasps. An oxygen mask covered his nose. He smiled weakly as he struggled for breath. Yannish sat down beside his bed and held his hand.

'I am so very sorry.'

'We are used to violence in my country, Maestro,' said Ariel, struggling to speak.

'But not in mine. You are in my care, Ariel. Please do not try to talk.'

'Do you know what happened?' Ariel rasped, ignoring his teacher.

'I haven't had the report yet from the Fire Chief, but I think it was an accident.'

'I do not think so, Maestro,' Ariel whispered. 'There is something else going on.'

Yannish looked at him keenly. 'Why do you say that?'

'A lot of strange things happening lately - in some areas, gossiping as though someone doesn't want you to succeed in bringing us all together.'

Ariel lay back on his pillow, exhausted with the effort. Yannish was astounded. He had to decide now whether to be honest with Ariel and admit he was right or to bluff it out. He decided the boy deserved the truth.

'You are right. Would you like to go home to your family and forget the project?'

'No way,' said Ariel wheezing. 'I'm going to stay here and encourage the others to do the same.'

Yannish saw the gleam of determination in Ariel's eyes.

'I can still play, Maestro. I will be better by the time we give the concert.'

Yannish laughed and kissed his battered face. 'So you will, my son.'

He turned his attention to Hannah. 'Hopefully, she will be able to play too. I must visit the others, Ariel, but I will see you tomorrow. Keep these thoughts to yourself for the time being. It is safer.'

As he spoke, Ariel closed his eyes in sleep.

The eight other students greeted him warmly. None of them were seriously injured, as they had been some distance from the explosion, but there were cuts and burns along with the smoke inhalation, which was the worst part. The nurse told them they could return to the academy in the morning.

Yannish spent time talking with each student and reassuring them that the project would carry on.

'In the meantime, you must rest and get well,' he said to them.

Driving back he thought about the evil energy behind the attack. Whoever was controlling the events did not care who got killed, as long as they prevented the academy from fulfilling its dream of bringing nations together. Evil and destruction was their business.

He must link with Calidus and the University of Light. He must also talk to Shakita. She must have more information. Inwardly he asked for protection for all his students and for his beloved friend, Carlos Sanandez. He prayed the professor would recover.

Back at the academy, he went straight to the Fire Chief. The chief had streaks of dirt across his face. The fire fighters had been there for hours.

'Is the building safe now?' Yannish asked.

'Yes Doctor, it is safe now, but we would suggest the students and staff approach the building from the back entrance. The main entrance is closed. It has been demolished anyway.'

'Do we know yet what caused the fire?'

'It is a very strange situation, unlike anything I have encountered. There was some kind of combustion but there is no evidence to show what it could have been. It wasn't a gas leak because it was the other side from the kitchen. There were no pipes or any connecting link that could have ignited this fire. No electric devices. No store room. Nothing. I am completely at a loss as to how it started.' He shook his head, puzzled.

'Was there a log fire in the reception area? Sometimes we light it on a cold day.'

'No, Doctor. There was no sign a fire had been lit. It'd been a hot day.'

Yannish looked at the chief sternly. 'What is your opinion, Chief?'

The Fire Chief lowered his voice. 'Unofficially, it was predetermined. Someone meant to harm your students. Whoever it was, expected them to sit at the nearest tables so there would be more damage and loss of life.'

Yannish gasped. 'But what started it, Chief?'

'Forgive me for saying this, Doctor, because I am a practical man. But this was almost supernatural.' He looked embarrassed.

Yannish said gravely, 'Did you detect a smell?'

'Well, now you mention it, there was a strange smell of something decayed but that was probably the smoke. Toxins are deadly in fires.'

'Thank you, Chief, you have been most helpful in all your duties. What will be the official conclusion?'

The Fire Chief looked at him sceptically. 'Accident, by unknown causes.'

Yannish nodded his head and shook his hand, then walked away.

The Inspector of Police confirmed the verdict. Yannish wondered if he actually believed it, but the Inspector face remained passive.

'How is the Professor?' he asked.

'Not good,' Yannish replied. 'The two students who have been badly cut and burned will have to stay in hospital a while longer. The others will be back tomorrow.'

'They have been very lucky. It's a miracle no one was killed.' He looked at Yannish. 'A nasty business. Will this mean they will all go home now?'

Yannish regarded him carefully. 'No, Inspector. This incident has made them all the more determined to go on.' He thought of Ariel's words.

'I see,' the Inspector said. 'They have great faith in you, I think.' He touched his cap and, as he went towards his car, he turned back. 'Be careful. If you have any more trouble or suspect anything unusual, call me.'

Yannish and the other tutors went back to the music room to find Daisy and the Colour Code Gang had completely taken over the students. They'd become the recovery team. Collette du Bois sat to one side, allowing them to take control.

The students were much calmer. Winna and Hiromi had decided

to arrange food for everyone. Francesca and Ronnie went to the kitchen with them. They were allowed back into the kitchen via the tradesmen entrance to make sandwiches from anything they could find in the fridge. They also found fresh soup prepared for the evening meal. The kitchen staff had cleared up and left after lunch. They'd probably been told by the police to leave and go home after everyone had been accounted for.

Making sandwiches for fifty people was no mean task, so Winna called Daisy on her mobile for reinforcements. Eli and Jonathan came to help with some of the more able- bodied students.

'Come on, guys, let's zing a little Rap. Get this show on the road,' Eli sang, swinging his hips. 'Let's set it up.'

They all fell into a hip hop dance as they made enough sand-wiches for everyone, stacking them on trays, finding bowls for soup, or mugs for those who might find it difficult to use a spoon. They used anything they could lay their hands on.

'Okay, guys, let's move.' Winna led the parade in single file, out of the back door towards the Music Room. They were greeted with shouts of applause from a bunch of very hungry people.

Hamish sat in the middle, telling them more stories about Scotland. He swore they were all true, but Daisy knew he was just bluffing. It didn't matter. He created a wonderful atmosphere that held the students fascinated.

She noticed Collette was quiet, as though she hardly heard the story. Perhaps she didn't understand the Scot's language or humour. She had tried her best to help the students and was most likely feeling exhausted. Finally, when Hamish finished his story, she stood up and told the students that as soon as they had finished their supper they should go to bed.

'I have to resume the Professor's duties now,' she said.

'Before you go,' Yannish said to the students. 'We need to clarify where we are after this terrible accident. We wanted to give you an opportunity to come together to enjoy different forms of expression. This accident may have changed your minds. You may feel unsafe here, so if anyone wants to return home you have my permission to go. Your money will be refunded, of course. I know Professor Sanandez would say the same.'

Daisy watched him address everyone. They all looked at him and then at each other in silence. Kyan Kahn stood up.

'I told you in class that I hated the noise of violence, but this academy has shown me such kindness and understanding. I believe in your ideal, that there is a better way to live, so I will stay.'

Dan and Jonathan whooped with joy. Aloysius blew a few notes on his saxophone. The room erupted with shrieks of 'Yes!' and 'Go for it!'

Daisy laughed with all of them, clasping hands that waved in the air.

'Thank you, my friends, on behalf of Carlos Sanandez and all our tutors. Now you may go to bed.'

Collette followed them with a smile to Yannish.

Yannish leaned over to Daisy. 'We must have a meeting in your room.'

Daisy nodded, then winked at her friends as she left.

The Colour Code

Chapter 24

Post Mortem of Events

As they filed out of the Music Room, they gazed in dismay at the devastation of the main entrance. Before the fire, there had been a beautiful wooden door hewn out of Spanish oak. Now, it lay in burnt ashes. The surrounding stone was intact from the outside but heavily blistered. The inside would be another story.

Black soot and heavy intoxicating smoke still hung around the building. Flowers that had once wound their way around the door were scorched and shrivelled. It was a sad sight for the students and for those who lived there, but the damage was limited and, with the help of local people, the place would be rebuilt.

After saying good night to everyone, Daisy and the Colour Code Gang returned to the girls' room to wait for Yannish.

They all felt very different from the carefree teenagers who had started out on their trip a few hours ago. Was it only this morning? It felt like a lifetime ago.

A single knock on the door brought their music tutor in, quietly closing the door behind him.

'You did a good job tonight, seeing to the students' needs,' he said, sitting wearily down on a chair.

'That was easy. We weren't the injured ones,' Daisy replied.

'Will Professor Sanandez be alright?' Dan asked.

Yannish sighed. 'It is too early to say. The doctor told me the next twenty-four hours were critical.'

'Was it an accident?' Marc looked directly at Yannish.

'No, it was not. There was evil intent behind this action. If the students had been sitting at the first two tables, instead of the last two, there would have been loss of life.'

'Do you think that Oleander thought they would sit closer to the entrance?'

'Yes, I do, Daisy. I am sure Shakita had something to do with that.'

'You mean somehow she changed what happened?'

He nodded his head.

'Why couldn't she stop it, then?' Winna challenged him.

'You must know that Light Servers are not allowed to intervene in any human action, but they may influence the situation where possible.'

'How very interesting,' said Marc. 'That's how I got my glasses back.' He smiled at the others, delighted at his good sense of deduction.

'Just think,' said Hiromi, 'We all went off happily for our day out, so we were out of the way, while Oleander was planning to kill the others.'

'No wonder Massoud was looking pleased with himself,' Daisy said bitterly. Then it suddenly dawned on her. His job was to get us out of the way.

'That explains at lot.' Yannish hit his fist in his hand. 'Now I remember. Carlos told me one of the students had suggested an outing to clear our minds from the spider incident. Carlos thought it was a great idea. We all did. It must have been Massoud.'

'At least we know now that Francesca and Ronnie aren't involved,' Jonathan pointed out reasonably.

'Maybe, Jonno, but how can we be sure? How long would it take to set up the fire, Yannish?'

'I am sure black magic was used, so it may not have taken long. Immediate, I would say.'

'Well, that rules out Francesca and Ronnie because they weren't there.' Jonathan stressed, looking at his sister.

'Not necessarily.' Marc argued. 'You said black magic must have been used. One of them could have used mind control.'

Jonathan shrugged irritably. 'You're certainly taking your detective role seriously, Marc.'

Ignoring him, he continued. 'That leaves us with Josefina, Isobel and Collette.'

'It's interesting Josefina and Isobel are missing,' Hiromi stressed.

'Collette helped to get the students out, which puts her in the clear, I think.'

'Unless she's very clever,' Marc said dryly. 'Sorry, but we've got to look at every possibility. It still could have been any of them.' He looked at them all in turn.

'Marc is right,' said Dan. 'We just don't know. Each of them had an alibi except Josefina and Isobel.'

'The kitchen staff were cooking lunch and were told to go home after the fire, so they're in the clear.' Daisy reasoned. They nodded their heads in agreement. 'Do you know where Josefina is, Yannish?'

'No, I do not,' he replied carefully. 'I believe Isobel was given permission to go to see her sister, so she wasn't even there. I am sure she has nothing to do with all of this.'

'So who do you think is?' Dan asked quietly. 'You are one of the Light Servers, so you must have some idea.'

Yannish sighed a deep sigh. 'I do have my suspicions but I cannot say at his moment. My telling you would not only endanger your lives, but Shakita's as well.'

'But we're all in danger anyway, Yannish. Some of our friends nearly got killed,' Hiromi protested. Daisy touched her hand.

'Are you afraid that if we knew, we might somehow let it slip, or she would know intuitively?' she asked.

'Yes. You cannot control your thoughts yet, so I am sure Oleander will be able to tune into them, even without you knowing. Please trust me on this.'

They all gaped at him, trying to understand what he had just told them. They knew the situation was serious. The events of the day had proved that dramatically, but somehow they were so caught up in Yannish's beautiful ideal to bring nations together they weren't prepared for the evil that was devastating their lives.

'This is what I want you to do,' said Yannish. 'Oleander's plan to frighten the students enough to leave the academy has backfired. I want you to continue your work with the Orange Ray by bringing peace and balance back amongst the students. The whole plan depends on this, otherwise we'll never make the concert.'

From out of his pocket he produced seven pieces of hexagonal gemstones, each set in a carnelian tube which tapered towards a point of about five inches long.

'Shakita sent one for each of you. They are called gemrays.' Holding one up, he turned it gently in his fingers so they could see how the light shone on one side and, as he turned it again, the darker colours flooded in.

'Shakita told me the energy of orange moves quickly from light to dark.' He continued, 'In effect, orange holds the balance between these two energies, a bit like a seesaw. Whenever the atmosphere is concentrated and heavy, turn the wand to the light. In this way, the energy becomes lighter and harmony is restored. This is why it is so important when we are dealing with so much darkness. It prevents the evil intent from affecting the students. Let this be your contribution. Remember, these are powerful magical tools which can change the environment. You work with the students. Shakita will deal with the rest and will instruct you how to use them.'

The gemrays felt warm in their hands, comforting and strong.

'Now I must go. Keep the gemrays safe in your pockets. Use them only when necessary to change the energy when it gets too negative, but be careful not to let anyone see them. Keep strong, my friends.'

So saying, he left with an encouraging smile.

'That's interesting,' Jonathan remarked. 'I like the lighter side of orange best because it's more yellow.'

'I like the deeper colours.' Aloysius sighed. 'They're warm and inviting.'

'I was just thinking about Calidus and what he first told us about this adventure. Do you remember?' Winna quizzed them. Daisy and Dan looked at each other. Hiromi raised her eyebrows at Aloysius. Marc looked blank. 'He told us this was going to be a wonderful experience which we would all love.'

'It is wonderful,' Aloysius replied defensively.

'For you perhaps, but I've had my moments.' Jonathan grimaced.

'Right. The poor students who got blown up weren't exactly having a wonderful time.' Winna mocked them.

'Come on, misery guts.' Daisy snapped her fingers. 'Don't go back into all that negative stuff you had in the Red Ray.' Winna stared at her, shocked.

'It's not like that. I was teasing, really, about what Calidus said. That's all...' she trailed off.

'Well, Shakita did warn us a negative force could try to prevent Yannish and Professor Sanandez from realising their plan. We knew this before we came.' Dan reminded her.

'Would you rather you hadn't come?' Hiromi asked curiously.

'No, of course not. I wish now I hadn't mentioned it,' said Winna tearfully.

'I think I know what you mean.' Marc came to her rescue. 'We've had great times in the orchestra, and with some of the dancing.' He giggled. 'And the art. But then there's been all this horrid stuff. Winna was just reflecting, that's all.' Winna squeezed his hand in thanks.

'You're right. It's a weird comparison,' said Daisy, relenting. 'We're learning about how to work together as a team, don't you think?'

'Sure.' Jonathan agreed. 'Oleander may have thought the spider thing would have stopped me and the other students, but she was wrong.' He beamed at them all with pride.

'Right on, Jonno. And with Marc's brilliant help, we're able to strengthen our team and help Yannish.' Hiromi tweaked his hair.

'What are you going to do tomorrow?' Daisy asked them. 'We should stay together.'

'I want to practise some jazz since Yannish seemed interested. I could use a good trumpet, Jonno, and what about you tinkling on the keyboard, Winna, my girl?' Al grinned. Jonathan slapped his open hand.

'I haven't tried the piano yet, Al,' said Winna. 'I'm not sure if I can play it.'

'Go for it.' Marc urged. 'Do you need drums, Al?'

'Bring it on, bro.'

'Good, that leaves Hiromi, Dan and me. What do you think, guys? Shall we explore the area?' Daisy asked the others. 'We must stick together though.'

'No probs.' They both agreed.

The boys left, calm but contented. The girls remained quiet, each reflecting on the extreme experiences of the day, from being carefree and enjoyable to the savagery of the explosion and the knowledge there was more to come.

Chapter 25

Intrigue and Forward Thinking

Oleander was furious. Her brilliant plan had failed. Then she suddenly realised - Professor Sanandez could die. She smiled slowly, flexing her fingers, admiring her long red nails.

It was through his actions to save the students that they had rallied round rather than destroy his plan,' she thought to herself, her face darkening. It wouldn't be hard to get into the hospital. No one was guarding him. What a tantalizing idea. I would get that fool to keep Yannish occupied whilst I paid the esteemed Master a visit. He's nearly dead anyway, so I would probably be doing him a favour! She sighed with pleasure. Life had a curious way of turning around.

She waited for Servant to arrive. The stupid boy was late again.

'So, you've deigned to come, my little soldier.' She pinched his cheek.

Massoud pulled back, blurting out he had been delayed by some of the students.

'So they are more important than me, are they?' Her eyes glinted dangerously.

'Of course not, Oleander, but I have to be seen to play my part.'

'How thoughtful you are,' she purred, stroking his face. Then suddenly she stuck her nails in deeply, clawing him from his eye to his chin.

He screamed with pain, clutching his face in his hands.

'Oh, sorry,' she murmured innocently. 'Silly me. I meant to file my nails.'

'I've done everything you asked me to do,' he wailed. 'I got Yannish and the students away.'

'So you did, you clever servant.'

'It wasn't my fault they changed their mind. I did my part.'

'Are you suggesting it was my fault, then?' Her eyes became glacial. He backed off, wiping his face as best he could.

Oleander calmed down. He had done his part. The rest was unfortunate but not irredeemable.

'You are right, Servant. I stand reprimanded.' Massoud goggled, not believing what he had just heard. 'I have a sweet plan to visit the Professor in hospital. He is not very well, you know, and may not recover.' She looked at him with concern.

God, thought Massoud. She's going to kill him.

'So you want me to keep Yannish away?' he asked.

'Exactly.'

'Monday would be good.' He suggested. 'That way we'll all be in the music room.'

'Yes, indeed. I have such a desire to see him as soon as possible. To pay my respects, you know.'

Massoud stared at her in horrified fascination. Oh, Mama, he cried inside. Why was I so ambitious to get away? I would do anything to go back to the poverty of my former life.

'Have you anything to tell me about the seven students?'

'Yes, something interesting.' He brightened up. 'I think it was Marc who disturbed us the other day in the woods. His face was terribly scratched, as though he'd been running through the trees and he had lost his glasses, although he has got them back now.'

'I see. He thinks he is clever, that one. That he is invisible. Maybe he will become so invisible he'll never appear again.' She laughed at her own joke. 'Very well, my little friend, it is time to go - and for goodness sake clean your face. It looks quite horrible.'

With this last remark she disappeared leaving him drenched in sweat, trying to wipe the blood from his scratched face.

***

Aloysius couldn't wait to begin his day in the music room.

Yannish had given him permission to practise jazz for the concert. Jonathan was willing to try and Eli Beke wanted to join them with his trombone and, of course, Marc on his drums.

Winna didn't know if she would be able to play the piano, so he agreed to meet her first so she could find out. He found her there already. Her fingers ran over the keyboard.

'I can't believe this, Al. I can actually play the instrument! It's as if my hands know exactly what to do. This is the most fantastical thing ever!'

'Great, girl. I can't wait for us to get to it.'

Jonathan arrived with his trumpet. 'Could be a bit slow to start with, Al.' He apologised. 'See how my mouth is.'

'No sweat, bro,' Al grinned back.

Daisy, Hiromi and Marc arrived at the same time as Eli. Dan joined them a little later. All had huge beams on their faces. It was going to be a good day.

'Right, we're off guys, so see you later.' Daisy was a little concerned about Jonathan's mouth, but it was up to him. Looking at his eager face, she knew he would enjoy every moment.

The sight that met their eyes when they came out of the music room was astonishing. A group of local farmers and workers were coming along the road, all armed with tools. They carried pickaxes, shovels, wheelbarrows with bags of cement, brushes, rakes and all sorts of general gardening equipment. Yannish went to meet them. One man stepped forward.

'We heard about the fire, Maestro, and we are here to help.'

Yannish was stunned at the generosity of his neighbours. These were ordinary country people with little money but, when a disaster happened, they came. They were anxious to help in any way they could. Yannish knew how proud the Spanish were. They would be offended if he declined.

'I am deeply grateful for your kindness,' he said, clasping the farmer's rough hand. He showed them the damage in the garden. The fountain lying crushed on its side, its walls smashed.

Pedro, the spokesman, nodded his head. He scratched his beard then clapped his hands. 'No problem. We will create new fauntin… Very beautiful.'

As foreman, he instructed each member of his team to take on various jobs. The women were to clear up the garden and to plant new flowers. The men would rebuild the path, gates and fountain. He was a formidable force of energy. For him, everything was possible.

'All you have to do, Maestro, is to bring many cups of tea and perhaps a little food. Yes?'

Daisy looked at them in wonder. 'Aren't they great! This is how we should all help each other.'

'Maybe they are helping the academy because of the work that Professor Sanandez and Yannish are doing?' Hiromi added.

'The students can help clear the rubbish, Pedro,' Yannish suggested.

'No. No. We manage. Enough people. We sing as we work.'

Yannish clasped his hand and thanked all his neighbours. 'We will play our music to you, my friends, and you can judge if we are good enough.'

'With you, Maestro, everything will be precioso.'

Yannish told the students to rest after yesterday's trauma.

'Do what pleases you,' he said to them. 'Josefina and the kitchen staff are here so they will provide lunch and supper as usual.'

Daisy looked at him sharply but daren't say anything in front of the students.

'Don't say anything.' She warned Hiromi and Dan.

'Come on, let's get out of here,' said Dan.

'So Josefina is back. I wonder what happened to her?' he whispered.

'Hang on a minute. I just want to check on something.' Daisy went over to one of the women who were gathering up the broken plant pots.

'Excuse me,' she said. 'Do you know the plant Oleander?'

The woman raised her head, pushing back her straw hat so she could she Daisy.

'Si. Oleander. Very pretty, but-' She raised her finger. 'Venenoso - very bad, morir.' She looked at Daisy with concern.

'Are there any herbs around here that would help if someone were poisoned?' Daisy asked as quietly as she could. Language was a problem and she didn't want to attract the attention of the others.

'Herbs – ah, hierba.' The woman understood. She thought for a moment, then beckoned an older woman over. Daisy tried to keep calm. She certainly didn't want a group discussion. The first woman repeated Daisy's question. The older woman pursed her lips. Her weather-beaten face suddenly brightened. She raised two fingers.

'Two hierba.' She scratched her head. 'Hey Pedro,' she called, beckoning him to her.

'Oh no!' Daisy nearly fainted with panic. 'It's okay,' she said, trying to get away.

'No.' The older woman held her arm. 'Momento.'

Pedro came over, wiping his hands. This was his mother. She asked him to tell Daisy what the two herbs were called.

He nodded and told her their names. They were rare but could be found in the hills, through the pastures and woods which was some distance from the academy. One was purple in colour, like clover with green spiky leaves, and could be found in crevices of the rocks. The other one was yellow with small leaves with white spots on them. This was more difficult to find, but to look in a trunk of an oak tree. Sometimes they grew inside, where birds nested.

Daisy thanked them all with a shaking of hands and smiles. Pedro asked her curiously why she wanted to know. Few people ever got poisoned by such a shrub. Daisy paused for a moment, then told him she was studying herbs in England and this was one of the shrubs she was writing about.

'It will take you all day,' he said to her. 'So wear strong walking boots.'

She thanked them again and ran. She prayed no one had noticed and that, if they had, they wouldn't tell anyone.

'I nearly wrecked the whole thing,' she said, groaning, when she found her friends. 'Let's get out of here. I can't believe what I've done.' She grabbed Hiromi's arm, pulling Dan after her.

'They're not going to say anything,' Hiromi said, soothing her. 'Why should they?'

'They might just talk among themselves, but why do you want to know about herbs?' asked Dan.

'If Oleander is like the shrub, it's poisonous, really bad, so we must know if we can find an antidote. I just have a feeling we should be prepared, that's all. Tai wa wa told me a lot about herbs and how to use them. He saved Little Wolf's life when he got bitten by the snake in Dan's initiation. I helped him.'

Tai wa wa was the Medicine Man in their last adventure, the Red Ray, and Daisy had worked with him as an apprentice.

'Well, I think that's very clever of you.' Dan praised her. 'Shall we go look for them?' Daisy hugged him with relief. 'It's a long way, so perhaps we'd better ask if we can take a few sandwiches and water with us, and Pedro said wear strong boots because it is rocky in the hills.'

'Good one,' Hiromi said. 'We'll get the boots while you go for the food, Daisy'.

'OK!' As she ran to the kitchen she almost bumped into Collette. 'Sorry, Collette. I wasn't looking where I was going.'

Collette laughed. 'So where are you off to, my little one, in such a hurry?'

'Nowhere special. A few of us are just going to hang around, that's all.'

'In the kitchen?' Collette laughed again.

'I'm just going to get a sandwich in case we go for a walk, that's all,' Daisy finished, as brightly as she could.

'Well, have a good time and don't get lost.'

Daisy swore under her breath. She decided not to tell anyone except Yannish in case they might be late back.

Chapter 26

The Quest and A Little Magic

Dan led the way down the dusty road, over the fields, towards the woods. The last time any one of them had taken this route was when Marc had followed Massoud. He very nearly got caught.

Daisy thought about this as they walked. 'Did Marc go further than the forest?' she asked.

'I don't think so,' Dan answered. 'He just mentioned the woods. This isn't the way we came in, but I have a feeling it goes on for miles.'

'Yeah, right,' said Hiromi, agreeing. 'I know there are pastures the other side. Maybe the hills come after that. Where do you think the herbs will be?'

'Pedro's mum told me they were both in the hills. One's in the rocks and the other is in the hollow of a tree. It sounds a bit weird. Hope it's not too difficult. Perhaps Tai wa wa will help me,' she said and giggled.

It was good to be out by themselves. Daisy rather wished Jonno and the others were with them, but they were having a good time playing jazz.

They approached the woods through a well-trodden path. It was a relief to get out of the hot sun. The oak trees were smaller than in some European countries, but what they lacked in height they made up for in width, with twisting branches and a canopy of leaves through which sunlight sparkled in flashes as they made their way through.

'We've got all day. We can do what we like and go where we like.' Hiromi breathed a huge sigh of pleasure. 'Do you realise this is the first time we've actually been able to explore without anyone being with us?'

They continued picking their way through the trees. The foliage was dense in places. The undergrowth teemed with life. Nature was abundant. Daisy remembered the experiment in the Music Room, when Yannish had opened the window and asked them to listen to the sounds of nature. She was aware of doing that now and was conscious Hiromi and Dan were doing the same, for they too were silent, savouring the peace. Birds were calling, some close, others above them, making more insistent calls to their mates. Insects buzzed. There was the rustling of something, a tiny insect or animal, as it darted through the foliage of moss and twigs. There was a sense of urgency as the law of nature responded to reproduce and regenerate its species. The teenagers were not so aware of nature's cycle. It was more they felt the activity around them.

Coming out of the woods, they passed into open grassland where sheep grazed and, in the distance, they could see cattle of some kind.

'Hey, look,' cried Hiromi.

They saw long-necked birds flying above them. Their wingspan was huge. They looked graceful, as if floating in mid-air.

'What are they?' asked Dan. 'They look like flying torpedoes with wings.'

'I think they're storks or cranes.' Daisy cupped her hands over her eyes to see better.

'They're beautiful,' Hiromi said with a sigh. 'Swans, I think.'

'Jonathan told me this is a great area for birds and butterflies, so I might be able to take a few photos on my mobile.'

'Climbing the hills is going to be hard work.' Dan warned them. 'But if we take it slowly, we'll be fine.'

'Well, I've got to find the herbs. I'm not going back without them. This could be the only chance we have without anyone finding out.'

'Do you really think it's that important?' Hiromi asked her.

'Yeah, I do. I just have this weird feeling there must be some nasty connection between Oleander and the shrub. Why does she have that name? Look what she's already done.' Her face was grim. Nothing would deflect her from finding the herbs.

'We're with you,' said Dan, taking her hand.

The climb was dusty with potholes in the path so they had to watch where they walked. The sun was hot. Dan had borrowed Jonathan's baseball cap. Hiromi had remembered to bring hers and Daisy's hats when she'd collected their boots.

As they walked the hills became steeper, the going tougher. Rocks appeared more often and were becoming craggy. In between the rocks were shrubs of hawthorn, elder and blackberry as well as many flowering plants. Daisy checked each one but couldn't find what she wanted. Then she suddenly saw a few crooked oak trees growing among the shrubs.

'This has got to be the right place.' She checked the first one. Her hands felt the trunk for an opening or hole where birds might nest. Finding nothing, she quickly went to the one in the middle. There was a bored-out opening with new shoots springing through. There were moss and twigs ready for bird nesting and, among the bits of debris, grew a tiny yellow plant.

'I've got it!' she shouted triumphantly.

'Check the leaves,' Hiromi shouted back.

'Green leaves with white spots. Brilliant.' Daisy scrambled down to them.

'One down. One to go.'

'Are we anywhere near the other one yet?' Hiromi asked.

'I think we need to go higher,' Daisy answered. 'The second one could be more difficult to find.' She was inwardly asking Tai wa wa, the medicine man, to help her. Please help me, she begged him.

The landscape started to change. The rock formations became bigger, and jagged boulders of limestone jutted out above their heads. Climbing was becoming increasingly difficult.

Dan told Daisy and Hiromi to go before him. It was better for him to be behind them in case of any difficulties. Some of the rocks were loose underfoot so they had to be careful where they placed their hands and feet. It seemed to take hours.

Each time they took a step, they had to stand still while rocks and gravel slid beneath their feet. The noise echoed down below as they fell. It was eerie and frightening.

'This is getting dangerous now, Dais,' said Dan, shielding his eyes from the dust. 'Let me go ahead of you. I can see if it's safe enough.'

'You stay there, Dan - both of you.' Daisy half-turned her head in his direction. 'I just want to check some of those crevices up there.

I promise, if it's too difficult I'll stop.'

'For heaven's sake, be careful!' Hiromi warned her nervously. 'Please don't do anything stupid. We've got one of the herbs. Isn't that enough?'

Daisy gritted her teeth. No, it wasn't enough, she thought.

Edging her way up, she stopped, not daring to look down. She felt frightened but tried to keep her breathing slow and steady.

'I have to get the other one,' she muttered through clenched teeth.

Both Hiromi and Dan watched in trepidation. If they moved, it might dislodge some of the rocks higher up near Daisy.

Just as she was about to move her hand again, a white stork appeared above her head. Daisy gasped but held on. The bird looked at her solemnly though small dark eyes. She had a graceful neck and long beak. Her wings rested lightly by her side, ready for flight. She didn't seem the least worried to see Daisy. It was almost as if she was expecting her.

Daisy was too surprised to do anything but hang on. The stork looked kindly into her eyes, telepathically reassuring her she was safe and that the bird was there to help her find the herbs.

'Who sent you?' Daisy asked within her mind, as Calidus had taught them.

'Shakita,' the stork answered. 'I know where the herb is. It is too high for you. I will get it, but first you can climb on my back and I will take you down to safety. Then I will return for the others.'

Daisy managed to climb onto her back. She was sure she must be too heavy, but the stork insisted. She sat astride the stork's narrow back and the stork's wings stretched out, like a weightless mantle. It was like floating on a cloud.

'Thank you so much,' Daisy said within herself, as the stork set her down on a safe ledge.

'Think nothing of it,' said the stork. She flew back to get Hiromi and Dan together, dropping them off like a stork taxi-service. With a nod of her beak, she soared high above them to find Daisy's herbs.

The teenagers gaped at each other in total amazement.

Daisy grinned at them. 'Shakita sent her. The stork spoke to me telepathically. It really works,' she said and giggled. 'She's gone to get the herbs now, so when she comes back just listen, because she doesn't talk.'

Dan and Hiromi nodded. 'Okay. We can do it.'

Not a word was spoken until the stork returned with the herbs safely in her mouth.

'You were right to get these,' she told them silently. 'Oleander is a dangerous person with a deadly poison. Keep them very safe and tell no one.'

'Thank you, Stork. You may have saved our lives.'

'Be careful, my friends.'

'Who are you?' Daisy peered more closely at the stork.

'Don't you recognise me?' The familiar low voice spoke to them. The stork's outline suddenly became blurred. Slowly, a figure who they all knew came into view. First the orange dress appeared. Then they saw brilliant red hair and finally the amber eyes, laughing at their startled faces.

'Shakita!' they shouted in delight.

'Where have you been?' Hiromi asked.

'Yes,' Daisy said. 'Yannish told us you were at the academy and that you would appear when you were ready.'

'I've been there all the time, but I couldn't let you know because it is very dangerous.' She looked at them quietly. 'All of you have been brilliant, really brave. You have thought through every action you have taken and Calidus and I are very proud of you. Now, you must be more careful and not give Oleander any reason to suspect you. She is so clever.'

'Do you know who she is?' Dan asked. 'I do, but I cannot tell you in case your knowing gives the game away.'

The three teenagers understood the situation. They accepted all she said.

'How did you know we were trying to find the herbs?'

'I was close by when you were asking the Spanish woman. I saw how upset you were when she asked Pedro's mother to come over.' Shakita laughed as she remembered Daisy's irritation.

'To think you were that close and I never knew.' Daisy sighed.

'No one knew. Then I took on the disguise of the stork to follow you here.'

Shakita leant over to touch each one lightly on their brows. Daisy looked at her, questioningly.

'Do you remember this chakra works with thought forms and memory?' asked Shakita.

Daisy nodded her head. Calidus had told them about this in the Red Ray.

'This will help you to keep your thoughts of finding the herbs to yourselves so Oleander cannot pick them up.'

'Good one.' Dan smiled.

'Now I must go and so must you. Tell Yannish to guard the Professor.'

She looked around, checking the area in case they might be seen. She hugged them all and resumed her disguise as the stork. With a quick tap on the ground with her long beak, she rose into the air and disappeared.

They sat for a while, savouring the moment. To see Shakita again was a huge lift to their morale. They had only seen her at the beginning of their mission but they had fallen in love with her beauty and warmth. Dan reached inside his bag for water and a little food.

'You'd better give those herbs to me, Dais, for safety.'

'Thanks Dan.' She wrapped them up carefully in tissues and handed them over. 'Guard them with your life.' She smiled but was serious. 'They may save someone from death.'

Dan tucked them safely into a pocket in his back pack.

'That reminds me. What did Shakita mean when she said guard the Professor?'

'I don't know.' Daisy sounded concerned. 'We'd better tell Yannish.'

Walking back was relaxing and fun. The sun was losing its heat so they felt more comfortable. They walked beside the river, the one where Marc had found his bamboo shoot to save his life. Taking off their shoes, they dangled their sore feet in the cool water.

'I wonder how Al has got on with his jazz?' Daisy mused. 'I can't wait to hear it. I guess you could have part in the band, Dan?'

'Maybe. I think he'll ask me later. I had a strong feeling I had to be here with you.'

'I couldn't have done this without you, Dan,' Daisy said. 'You give me strength.'

 *Chapter 27*

Letting Go and Being Careful

They arrived back in time for supper. Jonathan was concerned about Daisy, simply because she hadn't told him where they were going, but also elated about the day he'd had with Aloysius. His mouth had been fine, even though at first he'd been a little cautious about blowing his trumpet. But he'd loved every minute of it, finding that playing jazz was a real buzz.

Daisy, Hiromi and Dan went in search of them as soon as they'd returned. They found them still in the Music Room. The noise in the room was deafening.

Francesca and Hamish were there, clapping their hands. So was Yannish and Collette. Frank and Ronnie sat with the others, stamping their feet in applause. All the students whistled and shouted their appreciation.

Aloysius's face beamed his delight and gratitude. He bowed awkwardly. Jonathan stood by his side with Eli Beke and Louis Capello. Winna sat at the piano, smiling, her fingers still resting lightly on the piano keys. Marc looked as if would burst with emotion.

They all looked up as Daisy, Hiromi and Dan came in.

'Where've you been?' Jonathan asked.

'Oh, around. Pottering, you know,' said Daisy, smiling casually.

'We just wanted to hang out.' Hiromi added. 'Looks like you've been enjoying yourselves.'

'It was brilliant,' Jonathan said. His face was crimson with excitement and there were beads of perspiration on his brow. 'Did you have a good time?'

'Yeah, it was great. We saw some beautiful butterflies, Jonno, and some white storks. They were so funny with their long necks and huge beaks. I took a few photos for you.'

'Thanks, sis.'

The room began to empty as the supper bell rang. The tutors grinned as they went past.

'That brother of yours is good,' Ronnie told Daisy. 'And Al is a dream.' She rolled her eyes. 'Winna is great too.'

'It was a treat, I can tell you,' Hamish told them in his broad Scottish accent, nodding his head in appreciation. 'That wee brother of yours deserves a pat on his back for playing the trumpet after his ordeal.'

Francesca squeezed his arm, smiling at Daisy as she led her husband out.

'We were very upset by that accident,' she whispered.

'Thanks, Francesca.' Daisy was touched by their concern.

They waited for their gang to pack up their instruments amid laughter and relief their practice had gone so well. Yannish complimented them all. He told Aloysius he would talk to him later about the session and how to structure it for the end of term concert.

Daisy was able to whisper to Yannish that she needed to see him. She waited until everyone except her friends had gone. He looked at her keenly and nodded before walking out of the room.

Supper was a happier occasion, compared to the night before, when all the students had been so distraught. Those who had been in the explosion were feeling much better; they showed a few lacerations and abrasions, but generally their spirits were high.

The eight from the hospital had returned and were none the worse for their ordeal. But Ariel and Hannah still had to remain for an extra few days until the effects of smoke inhalation and glass cuts had healed. The burns to Ariel's body were still too painful for him to be moved. Thankfully Professor Sanandez was out of the critical stage and was said to be holding his own.

Since the dining room had been damaged, tables were moved into a room next to the laundry which was normally used for spare furniture, bedding etc. It was just big enough to house sixty students, with not much room for the kitchen staff to manoeuvre around the tables, but no one complained.

The food arrived hot and was delicious. If anything, the explosion had brought the students closer together. Adversity can often bring out the best in people. The professor had tried to rescue as many students as he could at the cost of his own life and this made an enormous impression on all of them. For some of them, they would never forget that they owed him their lives.

Aloysius told Daisy, Hiromi and Dan about their day. How first they'd practised among themselves, just to see how they could work together. Then Yannish asked him to play something for all the wonderful people who'd given up their time to clear the garden and rebuild the fountain and gates.

'It was fantastic!' Aloysius said. 'All the men and women, including Pedro's mum, danced and sang. Then Jonathan and Marc joined in. This was the first time I've ever played jazz, Dan. It was crazy.'

'What about me, then?' Winna said, her mouth crammed full of food. 'I've never even touched a piano before. That was unreal. I mean like unreal.' Her eyes almost came out on storks.

'Did you know Ronnie joined in too? She really is something.' Al marvelled.

Daisy sighed with pleasure and relief. Looking around, everyone was laughing and chattering. She felt great. The herbs were safe and Al's day had gone well.

'Come on, guys. Time for debriefing.' She realised that by using the term 'debrief', she sounded more like Marc. Maybe it wasn't the right word, but hey, it had the right ring, she thought to herself. She shrugged her shoulders, smiling as she led the way out of the music room.

***

The Colour Code Gang met as usual in the girls' room. It was becoming a ritual. Tonight there was a feeling of greater confidence and euphoria than any of them had experienced before. They were making a difference.

Aloysius's natural musical talent and exuberance for life had lifted everyone's spirits above the recent disaster. His sense of fun was infectious. Everyone responded. They couldn't help themselves. He truly represented the Orange Ray. He attracted everyone into his world of warmth with the help of his friends, Jonathan, Winna and Marc. Together they'd created an atmosphere of uninhibited delight.

Daisy, on the other hand, together with Hiromi and Dan, felt a compulsion to counteract a threat that she intuitively felt could come from Oleander. She'd had to find a remedy that would act as an antidote in case Oleander used the poison of the shrub.

Aloysius's jazz session had given Daisy the opportunity to slip away and put her plan into action. No one would have noticed.

When Yannish arrived, Daisy told them about their adventure, how they'd seen the white stork circling above them and later, when climbing had become so difficult, how the stork had appeared again to help her. She showed Jonathan a photo of the stork looking at her knowingly, with her head on one side.

'Hang on a minute.' He paused, looking thoroughly puzzled. 'This bird looks a bit odd.'

Hiromi and Dan burst out laughing. 'Guess who the stork was?'

He stared. 'How do you mean, who the stork was?' He put his hand to his mouth. 'Whoops! I see what you mean. It was Shakita!'

'You've got it, Jonno. It was Shakita following us all the time.' Daisy threw herself at him, giggling.

'We actually rode on her back,' Hiromi said. 'As a stork, I mean, not as Shakita.'

'You have the herbs now, Daisy?' Yannish enquired.

Dan produced them from his pocket.

'Well done,' he murmured. 'Of course, we don't know if Oleander will use poison, but it's best to be prepared. Fantastic work, all of you. Thank you so much.'

'One thing Shakita mentioned before she left, was to tell you to guard the Professor,' Daisy told him quietly.

He looked at her sharply, taking in a quick intake of breath, then letting it out slowly.

'I see.' His face paled. 'I will take the appropriate measures.'

He rose slowly. Daisy thought he looked tired.

'You have all achieved so much today,' he said, smiling.

'Is Josefina back?' Dan suddenly asked.

'Yes. She did receive some minor burns to her hands and face, and I think she must have felt a bit confused because she can't remember where she went.'

'Poor old bird,' Aloysius said quietly.

'It could also mean something else,' Marc said, squinting.

'Whatever.' Winna sighed.

'I need sleep.' Dan yawned. 'Back to Mozart tomorrow. Come on, you guys. It's been a great day. See you tomorrow, girls.'

'See ya,' the girls echoed.

 *Chapter 28*

Twists and Turns

It was good to get back to a normal routine. The reception area was still out of bounds. It would take time for the Police and Fire Departments to send in their final reports and conclusions about the cause of the fire. Till then, the area was sealed off, like a sick old friend who was somehow held in suspended judgment.

The students filed past, not wanting to look or to be reminded of what had happened.

Yannish tapped his baton. 'We will begin with the first movement.' He made no mention that Ariel or Hannah were missing.

It took a while for the students to concentrate.

'Pay attention,' he barked. 'Again, from the beginning. Keep up, oboes. You are playing into your feet.' He raised his palm up. 'Bassoon… you should be in a field!'

He was tough and exacting, whipping them back into shape.

'Stop!' He told them. 'This is too painful to my ears. I have heard children from nursery levels play better than this. Put all that has happened from your mind. This is where we are. Not languishing in self-pity or discomfort. We will not leave this place until you have reached the standard I know you can achieve.'

Daisy suddenly remembered her orange gemray in her pocket. Yannish had told them that if the atmosphere was ever heavy and depressed, to turn the wand more to the lighter colour of orange. That way the heaviness would dissipate and everyone would feel lighter.

She slid it out of her pocket so no one could see and turned it from dark orange to the lighter shade. In her mind she visualised the colour radiating out to everyone, including Yannish.

'Now, my friends, let us begin again.' He raised his baton.

***

Oleander smoothed her nails. She loved bright red nail polish. It was the same colour as the flowers on the shrub in the garden. Her shrub. The colour suited her mood.

It was going to be a delightful day. She sighed with pleasure at the thought of it. She was going to visit a good friend in hospital. Professor Sanandez.

Not many visitors were allowed, but she would be. He was out of danger now. She laughed quietly to herself. That means it would be easier to see him. Nurses could be difficult and bossy if a patient was in a critical state. Tiresome, fussing around like broody hens, but now restrictions would be lifted.

She smiled at the prospect of walking in unannounced. Yannish would be tied up for most of the day, so she could visit this morning or even this afternoon and then perhaps go into the town afterwards to drink hot chocolate at her favourite restaurant. Delicious! The thought pleased her.

The only problem was she had to check people's whereabouts. It wouldn't do to arrive at the hospital and find another visitor. She decided to wait for the coffee break to see where everyone was. Meanwhile, I'll prepare my present, she cooed to herself.

The preparation was almost as good as execution - but not quite.

***

'That is better.' Yannish lowered his hands. 'You are beginning to sound like an orchestra at last. Take a break and we will start again.'

'That man is heavy weather.' Chelsea grumbled to Daisy, rubbing her fingers. 'It's tough, but if we are going to be ready for the concert I suppose he has to be hard.' She then quickly changed the subject. 'What do you think about Jovan?' she asked, bending down to whisper in Daisy's ear.

'Jovan?' Daisy repeated, flabbergasted.

'Yeah, why not?' Chelsea put a piece of gum in her mouth and started chewing vigorously.

'Well, I think he's changed a lot.' Daisy began slowly, hardly believing what she was hearing. 'But what about Felippe Tonisoni?'

'Oh, that was ages ago and he's not much fun.'

'I wouldn't think Jovan was a bunch of laughs, either,' said Daisy, giggling.

Chelsea's eyes looked all dreamy. 'Maybe not, but he's, like, so moody and mysterious. Those dark flashing eyes of his are to die for.' She let out a deep longing sigh.

'Whatever, Chels. Does he like you?'

'Are you kidding? I've seen him ogling me,' she said, smiling to herself.

'What about his girlfriend? She's lethal, believe me. She shoved me aside once when I was too close to Jovan.'

'Let her try. Just let her try.' Chelsea's beautiful blue eyes grew hard and flinty.

'Well, good luck, Chels.' Daisy felt quite sorry for Jovan's girlfriend. Chelsea may look soft but she was formidable.

Coffee time was over and the place became quiet again. Yannish continued going through the music with his students.

Oleander went to find her car, satisfied Yannish was occupied. In her hand she carried a bag. She sang all the way as she drove, feeling relaxed and optimistic. To be absolutely sure she would be allowed to enter the hospital, she'd decided to change her appearance. It wouldn't do if she were recognised. Nurses might remember her afterwards.

What better disguise than to take on the illustrious Yannish Kablinski, Doctor of Music?

She parked her car in the general hospital car park and made her way through reception, up the stairs, along several corridors until she came to the private room where Professor Sanandez was being treated. She was about to open the door when a nurse came towards her.

'Ah, Doctor Kablinski. How nice to see you. I didn't expect to see you back.'

Oleander smiled her most charming smile as Yannish. 'I found a little time, so thought I would check on the professor.'

The nurse stood back, surprised. 'But we told you this morning where he was, Doctor.'

Oleander felt herself stiffening. 'Where he was?'

'He is not here,' the nurse said, baffled by Yannish's response.

Oleander turned the handle and pushed open the door of the Professor's room before the nurse could stop her. The room was empty. He was not there. The bed had been recently remade for a new patient.

The nurse stared at Oleander, upset by the apparent rudeness. Oleander managed to control her fury and smiled again to apologise.

'I am so sorry, nurse. I have so many things on my mind at the moment I totally forgot.'

The nurse remained where she was, slightly mollified by Yannish's apology. Obviously he had completely forgotten. She waited, looking at him.

'Now, let me see, where did you say the Professor was, nurse? My memory again.' Oleander touched her brow, acting out the forgetful Doctor.

The nurse smiled at him in turn. 'Why, he's been taken to the burns unit.'

'The burns unit?' Oleander spat through tight lips.

'Yes, Doctor. You have a very bad memory,' she said, laughing.

'Which burns unit?' Oleander hissed.

'Silly man, the one in Madrid, don't you remember?' The nurse watched his face darken. 'Now you're here, wouldn't you like to see the other two? I'm sure they would love to see you.'

Oleander turned, ready to strike her, but managed by supreme effort to hold herself together.

'Not now,' she snarled. 'I have other things to do.'

She turned her back on the nurse and marched off down the corridor, shaking with rage and disappointment.

If she had turned back she might have seen the nurse laughing. The nurse wasn't just any nurse who'd happened to be passing. This nurse had changed her appearance too, just as Oleander had transformed hers into Yannish. Shakita's amber eyes shone through.

She knew Oleander would try to kill the Professor and had told Daisy to warn Yannish. Together they'd arranged for the Professor to be moved to a private clinic, away from harm's way. Shakita was ready. She was a Light Server and could recognise the intention behind any action. She knew Oleander couldn't possibly come as herself. It was fascinating to see Oleander in the image of Yannish. She was so real, with exactly his voice.

This time they had outwitted Oleander, but Shakita knew she

would re-double her efforts at being tricked out of her victory. She would be brutal in her revenge.

Oleander returned to her car, mouthing curses as she walked. Some poor woman approached her, asking if she had change for the car park meter. Oleander pushed her aside.

'Get out of my way,' she snarled. Taking her frustration out of some innocent didn't solve the problem but it did help make her feel a whole lot better.

The Colour Code

 *Chapter 29*

Dance Time

A loysius felt great. Everything was going well. He loved playing in the orchestra, even though the clarinet wasn't his first choice of instrument. Still, he was learning and beginning to appreciate it more and more. Yannish had recognised some talent in him and had encouraged him to play a solo at the concert. Probably he had intended the solo would be something classical but, on hearing Aloysius play his saxophone, he must have changed his mind.

Al breathed a sigh of relief. Jazz was his first love. He wanted to share this honour with his friends. Already he had an idea in his mind and wanted to discuss it with Yannish. He would look for him after lunch, before the dance class.

Making his way out through the back entrance, he bumped into Collette du Bois.

'Aloysius, you are so clever. Your playing is magnifique.' She patted his arm. 'How are you all getting on after that bad experience?' Her eyes grew sad as she remembered it.

'We're all right, thanks, Collette. We were lucky, unlike the others. I feel guilty we weren't here.'

'Ah, you are so kind, but you give so much pleasure to all the students – no? You all do. I have seen how much you all help. You are special, I think.'

'We try out best, Collette,' Aloysius said, smiling.

'Where are you off to now?' she asked.

'Well, I'm just going to find Yannish to talk a few ideas over for the concert.'

'Of course,' she said. 'But why not practise with me first?'

His face lit up. It would be good to try something before going to Yannish. Just as he was about to follow Collette, Winna appeared and called after him.

'Hey, Al, where are you going?'

'I'm just going to try a few ideas with Collette.' He shuffled his feet, feeling slightly guilty at being found out.

Winna looked at them both. 'Sorry, Collette, we've got to go to Dancing class. Ronnie wants us to be there early. She said something about new dance steps.' She grinned apologetically, pulling Al away.

'Of course, you must go,' replied Collette, smiling at Aloysius. 'Another time.'

'What was that all about?' Winna hissed at him as they walked away. 'You know we're not meant to see anyone on our own, even though she's gorgeous!'

'Yeah, I know. But she's interested in what I'm doing and she plays the piano like a dream.'

'Does she play jazz?' Winna grilled him.

'Well, no, I don't think so.' He answered slowly. 'But she's likes jazz.'

Winna shrugged her shoulders irritably. 'Says you. You may be great at music, Al, but you're just a nerd when it comes to people.'

Aloysius backed off, hurt by Winna's remarks.

'I don't mean to be beastly, Al, but suppose Collette is Oleander? Once inside her room, alone with her, she might do something dreadful and we might never see you again.'

He gasped, shocked at the idea. 'I never thought.'

'Good.' Winna nodded her head with satisfaction. She thought Al needed a collar round his neck, like a pet dog. She would make sure she would look out for him.

'Anyway, if you were late, Daisy would do her nut, not to mention Ronnie.'

'Do we really have to go to the Dance class so early?'

'Not really,' Winna replied cheekily. 'I only said that to get you away.'

'Well, Yannish offered to see me, so I'll see you later, my fierce Guardian Angel.'

'You mean to tell me you would rather see Collette than Yannish?' asked Winna, giggling. 'I can't believe it. He's just as a pretty as she is.'

'I was on my way, Winna, but Collette just suddenly appeared and I forgot about Yannish.'

'Yeah, yeah, off you go. Looks like I've saved you from making a fool of yourself.'

He slapped her back as he went happily on his way.

***

Aloysius' meeting with Yannish took place in the Doctor's own private quarters. It was an open, sunny room. All the floors were of dark brown Spanish oak on which lay beautiful Persian rugs in deep warm colours. There was a large sofa in soft burgundy leather with sage green cushions.

A piano stood in one corner. Music scores lay open upon the stand as well as spreading over the top. Bookshelves covered one wall, while paintings covered another, mostly by local artists. Yannish's bureau was positioned beneath so that, whenever he looked up, he could feast his eyes on colour. Close to this, a desk housed his computer and all the various technical devices he needed. It was an elegant as well as a functional room.

Yannish made tea as he spoke about music. As Aloysius listened, his mind went back to his time with Tatanka, the musician from the Red Ray. There was a quality about Yannish that reminded him of the mystical man; the way he talked and the passion he had for music. He wondered if it was possible for Tatanka's spirit to enter another person's body in this life. All the time Yannish was speaking, Al was drawn to his eyes - dark brown in colour with a curious light shining through. Tatanka's eyes had been like these. The look concentrated, Yannish missing nothing.

'Have you heard anything I've said?' Yannish asked him.

'Yes, of course, Yannish. It's just you remind me of...' His words drifted away.

'Was this person helpful to you?'

Aloysius stared at him, startled Yannish could read his mind.

'He was a fantastic musician. You remind me of him.'

'I am honoured you think so,' Yannish said, smiling. 'Let us continue.'

***

Back at the Dance Studio, Frank and Ronnie had been practising special routines which they'd choreographed for those students dancing at the concert. The students hung around, some sitting on the floor, others leaning against the wall chatting amongst themselves.

'Okay, guys, Ronnie and I have designed three pieces so all of you will have a chance to strut your stuff. The first one is for those who like to Rap and Hip Hop.'

'Yeah!' said Marc to Jonathan and punched the air.

The second one is for the Street Dancers, while the last section is a more choreographed piece that Ronnie has designed for those who have a little more experience. We need about twenty in each section, so you decide which one you'd like to be in.

'I can't dance, Hiromi,' said Daisy, giving a lop-sided grin. 'I'm just not good enough.'

'Me, neither,' said Dan, grimacing.

'Come on, bro, hip your body. You'll never know unless you try.' Aloysius urged him.

'I tried, Al, and I just don't have the rhythm like you. You're the music man.'

'If I'm the music man, Dan my friend, you're the rock.'

'You're right, Al,' Daisy agreed. 'Dan is the rock. But you are my idea of what Orange is all about. I don't think I really understood what the qualities of each colour really meant until now. It's just beginning to dawn on me we have to use them to really know them.'

'I know what you mean.' Winna pondered. 'I guess Calidus knows what he's doing. I represented the Red Ray so had to learn how to handle my own anger and jealousy, and now Al has to learn how to use his creativity.'

'It's more than that, Winna,' Dan replied. 'We're all part of this. We all had to learn how to stand up for ourselves last time, and now we have to do the opposite - well, sort of.' He fumbled. 'I guess feeling stronger helps us to be more creative.'

The afternoon was fun. The studio wasn't big enough for everyone to dance at the same time, so first the Rappers and Hip Hoppers began their routine under the watchful eye of Frank. There would be about fifteen minutes for each session. Each one would have a few minutes to do their solo. Jonathan and Marc chose to dance together. Neither felt so confident that they wanted to be exposed by dancing by themselves.

Jovan skipped from one queue into the first one, wanting to

show off by himself. He didn't need or want anyone to out-dance him. This was his chance to show everyone how versatile he was. Chelsea groaned with disappointment. He proved to be brilliant, with a natural arrogance and attitude which made him stand out. Frank applauded. Chelsea gaped at him with admiration, while Daisy and Hiromi rolled their eyes upwards. 'Here we go again!'

'What else is new?' Daisy grunted.

Daisy was surprised to see Massoud had joined this group. How strange, she thought. She would never have expected him to be interested or even want to dance before the other students. He was too nervous. Maybe Oleander has told him to be here. But why?

Ronnie asked who had danced before. Hiromi and Yoshi held up their hands, together with Hannah. The others told her they were interested but had never had the opportunity. She looked at Massoud. He told her shyly that he loved to watch dancing, especially ballet. She smiled at him.

'You are a sensitive boy, Massoud, and I think you will be a good dancer.'

There was a smaller number of boys than girls in this group. The rest joined the other groups. Ronnie paired them up as she thought was appropriate. Hiromi should dance with Yoshi.

Daisy was inwardly shocked when Massoud asked if he could partner her.

'I'm not in this group,' she called back. 'I'm with the Street Dancers. I'm just watching Hiromi and Yoshi.'

Ronnie looked around the group. They were one girl short. She appealed to Daisy.

'Please, Daisy. There are more than enough Street Dancers. It would be great if you could join us. It's not difficult, I promise you.'

'But I'm happy just being with the others.' Daisy wailed. 'And I can't dance, not like Hiromi. Why can't Massoud join another group?' She glared at him.

'We just have too many in Rap and Street, Daisy. I promise you I will teach you myself, if only you'll help me now.'

Daisy was furious to be placed in such position. Why did she have to come to watch Hiromi? There was no way she wanted to partner Massoud.

'Oh, come on, Daisy.' Felippe encouraged her. 'You're such a good dancer. You just have to believe in yourself. Please, for us.'

'Okay,' Daisy replied. She struggled to get up, sighing deeply.

'But could I dance with you?'

Hiromi stared at her, alarmed. She knew how awful this situation was for Daisy. Felippe stepped forward.

'I'd love to dance with you another time, Daisy, but I want to dance with Hannah. We want to be together.' He smiled apologetically.

Ronnie took control. 'Come on, Daisy, this is not fair to Massoud. You will be very lucky to dance with him. He has a natural talent.'

Along with all his other talents, Daisy snarled inwardly.

Slowly she walked towards Massoud. She said nothing, not daring to look at him or at Hiromi's horrified face.

What could she do? How could she get out of it without being offensive as well as looking stupid? In the end she faced him and whispered.

'If you try to hurt me, I will tell everyone about you and Oleander.'

He gasped, turning pale. 'How do you know about Oleander?'

'We know and it is still not too late to tell us, Massoud. We know she makes you do terrible things. We can help you.'

Massoud laughed. 'You are so naïve, Daisy. Don't you realise she knows everything and will stop at nothing to wreck this project?'

'Is this why you're here now?' she challenged him 'To attack me next?'

'No, Daisy,' he whispered, looking around anxiously, in case he was overheard. 'I remember how you helped me. I don't want to hurt you or anyone. I just want to dance and have a little fun before it's too late.'

'Before it's too late?' Daisy repeated, alarm growing inside her.

'I mean for me,' he said dejectedly. 'I know I will never escape her. She will never free me.'

'Do you know who Oleander is, Massoud?'

'I can't say, Daisy. She will know.' Sweat began to form on his forehead. He had problems in controlling the trembling in his legs.

'Okay,' Daisy said. 'You will be my partner, but if you try to hurt anyone, including me, I will tell everyone you were to blame for the spiders and then Oleander will discover that we know.'

Massoud suddenly remembered the disturbance in the woods, when he was talking with Oleander. He knew it was Marc.

'I didn't...' he began.

'Yes, you did. You nearly killed my brother, so if you put a foot out of place, I'll tell. Got it?' Her green eyes blazed into his.

'I'm sorry, but I'm in an impossible situation. She will destroy my family if I don't obey.'

'In that case, tell me what she's planning and we will help you.'

He mumbled his thanks, wiped his face and took her hand as Ronnie shouted for attention.

She knew it couldn't be Ronnie, unless she had set the whole thing up with Massoud, to play on Daisy's sympathy. I must talk to the others and tell Yannish, she thought to herself.

She smiled thinly as she took Massoud's hand.

 *Chapter 30*

Daisy's Dilemma

Daisy was quiet over supper, although she tried her best to respond to Jonathan and Marc. They were so excited about their Rap Dancing. Winna listened to Aloysius. He told her about Yannish and how he reminded him of Tatanka. She nodded her head.

'Well, you never know. We went back in time, so why can't they come forward?'

He looked at her, his eyes glowing with pleasure. 'Well, if he has, he won't admit it.' He laughed. 'But I know and he knows that I know.'

'Well, don't get yourself into a knot. You're silly enough.' She grinned fondly. Winna felt a kind of responsibility for him and was beginning to understand how Daisy must feel about the whole group. She sighed, with a good warm feeling. She felt she was now part of the team.

Hiromi was concerned about Daisy. So was Dan. He always noticed if Daisy was worried. A frown appeared on her forehead and somehow her face looked pinched, especially around her mouth. He saw that now.

'Al,' said Daisy. 'When you saw Yannish, did he say if he was coming tonight?'

'No, Dais, he didn't say, Is it important?'

'Yeah, we all need to talk,' she said quietly.

'Would you like me to ask him, Dais?'

'Yeah, I think it looks more natural coming from you, Al. You could be asking him about your music.'

'Right you are. I'm on my way.' He grinned, pushing back his chair. On his way to Yannish's room he saw Josefina.

'Hi, Josefina. Do you know if Dr Kablinski is in his room?'

'Si.' She nodded toward Yannish's door. 'Go. Go.' She ushered him forward, beaming at him. 'He eese in room.'

'Gracias, Josefina.'

She shuffled away, laughing to herself. Aloysius knocked on the door. As the door opened, Collette came out.

'Ha. Here is your music boy, Maestro,' she said, stepping aside.

Yannish closed the door carefully as Al stepped into his room. He waited for a few seconds before turning on his CD player to drown any conversation.

'Can you come to see us tonight, Maestro? Daisy needs to see you.'

'No problem. I will be there one hour earlier than usual this time, in case anyone is watching our movements.'

'I don't know if this important, but Josefina was in the corridor when I came,' Aloysius said, watching his face for any reaction.

Yannish smirked. 'She is the nosy one. Yes? But means well.'

Daisy and her friends went back to the girls' room, as they always did, to wait for Yannish. He arrived on time, entering the room without knocking.

She told them about her dilemma of having to be Massoud's dancing partner.

'I only went to watch Hiromi and somehow I got hooked in by Ronnie. If only I'd left with the others none of this would have happened,' she moaned.

Her friends looked glum, closing around her with feelings of sympathy. She carried on telling them what had been said between Massoud and herself and what she had decided to do.

'The thing is, I don't know if he is innocent and really wants to dance, or if he's been put up to it by Oleander.' She looked at their silent faces as they waited for her to continue. 'He looked scared when I told him I would blab about what he had done to Jonathan, and if he tried to hurt me everyone would know. He was really frightened I knew about the spiders and, of course, tried to deny it. Honestly, I think he was shocked we knew. Maybe he's bluffing and it's all a big act?' Her green eyes grew dark with confusion.

Her friends shifted their positions, trying to find something useful to say.

'Did Ronnie see you talking to Massoud?' Dan asked her.

'Well, I guess so, but she was more interested in getting everyone together. She could be Oleander and pretended not to notice, I suppose. I don't know.'

'I just don't see her as Oleander,' Hiromi said.

'Nor do I,' said Jonathan. 'How could she hide it from Frank?'

'Unless he's part of it.' Marc blinked behind his glasses. 'I don't think this is a set-up, Daisy. I am sure Oleander is building up to attack Yannish or the orchestra. If Massoud was instructed to harm you, there are still the other two dance groups who can take over.'

'Great. Thanks, Marc. I feel so much better,' she said sarcastically. 'So you're saying that I should go ahead? What do you think, Yannish?'

'I think he's desperate. He knows he will never escape so he is more likely to trust you. It also means you can keep an eye on him.'

'I think it was a bit dangerous to tell him we knew about Oleander and the spiders,' Winna said. 'He'll tell her.'

'Somehow I don't think he will.' Daisy looked at them quietly. 'He told me he was grateful when I went to help him. I think he meant what he said.'

'I will alert Shakita. Meanwhile, try to hold your nerve, Daisy,' said Yannish, holding her hand. 'You are not alone. We are all here to protect you.'

'It's not just me,' Daisy said to him. 'It's waiting for the next attack and not knowing who is friend or enemy.'

'I understand. Stick together. Do not be beguiled by any offer from anyone which will separate you. Together you are strong.'

Aloysius looked at Winna with a guilty smile.

'Now try to relax. I will see you in the music room tomorrow.'

The only one who wasn't relaxed was Jonathan. He was worried about Daisy.

Massoud was the one who had cast a spell of spiders. He shuddered when he thought about it. He would talk to Marc and maybe they could follow Massoud together. If they were careful, perhaps they could find out if he was being honest, or if Oleander had ordered him to join the dance class to be Daisy's partner.

He felt anger fill him. Fear, too. This situation wasn't like the last time, when Daisy was in danger in the Red Ray. That was bad enough, but this was much more dangerous because they didn't know who they were up against. He had been attacked and survived, then some students and Professor Sanandez had been hurt. Who would be next? Daisy, Yannish, perhaps the whole orchestra? He made up his mind to ask Dan to watch over her whilst he and Marc quietly sniffed around. Better not tell Daisy though, he decided.

The next day, construction work began on the main entrance and reception area. There were only a few more weeks to go before the final concert, so it was essential to restore the academy in time.

Isobel, the receptionist, now worked in a room by the back entrance. She was a happy, busy soul, taking on extra jobs to help Collette du Bois who was standing in for Professor Sanandez at Yannish's suggestion. Collette had engaged more help so as to allow Isobel to deal with the more important jobs.

New computers had been installed and she was busily making booking arrangements for those wanting to attend the special day. Many of the people coming needed somewhere to stay so she was contacting local hotels. It was a huge event with many interested people coming, not just to hear their sons and daughters but because this academy was trying to make a difference in international relationships. Professor Sanandez was a well-known figure who was much loved and admired for his commitment to help young people from all over the world.

**

There was a song in the air as the labourers began their work of stripping down burnt walls, ceiling and floors. The sun was hot but these workmen were used to it. These men, like the local farm peasants, were the heart of Spain. They were strong, resilient and very proud.

After Oleander had tried to harm Professor Sanandez, Yannish had him constantly under surveillance. His whereabouts were secret and, as he slowly recovered from his ordeal, he was moved around to stay in different clinics until he would be well enough to come back and resume his duties. Shakita watched over him like the keen-eyed hawk or stork that she sometimes became. She missed nothing. Being invisible, she was free to observe and take any necessary action.

As yet, Oleander wasn't aware of her presence, though she knew there was a resistance, like a cross-current, inhibiting her efforts. She couldn't quite fathom it out, but she would. The explosion should have killed most of the students. Her plans had been carefully laid. Then something had made them sit closer to the kitchen. Why? She clenched her fingers in rage as she remembered, breaking one of her scarlet nails. She swore quietly.

And then there was the hospital visit. The Professor should have been there. He should be dead by now but, somehow, he had been spirited away.

'Very smart,' she hissed between tight lips.

She relaxed with a brief smile as she toyed with her new plan. She never allowed herself to be bothered for too long if things didn't go as she'd expected, though any miscalculation irritated her immensely.

She shrugged her shoulders, thinking of her next move. It would be a distraction to hide the real assault that would destroy Yannish's intentions. Maybe several distractions, if that idiot was up to scratch. There was little time now and every detail had to be fine tuned.

Servant was weakening. He'd been obedient to her wishes, though once this was over she would get rid of him. But first, he had to carry out his part.

She regarded at her broken nail. 'Never mind, this is nothing to the havoc I will create,' she said to herself.

She would call upon all the forces of evil and let the darkness come.

 *Chapter 31*

Creating a Barrier of Safety

'Don't you think it's funny we've taken for granted playing in the orchestra?' Jonathan casually asked the others as they chatted in the girls' room.

'Yeah, it's weird all right,' said Marc. 'Personally, I'd like it to go on forever, but playing in a pop group would be even better.' His eyes sparkled at the thought of dazzling screaming fans as he played in the biggest band ever.

'Hey, Marco, I'd never have had you for a pop star,' said Al. 'I see you more as the brilliant sleuth, like Sherlock Holmes, invisible but penetrating in your deductions.'

'Yeah, well I could do both, couldn't I, Al?'

'You're right though, Jonno,' said Winna unhappily. 'We do take it for granted now. I just love playing the flute and piano, and the thought of going back and not being able to is too awful. Don't you think so? It's okay for you, cos' you can already play, but for us it'll be devastating.'

'Performing in an orchestra is something else, Winna,' said Daisy. 'None of us were anywhere near that standard, so I feel the same as you. I guess we'll all go back to where we were before we came here.' She sighed. 'Still, it's been fantastic, hasn't it? Do you think you'll learn to play at school, Winn?'

'You bet. Well, only if my parents can afford the lessons, that is.

They don't have much money.'

There was an awkward silence and then Dan whispered, 'Do you know what we're practising today?' They turned to him, forgetting the moment of reality for Winna back home. Dan scanned their faces. 'Yannish said the orchestra is going to finish our part with music from Star Wars.'

'Wicked,' Jonathan cried, thumping the air.

'Are you sure, Dan?' asked Marc 'It seems a bit poppy for Yannish. Hardly classical music.'

'Maybe it will become a pop classic.' Hiromi suggested. 'If it isn't already.'

'You know what I think?' said Daisy. 'Al's to blame. He's the one everyone wants to hear with his jazz band.'

They all fell about laughing. Troubles seemed far away at that moment.

***

'Come on, Gang,' said Daisy. 'We've just got time to come together with the Orange Ray before we go. I think we should all try the gemrays out to see what they can do.'

'Good one,' said her twin. 'We haven't tested them properly, have we?'

They sat in their usual circle. Daisy took her orange gemray out of her pocket and held it up, pointing towards her friends. Each one did the same so that the point of each one touched the next. As they did so, it burst into an orange flame. The flame expanded before their astonished eyes flickering, enveloping them as it turned from the deepest orange, passing through every shade, into gold. Finally it rose above their heads, forming itself into the most beautiful seven-pointed star. Shakita appeared in the centre of the star. She opened her arms wide to greet them, smiling as she did so.

They gazed at her, bathed in the warmth of her ray, unable to speak. The beautiful apparition before them gently lowered herself effortlessly to the floor.

'Welcome, my friends.'

Daisy was the first to gather her wits. The others still couldn't believe what they had seen. It was though they had been touched by some Heavenly Being.

'We're so happy to see you at last, Shakita.'

Shakita smiled through the pulsating rays of orange energy. 'The University of Light is proud of all of you,' she said.

'Thanks,' they said.

'We were beginning to get worried you'd never come,' Jonathan said to her.

'I know. You've been through and witnessed many traumas. Are you all right now, Jonathan?'

'I'm fine, though it was scary. Did you come to help me, Shakita?'

'Did it help?'

'It was the best dream I've ever had.' He beamed at her, remembering the peace he'd felt. She touched his hand fleetingly.

'Now, my friends, we are reaching the end of yours and the students' time here.' They watched her quietly. Her face was still but serious, studying each one. 'You have done so well with your gemrays. When you unite like this, you create a barrier of safety around the students and academy.'

'Really?' Jonathan looked at the others with delight and astonishment.

'Really.' Shakita laughed. 'Haven't you noticed how much the students have changed?'

'Yes, but that wasn't due to us. It was because Professor Sanandez risked his own life to save theirs – that's what changed their attitude to each other.'

'Of course, Jonathan, you are right. The Professor was willing to sacrifice himself for them. But it was also your contribution that helped create the change.'

'Thanks, Shakita. We appreciate knowing that. What do we have to do now?' Daisy asked, coming back to practical matters. 'Yannish has advised us to stick together as much as possible.'

'That is right. The energy you hold together makes it more difficult for Oleander to penetrate.'

'It's not always possible,' said Hiromi, interrupting impatiently. 'Some of us are separated in the dancing class. Daisy is in an awful mess because she has to partner Massoud. She never wanted to, but Ronnie asked her to and she couldn't refuse. How does she deal with that?'

Daisy squeezed her hand. 'It's all right, Hiromi.'

'Daisy, my dear. You have some influence on Massoud and because of this you will be able to steer him in the right direction. These things happen for a reason. It wasn't an accident you were chosen.'

'Okay,' Daisy said slowly, trying to work out who manipulated this move in the first place. 'Was it Oleander who made it happen, or you, Shakita?' She looked at Shakita directly in the eyes.

'It was Oleander,' Shakita said quietly. 'But you weren't the one targeted.'

'I wasn't? Then, who?' She suddenly realised it was meant to be Hiromi, who'd had the same thought. They stared at each other, then looked back at Shakita, confused and disturbed.

'Oleander wanted to attack you through your friend Hiromi. She knew this would hurt you more, as it did with Jonathan. She knows you are the Initiator of the group so she is trying to attack those around you first. I placed the idea in your head to stay behind to watch Hiromi dance. Do you understand, Daisy, why I had to do this?'

'I guess so. You're right. I wouldn't want Hiromi to be used instead of me, but I just hope I can persuade Massoud to come over to our side, that's all.'

'This is just not fair!' Hiromi exploded. 'I am quite able to protect myself, thank you very much.' She was furious and felt stupid her friend had been manipulated by Shakita.

'Please do not feel angry or humiliated, Hiromi. I am not suggesting you are not able to handle this situation. I chose Daisy simply because she has seen Massoud at his weakest point. She has a connection with him which will influence his behaviour.'

'I'm still not happy about this.' Hiromi scowled at Shakita. 'Why does Daisy always have to be the one to be used?'

'Because she represents the Violet Ray and has put herself forward as the Initiator.'

'It's all right, Hiromi. I understand what lies behind Massoud's choice now, so I don't mind a bit. In fact, I'm quite looking forward to the partnership.' She gave Shakita a foxy smile.

'Now, each of you concentrate on keeping the balance between yourselves and the students. Imagine that every time you breathe in, you breathe out the Orange energy to those you meet and talk to. Visualise rays of healing and harmony radiating out from the Cosmos and the University of Light, and use your gemrays discreetly for the time being. There will be a time when you will discover the real power of these wands. They are tools that will transform destructive energy. I will instruct you all on this when the time is right. Meanwhile, just keep the balance and continue doing exactly what you are doing.'

'What happens if Oleander starts a full scale attack?' Dan asked her.

'I will be there to meet her. It will need my power and Calidus to stop her, but be warned. She is dangerous, very dangerous indeed. You will have your part to play in this.' She looked at them gravely and then, brightening up, she stood to leave.

'I will say goodbye now, my friends, but I am close to you, remember.' So saying, she faded within the flame.

The room became still, leaving a wonderful sense of warmth.

'I wonder what she meant when she said we would have our part to stop Oleander?' asked Jonathan.

'I guess these gemrays can do more than we think,' said Aloysius, wiping his forehead. 'I could fight an army now.'

'Let's hope we don't have to,' Hiromi replied dryly

Hiromi still felt slighted and generally irritated by Shakita. She felt like some stupid idiot who wasn't capable of anything important.

Daisy knew how she felt. She was sorry but could do nothing. Events were happening so quickly they had to learn to adapt to them and not quarrel among themselves. Or that was another way Oleander would score.

She wondered about the gemrays and what their part would be when they found out Oleander's true identity. All hell would break loose. She shivered inside at the enormity of the thought and then quickly turned her attention back to the present.

'Come on, Hiromi, let's forget it. You'll be in a good position to look out for me.'

'Okay,' Hiromi replied grudgingly. 'But I'm not a child.'

They linked arms as they left the bedroom. Today was another day.

Following close behind Daisy and Hiromi was Dan, Al and Winna. Jonathan and Marc kept some distance away. They whispered between themselves about their idea of stalking Massoud.

'We know now what his plan is, but we could still follow him and find out what other devious plots they're scheming. You're the detective," said Jonathan. 'I'll follow you.'

Marc beamed his thanks. 'We can do this but we'll have to be really careful.

If Daisy knew she'll go ballistic.'

Jonathan drew a deep sigh, wondering if they were being foolhardy. Both Yannish and Shakita had told them not to separate. Oh well, these are desperate times needing desperate action, he thought to himself, brightening up.

'What are you two up to? Plotting again?' Daisy tweaked her brother's ear.

'Not likely, Boss woman. We wouldn't want to incur your imperial anger.'

'Oh, shut up.' She pulled a face at him and walked on.

'Come on, girls, lighten up.' Al teased them. 'It's Star Wars' time.'

'Get on with you, Jazzman. Lead us to breakfast. I am as hungry as a lion,' said Winna, pushing him along.

Chapter 32

A Call to Arms

Yannish had taken his students through most of Mozart's Symphony No 40 to his satisfaction. There were four movements in total and he felt they understood all the nuances and varying shades of differences that Mozart had intended.

There was only the last movement to complete. This could be started the following week and then the whole symphony played as a whole.

Today he was introducing music from the film series Star Wars. The music was written by John Williams, a famous American composer. Yannish was looking forward to seeing the students' faces when he announced the morning's work.

As usual, the Colour Code Gang took their instruments into their rooms each night. Noticing this careful action, many other students began to do the same. Daisy and her friends seemed to show the way, almost as if they had a natural authority. It took longer for all of them to assemble their instruments the following morning, but Yannish approved their reasons and gave them the time they needed. In this way, another level of trust was formed.

'Now, my friends, we will give the Honourable Mozart a rest this morning and start a score from the films of Star Wars. I am sure most of you have seen these films.' There were howls and whistles from most of the students and blank faces from others. Yannish noticed this. 'This music is light and exciting. You will enjoy playing it, I think. The scores are before you, so let's begin.'

It was easy to play, and fun to relax with music that had so much visual imagination. Daisy and Jonathan grinned at each other as they remembered each film sequence as they played. She looked at Chelsea who beamed her pleasure, then at Jovan sitting next to her. He smiled back. He actually smiled back! Daisy could hardly believe it. Chelsea noticed him smile and winked at Daisy. I don't believe it. Chelsea's tamed the beast, thought Daisy, hardly believing what she saw.

'Daisy, where are you? Have you been transported away?' asked Yannish.

'Sorry, Yannish.' She apologised quickly. 'I got distracted.'

Later that morning, as they filed out of the Music Room, Hiromi sidled up to Daisy.

'So what happened to you?' she asked.

'You're never going to believe this.' Daisy burst out, 'but I think Chelsea's got Jovan's attention at last.'

'Never!' Hiromi laughed. 'You're joking, right?'

Daisy told her about her distraction during the morning and how Chelsea gave her a rather conspiratorial wink as if to boast she had conquered the arrogant Jovan.

'I wonder what happened to his girlfriend? Is she still alive?' Hiromi chuckled.

'Probably flattened somewhere!' Daisy giggled. 'Or maybe she's planning some terrible revenge.'

As they went towards the dining room, Chelsea caught up with them looking as fresh and as carefree as a newborn lamb.

'So, what's new?' Hiromi cooed. 'You look fantastic, Chels.'

Chelsea wound a strand of her platinum blonde hair round her finger. Her baby blue eyes shone with the compliment. She smiled with confidence.

'Jovan and I are an item now.'

'Really! You crafty girl. How did you get rid of the girlfriend?'

'She was becoming a bit of a drag,' Chelsea said dreamily. 'I think he was bored with her constant mothering. What he needs is someone more dynamic and exciting.'

'Well, you've certainly made a change in him. I've never seen him so friendly.' Daisy congratulated her.

'He's great really. I know he's pompous and arrogant, but so am I. That's why I like him. He's clever too.'

'Well, good luck, Chels,' Daisy said warmly, really meaning it.

'Gee, thanks you two. It means a lot to me that we're friends.' She quickly hugged them and ran to catch up with Jovan.

'Brilliant.' Daisy laughed. 'Perhaps we'll see another side of him.'

'Wonders will never cease,' said Hiromi as she ruffled Daisy's hair.

As they made their way to the Art Room after lunch, Francesca came running out.

'Someone's destroyed our artwork!' she shouted. 'It's ruined! There's nothing left.' She continued running into the main building to find Collette du Bois and Yannish.

Daisy and Hiromi hurried in to see what had happened. Devastation lay before them. The whole of the wall, where each student had lovingly drawn and painted their art, had been destroyed. Black paint had been poured over the whole mural. In some places, where they had designed a collage of added materials from natural fabrics, knives had been used to slice and savagely hack their work to bits. Pieces of coloured silk, ribbons, paper and wood hung off the wall, sadly drooping with nowhere to go.

Beads lay crushed on the ground. All the hard work and original ideas from each student and culture had been deliberately and cruelly destroyed. It was a frenzied attack. Nothing was left.

Hamish was there, trying to mop up the paint. It had taken weeks of hard work to not only get some of the more reluctant students on their side, but to plan a beautiful tableau of which they would all be proud.

'How could this happen?' Hamish cried. 'Who could have done this?' He stared at them, dazed. 'Why?'

Daisy and Hiromi gazed at the horror before them. Hamish, uncertain as to what to say or do, began to wipe down the paint. It was everywhere. Other students came in, eager to continue their designs, and then stopped, gasping at the scene of destruction. Mixed emotions flooded through them. Shock, anger, dismay.

'What on earth…? Who…? Why…?'

Francesca came back with Collette and Yannish, tears streaming down her face.

'You see,' she cried. 'What kind of maniac would do such a thing?'

Yannish looked with deep sadness. Collette waved her arms about, uttering disgust and anger.

'Francesca and Hamish, I am overwhelmed with grief' she said. 'I cannot tell you how shocked I am that someone should sabotage the students' work.'

Hamish stopped mopping up the sticky paint to put his arm round Francesca's shaking shoulders.

'Do people hate us so much?' she whispered to him.

Daisy stepped forward. 'Let's help clear this place up. With all of us working together, it will be done in no time.' She looked at all the students, urging them to help. 'We can then start the mural all over again.'

'That's right.' Jonathan joined in. 'We've still plenty of time.'

'Why not?' Aloysius slapped his hand. 'This was the practice run - the next one will be the real thing!'

'I'm with you,' Louis cried, looking around at the others. 'Bring it on.'

Francesca's mouth dropped open in total surprise. Hamish's face became red with excitement.

'We accept with all our hearts, aye Francesca?'

Francesca nodded her head, tears running down her face.

'I thank you so much. We can do it again, with your help,' she said.

Yannish watched the events with interest. Whatever Oleander did to try and ruin his plans, it seemed to have the opposite effect. The students wanted to help, not run away as she intended. He smiled to himself at the power of the human spirit.

Ariel put his hand up. 'You are right. This is some sick mind. I'm with you.'

After this, everyone clamoured to have their say and to offer their help.

'Why is this happening, Maestro? We know something is very wrong.' Kyan Khan questioned Yannish. 'We are not stupid or superstitious about bad omens. We live in the real world where it is hard enough to survive each day.' He looked at the others. They nodded in agreement. In this they were united.

Jovan stepped forward. 'There's been talk among ourselves, but now we want you to come clean. It's too late to brush us off with talk of accidents or freak spider storms that attacked only one person. We know there is more to this than you are telling us and we want to know the truth.'

Yannish faced them. 'I wanted only to spare you,' he told them quietly.

'We are not children,' Hannah Zimmerman said sharply. 'You encourage us to grow up and embrace each other's differences. Doesn't this mean you learn to trust us, as we have learnt to trust you?'

'Very well. Let us talk,' he said softly.

The Colour Code Gang sat to one side in fascination. They wanted to stay in the background, to let the students have their say. Daisy clasped Hiromi's hand.

Every nerve in Marc's body felt taut with apprehension as he squeezed in next to Jonathan. Dan, Aloysius and Winna remained quiet, watching the events. They knew there had been some rumblings among the students but didn't realise it had gone so far.

Yannish stood before them, searching for the right words to satisfy his students.

'Professor Sanandez and I have worked together to create an academy where students can share their talents together. You all know this. He told you about his dream the first night.' They all nodded their heads, remembering his words.

At that time, which seemed so long ago, many had scoffed or ridiculed the idea, but now, after playing together and discovering interests between each other instead of always finding differences, the situation was different. They'd also shared danger, pain, fear and laughter. They'd shared common interests that had allowed them to understand others' points of view and seek a new way of living. They were tired of violence, exhausted with war and attitudes of retaliation and revenge. Here, at the academy, they had discovered how one person could sacrifice himself to save their lives. Here they began to believe that hope was possible and a new trust could be formed.

Yannish said calmly, 'First, I must apologise for excluding you. It was not my intention to insult your intelligence, but to protect you. You are in our care in a country that is not your own. Therefore, it is our duty to see you are safe.' He paused.

Each student listened to their tutor, respect shining in their eyes.

'There is a negative element here that doesn't want us to succeed in our project to bring countries together. I do not know who is involved, but we have all experienced the results.'

'Was the spider attack on Jonathan part of this?' Louis asked.

'Yes it was. That was the first strike.'

'And the explosion?' Kyan Khan raised his hand.

'Yes. That was the most serious. Some of you could have been killed.'

Several students spoke at once, asking about Professor Sanandez.

'He is getting better, thank you, and hopes to be at the concert,' said Yannish.

Ariel regarded him quietly. All this he knew, because Yannish had told him in the hospital. He wondered how much Yannish would tell the students. Enough, he thought, to satisfy them. He kept quiet, watching the maestro.

Kyan Khan raised his hand. 'Yes Kyan.'

'Is this political?'

'Partly,' Yannish replied.

'Do you suspect who is involved?' Kyan asked again.

'All I can say is, there are those involved who gain more from division, and glory in destruction, than in positive results.'

'But we are only a small group. Why should anyone be interested in us?' Hannah Zimmerman asked, unbelieving. 'We're nobody.'

'You are wrong, Hannah. You are the future. We live in a world of extremes and polarities. Good and bad, heaven and earth, light and dark - often one state will, by its very nature, attract the opposite force.'

This sounds like Calidus, thought Daisy.

'Do you mean that some people want to destroy your idea of trying to find peace within nations?' said Hannah.

'There is a malicious force fueling violence within the world. It's up to us, as individuals, to take our responsibility and choose another way to live. Do you believe in this? Remember, there is a greater force for good than there is for evil.'

Daisy's heart swelled as she heard these words. Everyone there rose in unison. She watched everyone there. Hamish and Francesca clapped their hands, encouraged by the power of his words. Strangely, Collette stiffened slightly by Yannish's side.

It was only for a moment, but Daisy saw it. Collette glanced at her for a fraction of a second, then back to Yannish, applauding him. The colours of her aura surrounding her darkened like an oncoming storm. Daisy wondered if she was mistaken. It had happened so quickly, but she was left with a chill in the pit of her stomach, as though someone had pierced her. She caught her breath quickly.

'Hey, you okay?' Hiromi asked, sensing the sudden change in her friend.

'Yes, I'm fine. It's fabulous how the students are responding,' she whispered back.

There was no way she was going to say anything to the others. Thinking about it, it sounded silly anyway, but her intuitive reaction warned her to be on her guard.

'What do we do now, Maestro?' Ishmael from Israel asked.

'I appreciate your desire to help and your unfailing support, my friends. I believe you are more mature than all of us here.' All the students stamped their feet in response. 'So, on a practical note, we first clean up this mess.' Yannish laughed. 'Then we continue our work with our music and dance. I feel in some way this is a call to arms, but not in a military way. It is more a call of the spirit within us to overcome this aggression. We will not be beaten.'

There was a resounding cheer and whoops of triumph from the students.

'Now I know why this academy is called La Reunion,' said Ariel.

 *Chapter 33*

True of False?

Daisy didn't know what to do with her feelings or her impressions. She didn't want to tell Hiromi – well, she did want to, but she daren't. Firstly because Hiromi's thoughts might attract the wrong person and, secondly, she might accidentally tell someone and increase their danger.

She thought about Jonathan. No way. He would attack head on. So would Winna and Marc. Aloysius's head was far too full of music. But what about Dan?

She could talk to him about anything. He might even sense that something was bothering her. He never missed a trick but, at the same time, she didn't want to put him in danger either. Maybe she was completely wrong and Collette was just tired and worried about the mural being damaged – and yet why did she feel this sudden shock?

She decided she must see Yannish. He would know what to do. Meanwhile, she would channel her thoughts away from her disturbed feelings.

***

Supper that night was noisy with lively discussion. There were those who had the latest gossip and those who believed they held secret information. There was no need to whisper anymore. The unspoken was now talked about. The Colour Code Gang kept to themselves, not wishing to add their views. They chatted among themselves and left as soon as they could without attracting any attention.

Back in the girls' room, they swapped their own thoughts about the incident.

'Now we know that Francesca and Hamish are definitely not involved.' Jonathan pronounced.

'Looks like it.' Marc agreed, satisfied. 'It certainly narrows the field.'

'It was great you suggested we all pull together and paint the mural again,' said Dan, grinning at Daisy. 'That was a stroke of brilliance.'

'But I'm puzzled, Dan. Why was the mural destroyed now, when there's enough time to repaint it? Don't you think Oleander would have chosen a time closer to the concert?'

'Good point, Dais - unless it was just to keep us occupied to hide the real threat.'

'Hmm, could be. We have to consider that. It might also be that Massoud made a mistake and did it too early,' Marc said slowly. He looked at Jonathan briefly.

They knew what they had to do, but needed to avoid the eagle eye of Daisy. They needn't have bothered, because Daisy was angling how to see Yannish without creating too much interest.

'Do you know what?' she began. 'I'm going to see Yannish. I'll tell him that I'm not going to dance with Massoud.' She looked at them for their approval.

'You're right,' Dan agreed. 'I can't see why you have to do it, anyway. We know what he's capable of, so why take the risk?'

'You know what I think, sis?' said Jonathan. 'You'd have to be bonkers to dance with that mullet.'

'Ditto.' Winna rolled her eyes at Jonathan.

'Any more advice?' she asked sweetly.

'Would you like me to come with you?' asked Hiromi.

'It's okay, Hiromi, but maybe we could go for a walk afterwards. Meet me by the fountain, say in twenty minutes.'

Marc looked at Jonathan with a sly smile. They had seen Massoud slip out the back entrance after supper. That was about ten minutes ago. They would have to hurry.

Daisy went straight to Yannish's room and was just about to knock on the door when she heard raised voices inside. Uncertain, she turned to go, when the door was flung open and Collette stormed through, her eyes flashing with anger.

'No good comes to those who listen at doors,' she hissed as she passed.

Daisy recoiled. 'I wasn't listening. I heard voices and decided to come back later. That's all,' she protested.

Collette looked back, her eyes cold and mocking. 'Well, maybe you will be able to get more out of him than I could.' She marched down the corridor, leaving a chill in the warm air.

Daisy knocked tentatively again.

'What now!' The door swung open. 'Oh, it's you,' said Yannish apologetically.

'Sorry, I can come back another time,' Daisy said nervously.

'I beg your pardon, Daisy. Come in. Is there a problem?'

'Are you sure it's all right?'

Yannish let out a long breath and shook himself as if to free himself from an irritation.

'It is nothing.' He grinned. 'Collette wanted to know where Professor Sanandez was and when he was coming back. That's all.'

'Did you tell her?'

Yannish looked at Daisy with a twinkle in his eyes.

'No, I did not. Now tell me, what is bothering you? I can see there is something.'

Daisy told him exactly what happened in the Art Room and how she felt.

'I am sure Collette is Oleander, Yannish.' She watched his face for some kind of reaction. 'She was also vicious just now. She knows that I know.'

Yannish was quiet. 'She can be difficult.'

He obviously wasn't going to say anymore, so Daisy didn't pursue it. Instead, she told him that she didn't want to dance with Massoud.

'I can understand how you must feel, Daisy, but somehow I feel that if you are close to him we have a better chance of reaching him. He likes you and is grateful for helping him.'

'Thanks a bunch.' Daisy's green eyes flashed.' It doesn't matter if I put myself in danger then, as long as I can get information from him!'

Yannish laughed out loud. 'Daisy, you are a feisty girl. You are tres sauvage. I would have loved to have had a daughter like you.'

'Well.' She shrugged, feeling a little mollified.

'I cannot tell you what to do in this matter. The only thing I know is that it's better to be close to your enemy.' He paused for a moment. He's probably thinking about Collette, Daisy thought. If he can do it, then so can I.

'Okay Maestro. I'll try it for a while, but if he puts a finger out of place...' She paused. 'I'll kill him.'

Yannish nodded his head in agreement. 'I'll help you.' He grinned.

As Daisy moved towards the door, she turned back to him. 'By the way, you never said what you thought about Collette being Oleander.'

He smiled at her artlessly. 'I think you have a very good idea what I think, young lady.' He quietly closed the door.

***

Marc and Jonathan quickly beat a hasty retreat to follow Massoud's steps. They walked quickly down the dusty path towards the woods, hoping none of the students would see or stop them. This was the way Marc had been before. He hoped he was right and that Massoud hadn't agreed to meet Oleander in another place.

He saw himself as an accomplished scout. He sniffed the air and looked for clues on the ground, on the branches and all footprints. Jonathan had no idea if he deducted any information from this, but he trusted him anyway.

Marc drew him forward, quietly diving behind trees and flattening themselves when they thought they heard some sound. Often Marc would stop suddenly, his finger to his lips for immediate silence, his eyes wide behind his glasses, listening intently. But Massoud was an experienced agent himself. He was quick and quiet, leaving no trace of his tracks.

Jonathan was beginning to sweat with the pace. Marc pushed him, hauled him and shoved him behind tree stumps as they made their way deeper and deeper into the woods. The trees were lower and wider than in England, so it was easier for coverage, but the humidity was high.

Marc stopped suddenly, signalling Jonathan to bend down quickly. He heard a voice. The boys flattened themselves to the ground, terrified to be found out.

'Oleander,' Servant whispered. 'I am happy to see you.'

'Really?' she breathed in his ear, tweaking it sharply. He howled.

'Why is that then, my little Servant, when you never do anything I tell you? Perhaps you think I will forgive you and set you free?' She stroked his face, smiling at the fear in his eyes.

'Tell me why, you snivelling idiot, you destroyed the art mural now instead of when I told you?' She kicked him sharply in the ribs.

Grasping his side, Massoud cried. 'I thought you said this week.'

'You moronic imbecile, don't you see that now you have given them time to replace it?' Her voice rose to a screech.

'I can do it again, after they've finished.' He grovelled, trying to make up for his blunder. 'They won't expect that.'

'It is too late now, you pinhead,' she spat with disgust. 'Then you were meant to create an accident with the Asian girl and now… poof!' Her eyes grew wide with disbelief.

'That wasn't my fault, Lady. She chose the Japanese boy instead, but I have a much better idea.' Massoud appealed to her. Oleander looked at him coldly, waiting.

'I have managed to get Daisy to partner me.'

'You have asked her?'

'Yes and she has agreed,' he said triumphantly. 'She will be at my mercy, I promise you.'

Oleander smiled for the first time. 'You must make no mistake this time, Servant. You know what will happen if you fail, don't you?'

Jonathan, hearing this, made a lurch forward. Marc grabbed him with one hand, pulling him back. His clapped his other hand over Jonathan's mouth to stop him yelling out.

'Quiet!' he hissed. 'Do you want us to be killed, and then Daisy?'

Jonathan snorted with fury but lay still.

'Very well,' Oleander relented. 'This is your very last chance. I have too much to do to think about you. There is too much at stake. I have a grand finale planned.' Her eyes glowed with pleasure as she pictured what was to come. Then she remembered Massoud.

'I shall be pleased to be rid of you,' she said viciously. She then kicked him soundly in his side before leaving.

Massoud cried with pain and sobbed into the earth. Both the boys saw a darkness lift, like a thunderous cloud dispersing after a storm. There was a smell of something decayed and rotten. They waited for some time, not daring to move.

Jonathan was so shocked and angry that he wanted to go down and finish off Massoud, but Marc cautioned him.

'We have to get back and warn the others, Jonno.'

After enough time had elapsed, they crawled forward until it was safe to get up. Jonathan was sick with worry. Daisy was in danger.

And then Marc suddenly laughed out loud. 'Hang on, Jonno.

partner Massoud?'

Relief flooded across Jonathan's dirty and scratched face.

'You're right, Marco. But we'll have to watch him in case he plans something else.'

***

Hiromi sat beside the fountain, waiting for Daisy. It was beginning to grow cold. Spanish days were hot but the temperature dropped at night. She smelt the aroma of sweet flowers and herbs and listened to the birds as they began to settle down for the night. From the corner of her eye she saw a green lizard suddenly appear, lifting its head to see if it was safe, then quickly dart behind a plant pot. Hiromi sighed with pleasure. It felt as if they'd been at the academy for ever.

Daisy came to meet her with a strange smile on her face.

'Did you get what you wanted?' Hiromi asked, curious to know what the smile meant.

'Not exactly. Well, not at all, but we did come to some kind of arrangement. Yannish still wants me to be Massoud's dance partner so I can keep an eye on him. He thinks he'll come clean, or something.'

'I don't believe it,' said Hiromi, exasperated.

'Yeah, I know what you mean. I told him I would try, but if Massoud got nasty, I'd let him have it and tell the whole academy.' Daisy nodded her head vigorously to emphasise her feeling.

'Come on,' she said, 'let's hang out a bit before we go back.'

***

Out of breath, Jonathan and Marc slipped into their room. The idea was to escape an interrogation by the girls and catch up with them in the morning. Unfortunately, the gamble didn't work. Stretched out on the boys' beds, awaiting their return, were Daisy, Winna and Hiromi.

Daisy gave them a cool stare. 'Where've you been?'

Jonathan glanced at her casually. 'For a stroll.'

'Boy! Some stroll.' Dryly, she regarded their torn clothes, scratched knees and faces. Both boys were totally wrecked.

The rest of them exploded in laughter.

'Okay, we surrender,' said Jonathan, sighing deeply. 'You tell them, Marc.'

Marc described their experience in detail. That Massoud had destroyed the art mural too soon. He told them how Oleander screamed with rage, kicking him.

'It was blood curdling,' Jonathan said, paling as he remembered. Then Marc told them of Massoud's new plan, to injure Daisy while dancing.

Jonathan laughed in relief. 'But his devious plan isn't going to work now, is it? Because you've told Yannish you're not going to dance with Massoud. Right?'

No one spoke. The silence was deafening. Hiromi drew in her breath, looking with horror at Daisy. Jonathan searched her face.

'Oh, no. You can't! You told us you wouldn't, you stupid girl.'

'I know. Yannish told me I didn't have to do it, but he also told me that sometimes it is better to keep the enemy close.'

'That's just great! Yannish doesn't have to do it,' Jonathan shouted, furious at the change of events.

Daisy suddenly thought about how close Yannish was to Collette.

'Look. Massoud knows if he steps out of line, by a fraction, I'll tell all the others he's responsible for all the problems here.'

'I'll tell all the others he's responsible...' Jonathan imitated her in a sweet little voice. 'Don't you know, bozo, that by then it will be too late!' He spat at her.

'Come on, you two.' Hiromi reached out her hand to placate them.

Both ignored her efforts to pacify. They were too entrenched in their own battle.

'Look, I know what you're saying, Jonno, but both Yannish and Shakita will be looking out for me. It's a chance to get him to confess.'

'You didn't hear his miserable whining voice trying to please Oleander. He'll do anything to save himself,' Jonathan shouted, tears glistening in his eyes.

'Oh, Jonno. I am sorry. I know how you feel. '

'No, you don't, you pea brain. But if you want to do what Yannish's says rather than what I want, then you deserve everything you get!' Jonathan was beside himself with rage. His face was flushed red, almost to the colour of his hair, the scratches highlighted by his fury. They faced each other like too aggressive boxers in a ring.

Daisy forced herself to relax. 'Look, Jonno, what you say and do is more important to me than anything. If you ask me not to dance with Massoud - then I won't.'

He stared at her, not believing what he'd just heard.

'You won't dance with him if I ask you?'

'That's right,' she replied.

The rest of the gang looked on, not daring to speak or move.

'Then I ask you, Daisy, do not partner Massoud.'

'Okay, I won't,' she said simply.

Dan ruffled Jonathan's hair. Everyone relaxed. Somehow they all felt it was a momentous occasion. They weren't children anymore. These were fundamental issues, when each one had to take responsibility and stand by his or her choice.

Marc felt that somehow Jonathan had grown in stature and Daisy had understood the importance of accepting his reasons and, in her wisdom, allowed him to take charge.

'Good,' he said lightly.

 *Chapter 34*

Massoud

The construction of the main Reception and dining area was almost completed. The coloured geometric tiles for the Reception had been replaced. These were especially designed for the academy in orange, blue, scarlet and turquoise. Professor Sanandez wanted the building to be restored to its former beauty. The dining room floor had been re-covered. Two new, large tables lay to one side, ready to be moved into place. New windows had been installed in place of the ones that had been blown out in the explosion.

In the Reception area, new covered basket chairs, plus a wooden table, waited to be moved into place, together with collages and paintings donated by local designers and artists.

The local people gave what they could. They honoured the Professor and the ideal he represented. All of them wanted to help restore the damage. Yannish could hardly believe the level of generosity he'd received from them. Pedro and his family and friends had come, too, to rebuild the damage outside the main entrance door, the fountain and garden.

There was a light air of joyfulness about the place as workmen whistled and sang, knowing they were on time for the concert.

This uplifting feeling carried through to the students. Instead of being devastated by the damage done to the mural in the Art Room, the students spent whatever time they could repainting their art forms and some of them chose different themes this time round.

When they'd originally painted the mural, there'd been a lack of motivation and expression. Some had been enthusiastic, some encouraged by Francesca and Hamish and some had felt coerced. This time, however, they'd wanted to do it for themselves. They'd wanted to prove a point that a destructive force couldn't stop them from unifying together. They believed in Carlos Sanandez's dream and this time they painted with more meaning, because now they understood and were living the dream. Both tutors were ecstatic with the result.

Breakfast was filled with a feeling of friendliness and expectation. Jonathan chatted to the others, relieved he had changed Daisy's mind. All of the Colour Code Gang felt relieved. Kyan Khan came up to them, looking a little concerned.

'Have you seen Massoud?' he asked.

'No,' Dan replied on behalf of the others. 'Why?'

'Well, he didn't sleep in his bed last night.' Kyan shared a room with him. There was a guffaw of laughter from some listening nearby.

Daisy looked sharply at Jonathan, who in turn looked at Marc.

'Are you sure?' Winna said.

'Yes, the last time I saw him was at last night's supper. Do you think I should tell Collette or Yannish?'

'Hang on a minute, Kyan.' Daisy raised her hand to him. 'I have a feeling I know where he might be, and if I can't find him, I'll tell Yannish if you like.'

Kyan was clearly worried. 'Oh, thank you, Daisy. I hope he is all right.'

'He'll be fine.' Daisy smiled.

Quickly she turned to Jonathan and Marc. 'You said you heard him yell out, as if Oleander was kicking him?'

'Yeah, well, something like that,' Marc answered. 'But we couldn't wait because we had to get back.'

'She must've really hurt him.' Daisy looked concerned. 'I've seen what she can do. We'd better go and look for him. Maybe he's dead.'

'I tell you what,' Winna said. 'Why don't you, Marc and Dan go and we'll let Yannish know. Oh, and take your mobile with you.'

'Brilliant, Winn, thanks,' said Daisy, relieved.

'Come on, guys,' said Winna. They slipped out of the back entrance as quietly as they could.

'He'll probably need medical treatment,' said Daisy.

'Try not to worry. Yannish will arrange everything. What we've got to do is find him,' Dan said.

'But it's been nearly eleven hours, Dan.' She moaned. Even though she knew Massoud had done terrible things, she felt sorry for him.

Marc led them the way he and Jonathan had travelled the evening before. As they made their way towards the woods they saw a figure slouched against a tree. It was Massoud.

He could barely stand, so he had propped himself up as best he could. He had broken a branch off to use as a staff and hold himself up. He looked terrible. His face was very pale and twisted in pain as he held his left side. One of his shoes had come off and his sock was torn as he'd scrambled through the undergrowth.

They ran quickly towards him. Dan slipped his arm around his waist to take his weight. Massoud winced in pain. He managed a weak smile.

'Hi, Daisy. Thank you for coming to find me.'

'How did you manage to get this far, Massoud?'

'It's taken me a long time and I stopped to sleep in between.' He smiled weakly. 'Has anyone missed me?'

'Only Kyan when you didn't come home last night - that's all.'

Daisy's mobile rang. It was Yannish. He told her to come through the front French windows of his room so that no one would see them. She told him they had Massoud and would be there within a few minutes.

Yannish was waiting for them. He gently ushered them in and down the corridor to the sick bay where Sylvie, the Canadian nurse, was waiting for them. Dan gently slid Massoud onto the bed.

'Thanks, guys. I'll take over from here. Gee, what does the other guy look like?' Sylvie joked at Massoud. 'Okay, I understand. No one can come in except you and Daisy. Right?' She grinned at Yannish.

'Well remembered, Sylvie. I'll check on him later. Now, try to rest young man,' he said. 'Sylvie will take care of you.'

Sylvie smiled. 'Sure, but this is beginning to look like a bad habit!'

They made their way to the Music Room. Nothing was mentioned about Massoud. Curiously no one seemed to notice he was missing, except Kyan. Daisy smiled at him to reassure him all was well. She would tell him later.

Yannish took them through the last movement of Mozart's Symphony. This time the students were inspired and concentrated. Yannish didn't have to shout at them or cajole them for being out of tempo. Although Dan wasn't sympathetic towards Massoud, he did miss him as a musician. He was a good cellist and, together with Yoshi Atari, he contributed much to the overall music.

Daisy slipped back to the sick bay at lunchtime to see how Massoud was. Sylvie let her in after she whispered her name through the door. He looked much better - cleaner and more rested. Sylvie told her he had two cracked ribs and bruises down the whole of his left side. The scratches on his face and knees, due to dragging himself through the undergrowth, were thankfully superficial.

Massoud was eating lunch. He was ravenous, gulping down his food in between bouts of pain.

'I'm going to get my lunch now, so if you want to stay with him, that's all right.' Sylvie told Daisy.

Daisy sat close to him when they were alone.

'You can't keep doing this, Massoud. She'll kill you.'

'Not if I do as she says,' he answered stiffly.

Daisy ignored this remark, knowing full well she was the next target.

'Do you honestly believe she'll set you free?'

'She promised,' he said, his voice quavering, fear showing in his eyes.

'You made a hash of the mural and now you're going to fail in the dance routine.'

He gasped at her. 'What do you mean?'

'Do you really think we don't know about your plans to hurt me?' Daisy leaned forward, her green eyes glinting dangerously.

'You were there?' He seemed to shrivel within himself. Sweat began to form on his brow.

'I wasn't, but Jonathan and Marc were. They heard everything that was said and Jonathan isn't very pleased, especially after the spider thing.' She spoke slowly, drawing out each word.

'Please, Daisy. I'm caught in a trap.' He told her how Oleander had first come to his home in Afghanistan, offering him a chance to escape and learn music. How she'd given money to his mother and family. Then, later, she'd begun to blackmail him with the lives of his family so he would do what she wanted. By the time he realised, it was too late.

'Don't you think I would do anything to turn the clocks back?' His big brown eyes overflowed with tears.

'So let us help you so you need never be bothered with her again.'

'You don't know how powerful she is,' he said, pleading. 'She is awesome. The things she has made me do for her...'

'Don't you know we have powerful people too, far greater than Oleander?' She boasted, praying in her heart all the good guys from the University of Light were listening.

'I don't believe you,' he said.

'It's true, Massoud. Oh, and incidentally,' she said as casually as she could. 'I know who Oleander is.'

He gaped at her, panic filling him, terrified the walls had ears. 'Not through me,' he said, struggling to get up.

Daisy gently laid him back. She told him how she had inadvertently guessed and that Collette was aware she knew. Massoud held his face in his hands.

'Look, Massoud. She will never let you go and when she finds out I am not going to be your partner, she'll kill you anyway.'

'What about my family? She knows where they are.' He wailed in despair.

'We do too and will get them out before she even thinks about it,' Daisy said triumphantly, mentally crossing her fingers.

He sighed, all his energy completely drained. 'Very well. I have nothing to lose, if you are telling me the truth.'

Daisy nodded.

'What do I have to do?'

'I will talk to Yannish. We will keep you away from Oleander so she can't hurt you anymore. Try not to worry, Massoud. I promise we will protect you as long as you are true to us.'

He nodded his head in agreement.

Daisy stood, ready to leave, then looked down at Massoud. 'Do you know any of Oleander's plans?'

'No. She never tells me anything except that she'll do anything to stop the concert. And she did say she had planned a Grand Finale.'

'Okay. By the way, what is the connection between Oleander and the bush outside her window?'

'I don't know. She's always hanging around it.'

'Hmm. How very weird,' Daisy said, opening the door.

Outside in the corridor she met Josefina, and further along she saw Collette coming towards her. She smiled as she passed Josefina, trying to think of what to say when Collette came close.

'Hi, Josefina. How are you today?'

Josefina flashed her gold teeth. 'I am veery good, and you?' she asked, but Daisy's eyes were already on Collette.

'I see you coming out of the sick bay, ma petit. I hope nothing is wrong?' Collette sounded concerned.

'I'm afraid I've strained a muscle in my leg,' Daisy replied. She showed her the back of her thigh.

'Oh, no! That is terrible.' Collette touched her hand in sympathy. 'You will be able to dance, no?'

Daisy tried to look dejected. 'I'm not sure, Collette. I hope so. I will rest it for a few days.'

'Maybe I can help. I am very good at massage.'

I bet! thought Daisy. 'Oh, thanks, Collette,' she said. 'But Hiromi said she would help me.'

'Take care, my little one. We don't want you to miss the fun,' Collette purred and walked away.

'Nor you,' Daisy snarled.

***

Yannish congratulated her on her success in persuading Massoud to confess.

'What happens now?' Daisy asked him, after telling him about Collette outside the sick bay.

'You are off the hook,' he said, smiling. 'Now, Massoud will resume his position in the orchestra as usual, but when Oleander signals him to see her, Shakita will go in his place.' He laughed at Daisy's astonished face. 'She is very good at disguises, apart from storks. She has even pretended to be me. Oleander will never know and she will pretend to think of another plan to get to you.'

'There is just one thing,' Daisy said. 'Massoud can't play at the moment. Don't you think Collette will find out?'

'Shakita will see to his physical problems. Do you remember how she helped Jonathan?'

Daisy smiled, relieved.

'We just have to make sure he tells us when Oleander contacts him to meet her and doesn't go on his own,' said Yannish. 'I will talk to him now. It is his only hope.'

Daisy left him, feeling more relieved in one way but anxious in another. Time was running out and the dread of something terrible happening filled her with alarm.

She was beginning to feel scared and needed her friends.

 *Chapter 35*

The Source of Oleander's Power

'What's with the leg?' Winna asked, seeing Daisy limping. 'I've just seen Collette coming out of the sick bay, so I had to pretend I'd pulled a muscle in my leg and maybe won't be able to dance with Massoud,' she said to her. 'I promised Jonno.'

'Of course, so this will be your excuse to Ronnie, right?'

'Yes, but I'm not looking forward to telling her.'

'Come on,' said Winna. 'I'll come with you. Her bark is worse than her bite – I think!'

Daisy allowed herself to be guided by Winna. She had an air of confidence and self belief that was good to lean on. With head held high, Winna led the way to the Dance Studio.

Ronnie was busy organising her dancers. She noticed immediately. 'What's happened here?'

Daisy told her nervously. She hated lying, but she had promised Jonathan she would quit anyway. This gave her courage.

Ronnie sighed, clicking her tongue with irritation. 'All right. If you can't, you can't.'

'I am sorry, Ronnie.'

'Look, if this is the worst thing that happens we'll survive. I heard about the awful accident with the art mural. Don't worry,' she said. 'Just take care of yourself. Have you told Massoud?'

'Yeah. He's okay with it.'

'Gotcha,' Ronnie replied, her mind already on her other dancers. 'I've got to go now.' With a flash of a smile she was gone.

Daisy breathed a huge sigh of relief. At least that part was clear. She decided to spend a little time by herself in the garden while the other students were practising their dancing or painting the art mural. She needed time to think things through. Soon she'd have to tell her friends about Collette. Massoud was safe if he followed Yannish's orders.

She found a sheltered place in between the trellis work. It was like an open green-house with a brick wall behind it. On either side were climbing honeysuckles, blue bougainvilleas and lush greenery. She snuggled in like a little animal seeking shelter. It was the perfect hiding place where she had a good view of the garden but couldn't be seen by anyone.

She thought about all that had happened from the first moment when she and her friends walked up the winding dusty road to the academy. It seemed years ago. Pictures of the first night came into her mind, of Professor Sanandez, with his gentle smile and the way he told them about his dream to bring young people together with music and art and how the students had reacted to his words. She thought about the inspirational influence of Yannish and how he was able to enthuse each student, except Jovan at first, but even he had changed for the better.

She laughed to herself as she remembered how Jonathan and Marc had sneered at the thought of dancing and art and now they couldn't wait to show off on the dance floor. Then she thought about the sequence of events, when the attacks began.

First, Jonathan. She shuddered. Would she ever forget that image of the spiders attacking him? She shook her shoulders to free herself of the ugly memory. Then she thought about the awful explosion. Students could have been killed. Thankfully only a few were injured, but the Professor had nearly lost his life.

This was when the tide of feeling began to change. Many of the students' attitudes had already softened as a result of playing music together. Yannish had lifted them to another level of fulfilment. He'd said beauty was the way to touch people's hearts.

Daisy knew this. She had the gift of being able to see colours around people and plants. Calidus had told her how every living thing had an energy field around it, which was called an aura. She'd watched as the auric colours around some of the students changed from angry dark ones to lighter, softer colours that almost danced with vitality.

It was after this event that the students chose to stay and then, after the art mural was destroyed, they'd all wanted to be involved in helping to restore it. Daisy remembered what Collette had told Massoud – that there was going to be a grand finale. Would there be another explosion? What gruesome plan had Oleander got in mind? It was time she told the others about who she really was.

Just as she was about to get up from her hiding place, something caught her eye. It was Collette, coming out into the garden from the French windows of her room. Daisy drew back and watched. Collette looked carefully around, taking her time to check she was alone. Then, when she was completely satisfied, she quickly went towards the Oleander bush. It was in full bloom and bursting with exuberance, its scarlet flowers drinking in the afternoon sun.

She stood before it, raising her arms as though it was an altar and she was performing some ritualistic ceremony. She spoke some words but she was too far away for Daisy to hear. Then she plucked the blooms, sucking them ravenously with an ecstatic look on her face as she devoured everyone. Her face dripped with red juice.

Next, Daisy watched with horrified fascination as Collette tore off leaves and chewed them voraciously. She was extracting all the poison from the plant. Daisy clapped her hand to her mouth, trying not to cry out.

Collette quickly wiped her mouth on her sleeve, looking around once more. She seemed to grow in size. She was no longer the petite little French lady the students so loved, but a grotesque figure who vibrated unadulterated evil. The face was white and ghoulish with red eyes and a cruel mouth drawn tightly over yellowing teeth still dripping poison. The black covered figure exuded a decaying smell that Daisy had smelt before.

Daisy gasped, holding her breath and nose, hardly daring to breathe. She closed her eyes in sheer terror, squeezing herself into a small, tight ball.

'Please don't let her see me,' she whispered. 'Please, Calidus, help me.'

Slowly she opened her eyes. Oleander was changing again. Within a few moments the sweet form of Collette reappeared. With a flick of her fair hair, she went back into the building.

Daisy slumped against the trellis wall. She felt sick and horrified by what she'd witnessed. She stayed there for some time, trying to make sense of what she'd seen. She had asked Massoud about the significance of the Oleander bush, intuitively feeling the connection between them. Now she knew for certain. She had witnessed it. The bush gave her energy. The poison within gave her life.

Daisy shuddered, revolted. Just as the legend where vampires needed to feast on human blood, so Oleander needed the poison to become the monster of destruction. Daisy knew she had to tell the others quickly and that somehow they'd have to destroy the Oleander bush. If they could do that, then Collette would be powerless.

***

'You missed some fun.' Jonathan told his sister. 'Rap and Hip Hop are wicked.'

Marc flopped down beside him. 'I'm wrecked.' He yawned hugely.

They'd found Daisy waiting by the fountain. She'd wanted to catch them as they'd each come out of the studios.

'We need to talk. All of us.'

Hiromi saw how pale Daisy was.

'Let's get out of here and go by the stream,' she said, pulling Daisy up. 'It's quiet there.'

Daisy squeezed her hand with relief. Hiromi was always so calm.

They followed the path down the rough, dusty road, through the trees to the stream, talking about their day. Daisy chose the place where she, Hiromi and Dan had sat when they'd looked for the herbs. It seemed a long time ago now.

They gathered round Daisy as though, in some way, they needed to protect her.

She told them of her feelings about Collette in the art room, and everything since. They listened without saying a word. Aloysius was shocked when she told them how she'd seen Collette with the Oleander bush.

'I can't believe it.' His black face seemed to pale. 'I would have trusted her with my life.'

'I told you she was no good if she didn't play Jazz,' Winna said dryly.

'But she's always so kind to us and she's gorgeous.' Jonathan sighed. 'I can't believe it. Are you sure, Daisy?'

Daisy felt into her pocket and retrieved her mobile. She clicked the latest photos to show them pictures of Collette as she ate the flowers and leaves.

'Yuk!' Winna gulped. 'No wonder you look pale, Daisy.'

'I feel sick.' Aloysius moaned. 'I trusted her completely.'

'I thought she was too good to be true,' Winna said. 'A bit sickly really.'

'You can be so pompous, Winna,' retorted Dan. 'All of us liked her. I think you were a bit jealous of her popularity.'

'Rubbish,' Winna growled. 'I just felt Al was too trusting, that's all.'

'Are you sure she didn't see you, Daisy?' Hiromi asked anxiously.

'Pretty sure, even when I took the photos. It nearly freaked me out but I knew I had to get them for evidence. I tried to take some others but I was too frightened.'

'She looks weird,' said Marc, studying the photos. 'This is what she's really like, not the sweet little French woman we know.' He shivered with fear and revulsion.

'You should have seen her,' Daisy whispered. 'The more she ate, the more she changed.' Her eyes grew large with fear. 'She grew into a horrible monster. This is who Oleander really is.'

'Why didn't you tell us, Daisy?' Dan looked cross. 'We had a right to know.'

'I daren't, because any of us could've betrayed our feelings. But now it's much more serious. Now we know how she gets her power. The Oleander bush looks lovely, but it's poisonous. People have died from eating from it.'

'What about animals?' asked Marc.

'I don't know. It probably doesn't affect them.'

'So that's why you got the herbs?'

'Yes. I'd felt there must have been a connection between the name and the bush.'

'What about Massoud? What's the situation with him?' Dan asked.

Daisy told them what had happened in the sick bay and how he'd promised to help them. Jonathan snorted with disbelief.

'Yeah, until he sneaks off to see Oleander.'

She also told them how she'd bumped into Collette in the corridor, pretending she'd strained her muscle. Daisy began to giggle.

'You should have seen her face when I told her I might not be able to dance.'

'She'll be plotting something else then,' Hiromi said thoughtfully.

'Won't she be contacting Massoud?'

'He's agreed to signal us when she contacts him, but guess who will be going in his place in disguise?' Daisy smirked.

Jonathan thought for a moment and burst out. 'Not Shakita the stork?'

Daisy laughed out loud, the first time for days, at the astonished looks on their faces.

'That's right. Yannish says she's brilliant at disguise. She can do anything.'

'Can we trust Massoud?' Winna asked. 'He's been very dodgy, and I get the feeling he could sneak behind our backs and tell her everything.'

'He's terrified of her and knows - really knows - she will not only kill him, but his family too. I don't think he can take the risk.'

'I'm with Dais,' Dan said, agreeing.

'You're always with her.' Jonathan mocked him, raising an eyebrow.

'Not always, Jonno, but she is right in this instance, as long as Massoud keeps his nerve. I sit close to him in the orchestra so I can keep an eye on him.'

Hiromi let out a big sigh. 'There's a lot to take in and time is running out. Somehow I don't think the bush is Oleander's only source of energy.'

'What d'you mean?' Daisy gasped.

'Well, if she is part of the destructive forces against the Light, then there must be others to take her place. She's not the only one, is she?'

She looked at their stricken faces.

Daisy went completely white. 'You're right, Hiromi. I hadn't thought of that. But she's the one attacking us, so all we can do is try and find a way to stop her. Calidus and Shakita will have to deal with the rest.'

'There's another thing,' Marc said thoughtfully. 'You told us Collette knows that you know who she is – right?'

'Yes. I know she does. Whenever we meet she's sly and nasty to me.'

'We'll have to make sure you don't go anywhere alone, then.' His eyes blinked through his glasses.

Daisy squeezed his hand. 'Thanks, Marc. I would really like that.'

Marc checked his watch. 'Come on, guys, we'd better get back for supper.'

'Right.' Dan heaved himself up. 'Let's keep it cool, kids.'

Chapter 36

Yannish

Supper was quiet. Yoshi came to sit next to Hiromi, chatting about their dance routine, and Louis Capello signalled out Aloysius to enthuse about Jazz. Winna joined them, together with Eli Beke. They brought laughter and lightness to an otherwise restrained meal.

Jonathan looked up several times, adding the odd hilarious remark, but otherwise remained close to his sister. Dan and Marc sat next to Daisy like Roman centurions, guarding her safety. They understood the shock she had been through and the overall responsibility she must have felt, keeping her suspicions to herself. They would make sure she wasn't alone anymore.

Daisy noted Massoud sat with his friends and appeared none the worse for his 'accident'. Shakita had done her work. While he'd slept in the sick bay, she had worked on his body to repair the two broken ribs, whispering gently to him to be strong and to trust the goodness of his heart. He looked different somehow, happier, as he joined in with the others.

Feeling her gaze, he looked up and smiled. Daisy winked back secretly. They couldn't be seen to be too close to him in case Collette found out.

Shakita had impressed a thought within him that if Oleander contacted him to see her, he was to signal her. She'd shown him a picture of a stork. This was the password Massoud would automatically see and send to warn Shakita. The rest would be taken care of, but he must go quietly to his room to protect himself.

***

The meeting was to be in the boys' room, a little later than usual. They'd decided it was safer to change the times. Leaving the dining room, Daisy suddenly had the strangest feeling. She stopped in her tracks.

'Hang on,' she said to Hiromi. 'There's something wrong.'

'What's up?' said Dan, leaning down to her.

'I've got to check Yannish's room. I know he's in danger.' She turned quickly, hurrying down the corridor. She dropped her voice so no one else could hear. 'Hiromi, go to Marc and ask him for the herbs, quickly! Dan, you come with me.'

She made her way to Yannish's room, quietly opening the door. He was nowhere to be seen. Dan suddenly gave a shout. He found Yannish slumped by the side of his bed, unconscious.

As Dan carefully turned him over, Daisy could see he was deathly pale. Quickly she examined his body and found a bite mark on his right arm.

'Dan, your penknife,' she cried.

Feeling inside his trouser pocket, he gave her his knife. The wound was beginning to fester, Yannish's arm was starting to swell. His eyes glazed as his life ebbed away. Dan pushed the bed aside to make space for Daisy to move around Yannish. She ripped Yannish's sleeve, cut the bite wide open and began to suck out the poison as she had seen Tai wa wa the Medicine Man do with Little Wolf in the Red Ray.

Again and again she sucked and spat the poison. Hiromi came back with the herbs. Daisy instructed her to crush one of the herbs into a powder and to pack into the wound. The other one was to remain in its whole state, to lie over the other. The first was to cleanse and absorb the poison from the wound. The second was to heal Yannish's body.

'Can you get me a bandage from the sick bay?' she asked Hiromi again. 'If you see Sylvie, tell her I'll explain later.'

She checked Yannish's body to be sure there were no other visible wounds. Her face was flushed with the exertions but her eyes remained calm. Somehow she felt help was with her. What would Tai wa wa do now? she thought.

'Let's get him on to the bed, Dan.' Both of them managed to lift him on to the bed.

What now? she thought. He looks so terribly pale. Tell me what to do. Then the words came into her mind. 'Work on his heart chakra. Give him energy.'

Calidus had explained in the Red Ray how human life was maintained and regulated by seven invisible energy centres. They acted like wheels of light, revolving in and through our energy system, looking after our physical, emotional, mental and spiritual levels. Tai wa wa showed her how to stimulate them in healing.

Now she placed both her hands on his heart. She asked Dan to place one of his hands under Yannish's body at the bottom of his spine, and the other one on top, to send red energy to strengthen his life force. Dan had a natural feeling with his hands. It was almost as if he knew what to do. He didn't ask any questions but just obeyed her every word.

Hiromi returned with bandages. 'Sylvie wasn't there,' she said grinning.

Her fingers were light and quick as she gently rolled the first one over the sealed pack of herbs. The second one supported the arm. She then sat on the bed, watching the others.

'Take over here, Hiromi, please,' Daisy asked. She went to Yannish's head to place her hands over his crown Chakra. Then she asked Dan to take off Yannish's shoes and hold the soles of his feet.

'We have to concentrate now on holding our energy together for him.'

'What about the others?' Hiromi asked. 'Wouldn't it be better if all of us were here?'

'It might attract attention,' Dan said cautiously.

'I agree. We don't want Collette storming in here.'

'Agreed. What about me texting Jonathan to tell him what's happened, so he doesn't come looking for us?' suggested Hiromi. 'We're meant to meet, so he's bound to be anxious, isn't he?'

'Good one. Do it.' Daisy and Dan agreed.

'We've to hold Yannish's energy enough for his body to fight the poison. It might take hours,' Daisy said, looking at them anxiously. 'Then he'll probably go into a fever. That will be the next critical point, but if he gets through it, he'll recover. At least that's what happened with Little Wolf, but...' She hesitated. 'that was with Tai wa wa though...' She looked at the others miserably, unsure of herself.

'Come on, Daisy,' said Dan. 'Don't you think Tai wa wa will help you? It doesn't matter how long it takes. We're not going anywhere.'

'Yeah, that's right and we'll call upon all the good guys to help us. We've got the University of Light behind us, haven't we?' said Hiromi, grinning.

Daisy let out a deep breath of relief. At least she wasn't on her own. She had Hiromi with her Indigo Ray to clear away any negative disturbance around them and Dan, who was the rock of strength and love. What better allies could there be?

Hiromi sent a message to Jonathan explaining what had happened. He was not to look for them but to carry on as normal. She said they would come back when Yannish was out of danger. She told him to delete the message immediately so it couldn't be picked up.

They sat together for hours, holding their hands over each chakra of Yannish's body. Daisy intuitively laid her hands around his injured arm. She felt heat coming from the wound. Then it was as though someone lifted her hands to draw the heat away to disperse it into the air. It was the oddest sensation. Her hands returned again and again until the burning heat lessened.

'Tai wa wa is here,' she whispered to herself.

Yannish began to shake and shiver. Sweat poured from his body. He jerked in violent spasms. Quickly, Dan removed his clothes. They helped him by swiftly wrapping Yannish in a warm duvet before putting him into his bed. The fever had started. Yannish's eyes stared wildly, not seeing anyone. He gnashed his teeth, mumbling words they couldn't understand. Hiromi soothed his fevered brow with cold wet flannels. Yannish thrashed around, throwing off the bedclothes.

'We've got to keep him warm,' Daisy said urgently.

'I know, but I can't keep him still.' Dan pushed him back gently again. 'It's like restraining a wild animal.'

Daisy sympathised. 'Do your best, Dan. It's going to be tough for a while.'

'Tell me about it.' Dan pushed him back again.

Hiromi continued applying cold compresses. For a while they soothed him and then the sweating began again.

Hiromi wiped her forehead. Both she and Dan looked exhausted.

'He seems quieter now,' Daisy said to them. 'We'll know more in the morning.'

Yannish's breathing was easier. The sweating was lessening and he sank into a restless sleep, twitching sometimes, but remaining still.

All of them breathed sighs of relief. Their concentrated efforts had left them exhausted.

'Why don't you both go to bed?' said Daisy. 'There's nothing more to do. You've been brilliant. I couldn't have done this without you and now I think he's going to be all right.' She hugged them, tears streaming down her face.

'Okay, Dais,' Dan said. 'What about you?'

'I think I'll stay here, just in case he wakes. I can sleep in a chair.'

'If you're staying, we will,' Dan said firmly.

'Dan, it's okay, really it is.' She held both their hands in hers. 'I think he'll sleep until morning, so you might as well get some kip too.'

A frown came over her face as she suddenly thought of Collette. What if she comes back to check on Yannish, to see if he's dead?

'I'm going to call on Shakita to come and protect Yannish in case Collette comes back. That's the only part worrying me.'

'Of course, Daisy, that's the answer. Do it now.' Hiromi pleaded.

Within a few seconds, they heard a tiny knock on the door. They stared at the door, not daring to open it. Maybe Collette had heard them? Dan put his finger to his lips as he moved forward. He signalled them to hide behind the bed then, lifting a heavy candlestick, he tiptoed towards the door and flung it open. He was just about to bring the weapon down with all his might when Josefina ducked under his arm.

She took the heavy object from him.

'Hola!' she said, smiling broadly at his astonished face as she set the candlestick back on the table.

'Josefina! What are you...?' Dan gazed at her, struggling for words.

Daisy and Hiromi peered over the side of Yannish's bed, relieved it wasn't Collette, but confused as to why Josefina should be up at this time. Josefina gave them her best gold-studded, toothy grin.

'You called me, I think.'

They were speechless, staring at this irritating, grumpy old woman who always seemed to be hanging around. Nobody particularly liked her except Aloysius who was always polite to her. Jonathan couldn't stand her simply because she had called them children. He still held a grudge about it.

'Why are you here?' Dan asked, taking command.

'You called me.' As she walked towards them, her form began to change from the old woman she pretended to be into the lovely glowing figure of Shakita.

Dan staggered back. He might have killed her. 'I'm so sorry!'

'You've good reflexes, Dan,' she said, smiling. 'Now, let me see Yannish.'

Daisy and Hiromi ran quickly from their hiding place to hug her. Shakita then looked at Yannish and the treatment they had given him.

'You have saved his life. I thank you with all my heart.'

'We did it together and I am sure Tai wa wa helped us,' Daisy said to her.

'Did you know what had happened?' Hiromi asked, curious that Shakita hadn't come before to help them.

'Yes, I knew. You were doing everything you should, so I decided to leave you.'

'Really!' Daisy gazed at her, amazed at her trust in them.

'You were perfectly able to deal with the situation and I had a pressing engagement with Oleander as Massoud,' she said, smiling cheekily.

'What happened?' Dan asked, doing his best to stifle a yawn.

'I will tell you another time, my friends. You all need sleep. Let me just say, I gave her something to think about. Now go. I will watch over Yannish and make sure Collette sees only what she wants to see.'

Quietly they slipped away, happy and relieved Yannish was safe and they had all done their best. Tomorrow would be a better day.

***

Shakita checked Yannish over, satisfied he was out of danger. Neither she nor Calidus had interfered with the treatment Daisy had given him. They were not allowed to. She had to find her own power from within, to use her experience of healing that she had learnt with Tai wa wa. He'd guided her, but refrained from doing it for her. Daisy was learning to access her natural intuitive insight using the invaluable help of Hiromi and Dan.

Without these two, who'd helped create the circuit of energy, he might have died. Each one had contributed their own special quality. This was why they were here, to learn how to use the qualities within the Colour Code.

Shakita smiled to herself at the astonishment on their faces when Josefina came in. She was good at disguises. Then she remembered her meeting with Oleander. Massoud had warned her, so she'd appeared as him. Oleander had never guessed. Shakita was also careful to protect herself against the physical blows Massoud always received. She'd pretended to cry and whimper as blow after blow rained down upon her. The energy field surrounding her had saved her.

As Massoud, Shakita had told Oleander that Daisy had badly strained her leg so wouldn't be able to dance. That had sent Oleander into a savage rage. Shakita was fascinated how quickly she could change into a frenzy of an inferno within seconds and then change back into her normal self. She was a powerful and dangerous force of destruction and Shakita would have to be very careful.

When Oleander had calmed down, Shakita (as Massoud) had told her of his idea.

'In the desert where I lived, there are deadly scorpions.' He paused. Oleander's eyes glittered with interest. 'You have taught me so much, Oleander, and I know how to get one. It will be a special surprise for her - and you.'

'How clever you are, Servant,' Oleander purred. 'Of course you can. It will be a pleasure. What will you do then?' She caressed his face fondly, wanting to know every detail.

'I will place it in Daisy's bed,' Shakita said, smiling.

'Ah! How delicious. I hope it will be an agonizing death.'

'How is your grand finale going?' Shakita asked tentatively.

Oleander looked sharply. 'It has begun. First we use a rapid attack to kill the source.' By this she meant Yannish. 'Then we bring in all the destructive forces to obliterate the academy.' She laughed with sheer delight, like a child who had received a beautiful present. 'You have pleased me, Servant. If you do this, I will repay you.' 'Thank you, my Lady.' Shakita bowed, knowing Massoud would never survive, however much he pleased her.

***

Shakita looked at Yannish again to check on his breathing. He was peaceful but it had been a battle to keep him alive. She knew Collette wouldn't be able to resist checking to see if he was truly dead. She would return and Shakita would create a scene where a hologram of Yannish would be found on the floor, dead. It only needed part of the object or person to produce the whole image. That is what she would see, when in fact he would be safe somewhere else.

First she transported Yannish to Professor Sanandez's room.

Then she prepared Yannish's own room, scattering objects on the floor as if he'd fallen to the ground, with the image of Yannish lying dead. Satisfied, Shakita closed the door.

A few hours later, Josefina was shuffling along the corridor when Collette passed her.

'Have you been here long?' she asked.

'No, no. I just come.' Josefina answered.

'Go and help in the kitchen.' Collette ordered her.

'Si, Senorita.' Josefina grunted as she made her way towards the kitchen area.

With a quick check to make sure she was alone, Collette opened Yannish's door. Inside, the room looked as if it had been hit by a bomb. Books and objects were strewn about the floor. Chairs had been overturned, as though he'd struggled to get up. It must have been a terrible effort to clutch at anything as he'd dragged it down. She smiled at the disarray.

Then she saw him, lying on the floor beside his piano. He was dead, quite dead. His face was swollen. His mouth was set in a grimace of agony as he'd gasped for breath. His body was contorted as he'd thrashed about in pain. His eyes were staring, terrified, as he'd realised he was dying. Collette chuckled with delight. The concert would never take place now. She had won.

She then thought quickly. It would be too soon to say he had died. It would be so much more satisfying to tell everyone on the morning of the concert. For now, she would say he was indisposed - perhaps a bad tummy upset. She giggled when she thought of it.

Yes, that would do nicely. She left, quietly locking the door behind her. This was going to be a splendid day.

 *Chapter 37*

Duplicity

There was excitement in the air. Everyone was preparing for the big day. The dining room and reception room were now finally completed. Fresh flowers would be displayed, crockery and cutlery stacked and ready for use. Food was ordered ready to be delivered early the following day. Outside, torches were positioned along the road approaching the academy so that, as people arrived, they would be met by an avenue of glowing lights. At the entrance itself, a huge wrought iron basket had been centrally positioned. It was filled with wood ready to be lit to welcome the guests.

Francesca and Hamish were content with the mural. In a way, they were surprised at the difference in the new one. They couldn't wait to show the public what their students had achieved.

The Colour Code Gang met before breakfast. This time the girls went to the boys' room, to confuse Oleander. They had to be alert, especially now. She wondered how and where Yannish was, but Shakita would have taken care of him, as well as Collette if she'd gone back to check if he'd died. Daisy shivered. So much was happening and so quickly. There was hardly time to think.

The boys and Winna fired questions about Yannish. The whole incident was frightening as he would have died if Daisy hadn't felt something was wrong and gone to his room.

'Gee, Dais,' Al said. 'You saved the man's life.'

'We all did.' Daisy protested. 'I couldn't have done it without

Hiromi and Dan. There was too much to do and it wasn't just one person, Al. We all had to give him strength to fight the poison.'

'Of course.' Jonathan agreed. 'You all did a great job, sis.' He grinned at the other two who, by now, were feeling a little embarrassed.

Daisy then told them about Josefina being Shakita.

'So that's why the old bird seemed to be everywhere,' said Jonathan, bursting into laughter.

'She was the one who found my glasses.' Marc reminded them. 'I thought it was a bit odd. Now we know why. She probably became the stork again!' he giggled.

There was a discreet knock on the door. Aloysius opened it to find Josefina standing there. She quickly slipped in, telling them what had happened after the three of them had left Yannish's room.

'So Collette thinks Yannish is dead?'

'That's right. I am afraid she's going to have a nasty shock when he appears this evening.'

'What about the dress rehearsal?' Aloysius gaped in disbelief. It was essential Yannish was there. The others waited, not knowing what to think.

'It's his idea. He wants her to think he's out of the picture for a few hours anyway. He says you must all practise quietly, even though he is absent. Then he'll present himself later.'

They sat silently, looking nervously at each other. It would be difficult without Yannish. Daisy suddenly remembered she hadn't told Shakita about seeing Collette with the Oleander bush. She showed her the mobile photos.

'Destroy them. Now,' Shakita said to her. 'You are right - the bush gives her power and we have to destroy it.'

'How can we do it? She'll see us,' said Dan, glancing at the others uncertainly.

'I will draw her away and will get the gardener to remove it,' she said with a satisfied grin. 'When we get back, it will all be over.'

'There is just one other thing I've been worrying about,' Daisy said. 'If Collette tells us Yannish is unwell, won't Sylvie want to take him into the sick bay?'

'Sylvie understands the situation. She knows there are strange things going on, so I have warned her to keep quiet if Collette tries to stop her.'

'Well, that's a relief.' Daisy said.

'So what do we do now?' Winna asked.

'It is going to be hard for you, but you must hold your nerve,' Shakita said quietly. 'You know Yannish is all right. He thanks you with all his heart for saving his life.'

Daisy grinned at Hiromi and Dan.

Shakita continued. 'Collette thinks the concert will be cancelled. Her plan is to wait until the last moment to announce he is dead. That means Professor Sanandez and Yannish's dream to bring the East and Western countries together will fall apart and the whole project will collapse. No one will come just to see the dancers or bother about the mural. The orchestra is the main attraction. That will be her triumph, to see Yannish's dream collapse.'

'Great.' Marc hissed through his teeth.

'What happens when Collette finds out her Oleander bush has been chopped down?' Hiromi asked anxiously.

'Wait and see,' said Shakita, smiling. 'But there will be an eruption, especially when Yannish appears. She will call upon all the forces of darkness, so beware.' She looked at their frightened faces. 'Yannish and I will be there to stop them. I will call you when I need you, so be ready to act. Remember to hold your gemrays out together as I showed you. Turn them towards the lighter colour. In this way they have the power to transform. Try to keep in a circle together, or at least as close as you can.'

'Terrific,' mouthed Winna to Jonathan.

'I will see you later.' Shakita left quickly. She had to arrange a phone call to draw Collette away.

***

As the students filed into breakfast, Collette came in, followed by the tutors. She faced them all solemnly.

'Mes amis,' she said and smiled. 'I am afraid Dr Kablinski will be unable to attend the dress rehearsal today. He has a little food poisoning. He hopes to be with you later.' She smiled prettily, seeing the students' worried faces. 'He asks you to practise without him. I will let you know how he is later. Let us hope our dear Maestro is soon well.'

The students were distraught over the news. It was the day before the concert and it didn't give him much time to recover. As Collette turned to leave the dining room, Isobel whispered in her ear. An ecstatic smile lit her face.

'Of course,' she said. 'Tell him I will be there.'

The students were dismayed but determined to practise as normal. They gathered together in the music room. Each one sauntered over to their chair, unsure what to do next.

'Who's going to be in charge?' Louis Cappello asked.

'What about you, Jovan?' Daisy suggested. This would be his great opportunity to show them what he could do. When she'd first thought of it, it was a bit of a joke, but then she decided he would probably be the best choice.

He looked at her, shocked and thrilled she had signalled him out. 'Are you sure?'

'Go for it, Jovan.' Some of the other students encouraged him. 'If you're rubbish, we'll throw you out.'

'I will do my best,' he replied, and bowed.

'Come off it, you're not Yannish!' Eli Beke exclaimed.

Chelsea beamed with pleasure. She was so proud.

Jovan tapped his baton and led them through the first movement of Mozart's symphony.

***

The message Sylvie had given Collette was supposedly from Professor Sanandez. He'd asked her to fetch him from the clinic so he would be in good time for tomorrow's concert. Collette could hardly contain herself. Originally he had wanted his friend Yannish to come but, hearing he was unwell, he'd asked for her instead, if it wasn't too much trouble.

'Of course not.' She had told him. 'It would be a pleasure.' She'd just got rid of Yannish and now the meddlesome Spaniard would be in her grasp. She shivered with excitement.

She told no one, only that she had to go out for several hours.

Shakita watched her as her car sped up the drive. Disguised as Collette, she'd asked the gardener to cut down the Oleander bush and burn it. In its place, he could plant something different. The gardener was amazed. He'd told her the Oleander was spectacular and had taken many years to grow to that size. Also, it was in full bloom.

'I am tired of it,' she said petulantly.

'Very well.' He turned away, thinking she was a very silly woman.

***

Jovan had authority and a general understanding of what was needed to hold the orchestra together. It was an amazing experience to be in control of all the musicians and exhilarating to read the score for every instrument rather than just his part. He also felt a great sense of responsibility. So far the music sounded good and each musician responded exactly as he or she should. As the first movement drew to a close he paused for anyone to complain but, hearing no derogatory remarks, he raised his baton for the second movement. The music was beautiful and lyrical. He hoped Yannish would approve of his conducting.

***

The gardener chopped down the Oleander bush. He wore gloves because he knew it was poisonous. Even so, it was a shame to destroy the plant. It took a long time because it had been there for years and was well established. Finally he dug up the roots. They were deep and had spread wide.

'You're a tough one,' he said, puffing with exertion as he dragged it over to the bonfire. He wanted to prepare and feed the soil before he planted a new bush, this time one that attracted butterflies. The soil looked drained of any goodness. The Oleander bush must have been diseased. Most of the roots had been rotten. Strange, he thought, how a plant can look healthy on the outside but deep inside it could be decayed.

He removed the earth and shovelled in fresh compost to vitalise the old soil. Best leave it, he thought, and let the mould sift through. He shifted pots of geraniums in front of the area, to hide the empty place. He wiped his eyes as he poked the remaining branches into the fire. The bush exuded a putrid smell. He would have to get rid of it before the day was out or he'd be in big trouble.

***

'Very good.' Felippe Tonisoni congratulated Jovan on his performance after the symphony had concluded.

'Not bad.' Eli Beke grinned.

'He was awesome.' Chelsea linked her arm through his, as if he belonged to her.

Dan slapped him on the back and most of the other students

nodded with approval as they walked out of the music room for lunch.

The morning had gone well. It had been a relief to them all. At the start, they'd felt uncertain without Yannish's direction, but Jovan had conducted well and playing together had given them greater confidence in themselves as musicians. They were able to cope on their own.

Collette arrived at the clinic. It had taken her three hours to get there but she didn't mind. The thought of what she'd do when she saw him was so intoxicating it took her breath away. She parked the car and went straight to reception, explaining she was there to pick up Professor Sanandez. The receptionist asked her to take a seat while she located the Professor. Collette sat down, relaxed, enjoying the moment.

She didn't care if anyone saw her because the academy itself would soon be demolished. The Professor walked towards her, smiling, carrying his bag. He kissed her lightly on the cheek.

'Gracias, Senorita. It has been a long time.' She hugged him and, with tears in her eyes, told him how much better he looked and how they'd all missed him.

'Have you eaten?' she asked. 'It would be good to take a little refreshment before we leave, don't you agree?'

'That would be nice,' he said, smiling gently. 'We could eat here. They have a delightful little café.'

She squeezed his arm, telling him she knew of a sweet café on route where they could relax more comfortably. She couldn't risk the danger of him collapsing close to the clinic.

'I am in your hands, Senorita.'

'You'll be quite safe,' she said, beaming.

The café was charming. It was also empty. They sat outside under a large umbrella out of the hot sun and discussed Yannish.

'How is my friend?' he asked. 'Was it something he ate?'

'I believe so, but you know how food poisoning can be?' She glanced briefly at him, toying with the stem of her glass of water. 'It can be unpredictable.'

He frowned. 'Is he more serious than you led me to believe?'

Collette patted his hand. 'No no, he was holding on when I saw him this morning. The doctor had given him medication and the nurse was looking after him.'

'Well?' he said, raising his eyebrows.

'All I'm saying, is he might not be well enough to conduct tomorrow.'

The Colour Code

'He would have to be dead before he'd let any sickness stop him from conducting,' Carlos replied through tight lips. 'Come, we must go. I need to get back without any delay.'

'At least finish your drink, Professor, and eat a little. It is quite a long journey and you need to be strong.'

Carlos hesitated. He was concerned about his friend. Collette had suggested Yannish could be worse than she'd first said and was now trying her best to reassure him.

They had ordered grilled fish and a simple salad. Carlos felt uncertain. He rose from the table, saying he needed the bathroom. This was the moment for which Collette had been waiting. As soon as he was out of sight, she took a bottle from her bag and inserted a few drops into his water. There would be no taste. He would never know what hit him. This dose was even more lethal than the one she'd given Yannish.

She wanted him to die slowly, in agony. With Carlos, a quick death was needed before anyone noticed.

'Shall we go then?' he asked upon returning, picking up his bag.

'Let's just salute Yannish with a toast,' she said, smiling as she raised her glass to her lips.

Carlos nodded as he drank the remains in one gulp.

Collette regarded him with interest. For a moment he stared at her. Then he clutched his throat and fell across the table, dead. Quickly she propped him up, so it looked as if he was resting on his elbows across the table, his hands under his chin. She sweated as she did so. He was a big man but she had super strength when needed. She rapidly checked the scene and left with a smile on her face.

Really it had been the most glorious two days. Now she must hurry to begin the grand finale.

Chapter 38

The Grand Finale

Ronnie and Frank were satisfied with their dance routines. Dresses for the girls and costumes for the boys had been pressed and were now hanging up. A make-up table was ready with all the stage paint. They were excited. This was the kind of work they loved - live performances. The students couldn't wait. After the concert, it would be cool to unwind with a little Street Dance, Rap and Hip Hop.

The music room had been transformed into a concert hall. Empty chairs within the auditorium rose from the front to the back. There was a curious silence as they waited to be filled. Then they would come alive with the audience, excitement growing for the performance to begin. The concert hall held many memories of glorious sounds which echoed in the atmosphere. For those who loved music and were sensitive, musical notes could be heard floating in the ether.

The orchestra chairs were rearranged carefully. The only instruments on view were those that were too big to move - the drums, harp and double bass. The rest would be brought in with the musicians. Musical scores lay open on the stands for each student. The conductor, too, waited in the wings, ready to spring into action.

There was a golden warmth lighting the hall as the sun came shining through the windows. Outside the concert hall, in the cobbled square, tables and chairs had been placed under umbrellas for those who couldn't find seats inside. Loudspeakers were erected and even a television screen, so everything could be viewed comfortably.

Yannish knew the local workers would prefer to be out in the open rather than shut up inside. Also, outside in front of the Dance Studio, a large dais had been erected for the dancers to perform. The studio itself was large enough for practice but there wasn't enough room for an audience, so Frank and Ronnie had created a beautiful stage so each group could entertain the public.

Leading from the entrance of the studio, Frank had designed a covered archway where the students would appear for their individual dance. It would be an open, creative extravaganza to please all tastes.

Daisy longed to find out how Yannish was, but knew he would emerge when Collette pronounced his death. One part of her couldn't wait to see the look on Collette's face, yet the other was terrified as to what she would do in revenge. The old proverb 'Hell has no fury like a woman scorned' would be very apt in this case. It would be a day of reckoning and retribution.

Collette drove fast. She was anxious to create as much distance from the café as possible. The car was travelling well but she felt a curious sense of weakness in her limbs. She smiled at herself. What could she expect? She had been living on adrenalin for the past two days, without any let up, and now she was beginning to relax, that was all. She wondered if that idiot Servant had managed to find his scorpion. Probably not. She really didn't have much confidence in him. Still, it would be amusing if he did manage to get one and put an end to that obnoxious girl. If not, she would gladly deal with the girl herself…and him too.

Her fingers on the wheel began to cramp. She rubbed them against her arm. They looked white and stiff.

'Come on, you stupid girl. You can't be sickening for something.' She turned on her CD and began to sing to the music at the top of her voice, but she found the music irritating and singing was a struggle.

A strange lassitude began to creep over her, as though she was sickening for something. She shook herself, trying to stimulate her body into action. Her muscles were beginning to ache and her brain felt stale, as if she had been awake for days.

She stopped the car and got out, slamming the door.

'This will not do,' she told herself sternly, beating her hands on the car.

'I will not accept this. I have the power. This is my moment of triumph,' she screamed. Why was her energy draining away? She had filled herself from the Oleander bush. The act of destroying Yannish and Professor Sanandez should have increased her energy, not depleted it.

Opening the car door, she reached inside for her bag. Maybe there were still a few drops of poison left in the syringe. She had taken the poison from the leaves of the plant because they were more deadly and fast working than the flowers. There was a little, perhaps just enough, to get her back to the academy.

She injected the few drops directly into her tongue with a huge sigh of relief. Within a few moments, she felt a surge of energy flow back into her body. Her blood began to pump again.

'That's it!' she shouted. 'Give me my strength.' She stamped her feet and rubbed her legs, forcing her muscles to overcome their tiredness. 'Nothing can prevent my success.'

As she started the engine, she began to sing.

***

Supper was to be served within the next twenty minutes, when Yannish would suddenly come back from the dead. The impact on Collette would be terrifying. Daisy trembled inside when she thought about it. She had witnessed the monstrous spectacle the woman could become. The Colour Code Gang checked they had their orange gemrays.

'Okay, we know what to do.' Daisy prayed to herself and looked at them in turn. She held her gemray in her hand and pointed it at the others.

'We form a circle, right?' Marc questioned.

'I don't know,' Daisy replied thoughtfully. 'It may not be possible.'

'I guess it will happen at supper, so we'll either be sitting next to each other or opposite each other.' Dan reasoned.

Daisy nodded her head. 'We'd better sit three on one side and four on the other, so at least we can form a semi circle.'

'Will that be enough?' Winna looked worried. 'After all, we usually sit in a circle.'

'It's the best we can do, Winn. I'm sure it'll be all right.'

Marc wasn't sure if this would be a blessing or a disappointment. He was rather hoping they would sit in a circle and he could face the others rather than Collette. Her wrath would be dramatic and horrendous but, as a detective with an inquiring mind, part of him needed to see the gruesome details. The other part simply wanted to run away. He was torn between a growing fear of witnessing the spectacle and a morbid fascination in seeing it.

'What's the matter, Marc? Don't you want to face the enemy?' Daisy smirked.

He looked confused, blinking behind his spectacles.

'I'm not sure really...' he replied. 'Can I stand next to you, Daisy?' He finished weakly.

'Me, too.' Winna sniffed. 'I don't particularly want to see the grotesque figure of Collette anyway.' She shot a look at Aloysius.

'Thanks, Winn,' said Daisy, giggling. 'Let's practise now.' She held her gemray out in front of her. They all did the same, turning them from the darker orange to the lighter golden colour.

'Do you know what will happen?' Hiromi asked nervously.

'No idea.' Daisy breathed deeply. 'All I know is we have to work together as a team. Do you realise this is the first time we've really had to connect together as a whole? Everything depends on it, even our lives.'

Aloysius let out a deep breath. 'Come on, you guys. We gotta crank up a little. Not so much of this depressing stuff! Right?'

'A little speculation is all right, Al,' said Dan, ruffling his hair. 'After all, this is a new experience.'

'Tell me about it,' said Jonathan with a snort.

'Are we ready?' Daisy placed the palm of her hand out. Jonathan put his hand on top with a brisk slap.

'Yeah, sis. I'm ready.'

'So am I.' Dan came next.

'Me, too.' Al joined in.

'And me.' Hiromi and Winna echoed.

Lastly, Marc sealed their friendship, placing his hand on top of them all. They held their hands together, feeling very close and connected.

'Okay, gang, time to go.' Daisy opened the door and led the way.

***

Collette parked her car and struggled out. The few drops of poison had given her enough energy to get back, but no more. She would have to revive herself quickly. The students would have just gone into supper so there would be no one around to see her.

She had adequate time to get to the Oleander bush before she gave them the 'good news'.

She froze. There was a pungent smell in the atmosphere which she recognised immediately. In trepidation, she approached the space where the Oleander bush had flourished for so many years. Her heart thumped with a growing sense of dread. The Oleander bush had gone. There was an empty space with two pots of geraniums in its place. Fury raged through her. She smashed the pots with one hand in an act of total aggression, spittle flying from her mouth. Then she turned to find the remains of her life-support bush charred in the dying embers of the fire.

She screamed with grief, swearing vengeance, shaking her arms to the elements. Questions flooded her mind. Had anyone seen her? Who was responsible? Both Yannish and Carlos were dead. Could it have been that dreadful girl? Or Massoud? No, he wasn't clever enough. But the girl was.

Slowly she regained her composure. She had an emergency bottle kept for such an occasion. That would give her the power she needed to invoke all the destructive forces at her disposal. Whoever was working against her would pay. They had seen nothing yet! She would pulverise the place into dust. She shook herself, making her way back to room. The best was yet to come.

She drank deeply of the poison. Her colour and beauty came back immediately. She flicked her hair and added a little lipstick to her generous mouth. She changed her clothes. A smell of burning still clung to them. She decided to get rid of them, as they would always remind her of her beloved Oleander. She smiled at the reflection in the mirror. She was ready for the prime time of her life.

***

The noise level in the dining room was deafening. Tomorrow was the concert and all the students were excited about the coming event.

Daisy and her friends chose to sit at the top of the middle table. Somehow she thought that sitting opposite the window where the tutors usually spoke to them would be the best position (or worst – she wasn't sure which) as that would be where the initial action would take place.

Collette strolled in, waving at the students as she passed by. She stood at the top of the middle table, not far away from where Daisy and her friends were sitting. She was dressed in a pretty pale blue dress to match her eyes. Her short blonde hair was brushed back. Her mouth and nails, as usual, were blood red.

For a moment she glanced at Daisy with a hint of amusement in her eyes, and then she visibly composed herself.

'Mes amis.' She began solemnly. 'I'm afraid I have very bad news for you.' She paused. The students stopped eating, gazing at her with alarm.

'Our wonderful Maestro, Dr Kablinski, took a turn for the worst and didn't recover from the food poisoning. He passed away at two o'clock this morning.' Tears ran down her face. 'We did all we could.'

There was a deathly silence in the room. First, the students couldn't take in what she'd said, and then the whole room erupted with shouts of disbelief. How could this be happening? They stared at each other in total confusion and sorrow. How could their beloved Maestro be dead?

She banged a spoon on the table for attention.

'There is more, my friends. I have to also tell you of another tragedy, so you must be brave.'

The students regarded her in horror.

'Professor Sanandez's burns were too serious. He died. I believe it was the severity of the shock that killed him.'

Then boys and girls began weeping with grief. The joy they'd all experienced had gone. They sat at the tables, deadened by the news.

Then, quietly, two figures came into the dining room from Reception. Yannish and Carlos. The students couldn't comprehend what they were seeing. They'd just been told both men were dead, and yet here they were. Was this some sick joke?

Collette, who'd been sympathising with one of the boys, suddenly looked up to see the men walk in. The horror of the revelation hit her like a bombshell. She was paralysed with shock.

Yannish strode swiftly to the front of the dining room to address the students, closely followed by Carlos Sanandez.

'I am deeply sorry for the trauma you have just received,' said Yannish. 'As you can see, I am perfectly healthy. Nothing could keep me from the concert.' He looked at Collette with amusement. There was a thunderous applause from the students.

'I am also happy to tell you I have recovered well, too.' Carlos saluted them.

They both turned to face Collette. Disbelief and explosive anger tore across her face. Her moment of sweetness had gone.

'You think you are so clever, but you are nothing!' she screeched at Yannish.

Her body began to change. It grew darker and bigger as it began to fill with the forces of malevolence and all the negative poisonous energy feeding her. Her face turned white, the eyes red, her mouth two slits of venomous gristle spewing out abuse.

'I invoke the Lords of Destruction! My demons! Come to me now! Devour all my enemies with your voracious appetites.' She laughed with sheer delight as she raised her arms, beckoning her evil spirits to her.

'I will annihilate you all, especially you!' she screamed at Yannish.

Some students ran from the room, terrified. Others were paralysed with fear at the apparition before them, unable to comprehend what was happening. Some dived under the tables, hiding from the macabre spectacle that was once Collette. Daisy and her friends remained shaking and pale, still clutching their gemrays, waiting for the moment to use them.

Collette faced Yannish, ready to strike him down, when Shakita appeared in front of him pushing him gently aside. It was his part as a Light Server to inspire his students, hers to protect his plan. A blaze of orange illuminated the room. She stood facing Collette, her orange hair flowing behind her, her amber eyes blazing light.

'Ah, so it was you,' Collette whispered.

Shakita showed her how she had deceived her all along, first pretending to be the nurse at the hospital, then Yannish when Collette had tried to poison him, and lastly as Carlos.

Collette screamed with rage as she thrust her fingers at Shakita. Poisonous acid flew from them straight towards Shakita's eyes. With a flick of her hands, Shakita unleashed a powerful liquid substance which immediately neutralised the poison as it sped towards her, making it fall to the ground harmlessly.

Collette turned towards her, lips grimacing, eyes glinting as she recognised a worthy opponent. The smell of decay the children had noticed before became stronger as she drew deeply from the poisonous substance that fuelled her.

Recognising the change within her, Yannish shouted to the students to lie down.

'Find cover quickly. Prepare yourselves.' He instructed the Colour Code Gang.

Then he stood side-by-side with Shakita. He was calm and dignified while she emitted waves of peace. They were there to meet the destruction that was about to be unleashed.

Collette eyed Shakita with distain at her passive response. She felt the waves of harmonious energy and laughed. She had expected more retaliation, not this stupid non-active response. With a cry of disgust, Collette raised her hand upwards to the ceiling of the dining room. Shakita was not the worthy opponent she'd first thought.

A thunderous roar like a tornado lifted off the roof of the academy. Coming towards them was a dark and ominous mass. Collette's creatures swarmed closer and closer in increasing numbers. They devoured everything in their wake, moving on relentlessly like a dreaded plague that couldn't be stopped.

These were her creatures, whose souls she had trapped in the underworld over aeons of time and had become subject to her will. Now she used them as her flying monsters. Their large bodies and heads were covered with black scales. Their steely grey wings outstretched as they approached swiftly, their red eyes like two drops of molten lava ready for the kill. The hordes filled the sky, cancelling out any light suddenly and frighteningly, casting everything into darkness except for the glinting red points of their eyes. The sound of their hissing increased as they drew closer, enveloping everything in their path.

'Destroy them!' she screamed. 'Grind them into dust.

Shakita firmly stood her ground, holding in her hands a shield of light that she wielded like a sword, warding off her attackers. Her protective shield shone light directly into their eyes so that, as the flying monsters dived towards them, they were blinded by the intensity of the blazing sunlight.

With screeches of confusion, each creature crashed into each other as they stalled and retreated, trying to free themselves.

'Ah, ha!' Collette laughed. 'So you can fight, after all? Well, take this.'

With a lightening bolt she hurled a spear at high speed to break Shakita's shield. Shakita felt the air move in the darkness and deftly stood aside. With a flick of her wrist she sent the spear spiralling back towards Collette. Collette screamed with surprise and some delight as she caught it in her hands. This was turning into a battle worthy of her talents!

In retaliation, she cleverly created screens around the eyes of her monsters to protect them from the blinding light. They resumed their assault, this time with more precision, attacking Shakita herself before moving onwards to destroy Yannish and the students. Shakita's amber eyes became like two laser beams of fire directed into the creatures, melting them away. Once more they fell away, unable to carry out Collette's destructive orders.

It was a battle of giants but, even as Shakita retaliated with her extraordinary power, the sheer numbers of the attackers kept growing, and they snapped with their sharp teeth from every angle. The sheer might of them was wearing down Shakita. Daisy could see her strength lessening.

'We're coming in, Shakita!' she yelled.

Shakita nodded with thanks.

Daisy and her friends were ready. They knew this was the moment they'd been waiting for. It was the point of their being there - to support Shakita and to disable Collette's destructive forces.

'Now!' Daisy shrieked. The Colour Code Gang stood up, trembling in their shoes.

'I can't see anything,' Marc screamed.

'They're nearly on us,' Winna shouted, thrashing her arms across her face.

'Point to their eyes as Shakita did,' Daisy told them. 'Hold on, whatever happens.'

'I can't.' Marc was terrified.

'Yes, you can, Marc.' Jonathan touched him in the dark. 'Feel my hand and do what I do.' He guided Marc's sweaty hand, clutching his gemray to his and together they pointed them directly into the red eyes of the insects.

'Come on, guys, we can do this!' Dan cried. 'Look, it's already working.'

They held their orange gemrays out, each pointing together like a star of light.

Shakita shouted to them. 'Hold the light, whatever happens!'

Daisy and the Colour Code Gang held their gemrays pointing towards the approaching mass. They were terrified, feeling the hot breath of the monsters as they grew closer.

'Oh, God, I can't do it,' Aloysius shouted. 'My hand's shaking too much.'

'Come on, Al, you've got to. They'll kill us otherwise.' Winna urged him.

'I'm damned if I'll let them kill me,' shouted Jonathan. 'Look out, you bug-eyed creeps. Your time is up.'

'Hang in there, guys,' shouted Dan. 'The light is increasing. Something's happening.'

'I'm getting cramp in my hands.' Marc whined. 'My fingers are slipping.'

'I'll hold your hands, Marc.' Hiromi grasped both his hands in hers so their gem rays became fused together.

'Hold on,' Shakita told them. Her voice sounded weaker. The sheer force and weight of the army was draining even her energy. She needed the extra power from her young friends. The strain was almost too much to bear.

As Shakita called out to them, Collette began to laugh triumphantly, feeling success close at hand. But even as the moment of victory was within her grasp, her creatures began to screech with frustration as their numbers dispersed and they lost their power to stay together.

The intensity of the radiation from Shakita and the Colour Code Gang took effect. The blaze of light began to change the chemistry of her monsters. First, the outward form of their bodies began to shudder and disintegrate. They thrashed about, wings flapping helplessly as their tails detached themselves, flying off into space so they lost their sense of balance, like a helicopter that had lost its rudder, spiralling out of control. Then, as the compassionate quality of the light enveloped them, the evil intention which had imprisoned them for so long, was also transformed. The lost souls sighed with relief as they returned once more to their state of higher beings.

Collette watched in fury, snarling as she saw her army disband and disappear. She slowly turned to face Yannish.

'Sounds can be unpleasant too, can't they, Maestro?' she spat at him menacingly. 'See how your precious students like this!'

Closing her eyes, she placed her fingers on each side of her head. A sound grew deep within her throat, growing stronger and stronger. It sounded like an ancient discordant turbulence that had lain dormant until Collette's call had awakened it.

The students were transfixed in horror as they felt it first through their feet, a low rumbling noise that quickly moved through the bones of their legs. The sound increased in intensity and the pain began as it travelled up through their spines and into their heads. Many of the students screamed as the noise hit their ears. It was a whining, droning noise that obliterated every thought and feeling except their overriding panic to escape.

Collette brayed with delight to see the students clutching their heads, screaming with agony as they tried to crawl away under the tables and out of the dining room.

The sound was so intense that Marc, Jonathan and Aloysius dropped their orange gemrays as they frantically tried to close their ears. Daisy tried to hold onto hers, as did Dan, Hiromi and Winna but, like the others, the ear-splitting noise grew unbearable.

'Hold on!' screamed Daisy. 'Point them to the ground. Turn them to the light. It's got to make a difference.' Tears streamed down her face and finally she had to let go.

Marc scrambled onto the floor, trying to find his and Jonathan's. Poor Al lay on the ground almost senseless. There was chaos everywhere. Tables were overturned and crockery smashed as the students stampeded to get away.

As Daisy looked up, she saw Shakita was trying to deflect Collette's sheer volume of attack onto herself whilst trying to defend Yannish, but her energy was failing. Shakita was losing her power.

'Come on, Gang, we need to be together now. Shakita can't hold on forever,' Daisy cried helplessly.

She saw Chelsea whimpering pitifully as she held on to Jovan.

'It's all right, Chels,' she called to her. 'Come behind me.'

'I can't move,' she whimpered.

'Yes, you can.' Dan encouraged her, pushing himself up. 'Grab hold of Jovan and get behind us.'

Jovan stared at them both, terrified, then silently he grabbed hold of Chelsea and dragged her out of harm's way behind Daisy.

'It's no good, Daisy, the pain is too strong.' Dan grabbed her hand in a frantic effort to lift them both up but fell back, writhing in agony as the jarring sound tore his nerves.

Hiromi lay unconscious on the ground, next to other students who had tried to escape, panic written over their faces. It was a scene of carnage, with young people losing their minds. Everything they had worked for and had grown to believe had been blown away in a matter of moments.

Suddenly another sound penetrated the piercing noise. At first it was almost imperceptible. Was it their imagination? Aloysius recognised it first, as he lay upon the ground. He was almost unconscious and it came to him in a dream state.

The sound grew stronger. It was pure and magical, soft and lyrical, and harmonious in its beauty. He struggled to sit up.

'Tatanka!' he yelled.

Standing quietly beside Shakita, Yannish played the flute Aloysius had made in the Red Ray. Yannish continued playing his soft melody with all the Light and love that filled his spirit and that of creation. The penetrating noise invoked by Collette lessened and grew weaker, changing as it felt the irresistible sounds of harmony it had longed for to make it whole.

Shakita stood to face Collette, or rather the monster she had become.

'Your time is up,' Shakita told her quietly. 'Did you not know that goodness will always overcome evil? That love is greater than fear?'

Collette screamed abuse at her and Yannish.

'Never!' she spat at them.

'Love is the source behind all of creation. Fear is a temporary force through which we discover the Light. It is meant to serve the Light itself.'

'We are a powerful force that will never go away. Never!' Collette hissed as Shakita began to shine the full extent of her energy upon her.

'It is time you returned to the Light. You have served your purpose well,' she whispered softly, as the darkness of Collette's form began to fade, becoming lighter, and expanding so it lost its contours. Her body spread outwards and upwards so her features disappeared. Her voice became a whine, then a whisper in the wind, until she was no more. There was just a blaze of light as she evaporated into the air.

Silence filled the room. It had been a terrible and devastating experience. Everyone was drained and totally shocked. They looked at each other uneasily, fearing something else could go wrong and that another onslaught would occur.

Yannish and Carlos pulled out two chairs and sat down, facing the students who crawled out of their hiding places, like small animals when danger had passed.

'My dear friends,' Carlos said. 'We are safe now. The enemy that has dogged our time together has gone.'

The students looked at each other uncertainly.

'Who was the lady with the orange hair?' Louis Cappello asked. 'She was awesome.'

'Yes, you are right. She is a very special lady who works for the good of the world.'

'She can come back anytime. She was gorgeous!' Louis sighed

with pleasure.

'Are we safe now?' Kyan Khan asked.

'Yes,' Yannish answered. 'We will have no more disruptions, I promise you. Our concert will go ahead as planned, and Professor Sanandez is back with us.'

Kyan touched his arm.

'When you asked us what sounds we disliked and I told you I hated the noise of violence…' he said. It seemed so long ago now. Yannish nodded looking at him carefully. 'Well, now I know why music is so important. It can change destruction into peace,' he said.

Yannish sighed deeply. 'Yes. Music brings harmony. Playing my flute enabled discordant sounds to be reunited into the whole. Perhaps now you understand why this project is so important to me? And to you?'

'Thank you, Maestro,' Kyan said.

'What happened about the food poisoning?' Jovan asked.

'We knew Collette was a force for evil and that she didn't want our dream of reunion to happen. She thought if I and Carlos were out of the picture, then the concert wouldn't happen, so we got Shakita to disguise herself in our place. She is impervious to poison and pretended to be dead.'

'Wow, who'd have believed that sweet-faced French lady could be so foul?' Ariel spluttered. 'She was so kind.'

'Try not to be so hard,' Yannish said quietly. 'So often we have to experience negative forces before we can really understand the qualities of love. Light and darkness serve each other. Collette was part of this.'

Aloysius didn't say anything. Winna touched his hand in sympathy.

'What happens now?' Hannah asked, looking around at the tables. 'At least nothing's broken and the floor seems to be okay.'

Josefina came out of the kitchen, smiling broadly as if nothing had happened.

'Eeese everyone ready for supper?' she asked.

'Yes, yes, dear Josefina,' replied Jonathan, who leapt up and hugged her.

Dan laughed loudly and was joined by Al. 'What a change of attitude. Anyone would think she was his best friend!'

Food was served to the very hungry students. This time they ate with a new knowledge that nothing unpleasant would ruin their concert. They had come a long way together, as students and as friends. Few people would have experienced such a test of character and it was because of their trust, courage and belief in the project that had helped them survive.

Yannish and Carlos walked out into the garden. The air was fresh and clear. It was as though nothing had ever happened to disturb their peace.

Yannish would speak to the Colour Code Gang later to thank them for all they had done. They were remarkable and brave. He would never forget them.

 *Chapter 39*

The Concert

It was the day of the concert. Daisy felt exhausted and didn't want to get out of bed. Hiromi had been up for some time, practising her movements outside.

Winna awoke quickly, thinking about the Jazz. She giggled at the thought of the fun they would have.

'Come on, Dais,' she urged. 'It's time to move.'

'You go, Winn. I just want to think a while,' she murmured.

When the room was quiet, Daisy went over the previous day's events. In some ways it had felt like a nightmare in which she was unable to get out. She saw all the horrible creatures appearing, ready to devour them, even though Shakita had told them they would be all right. But would they? Nothing like this had ever happened to them before and again she felt responsible for her friends and the students. She had managed to hold them together but it was so awful.

On the other hand, it had been amazing to see how the gemrays worked. It was weird when the demons just lost their power and disappeared. They'd became harmless. It was so strange. And to see Shakita in action! She was formidable and totally awesome. How do you get back to normality from that! she thought.

She then considered Yannish and how he'd thanked them for all they'd done. Shakita had joined him, together with Carlos. They were all so great, but now she felt low in spirits. The others were fine, but somehow she was left in a void of nothingness. Her mum would say it was simply the after affects. Suddenly she realised it wouldn't be long before they would be going home again.

It would be great to see her mum. She wished she could see her now.

The boys were already up and about. They'd decided they didn't need to make their link with the girls now, as all was well. They were anxious to go through the symphony with Yannish and then to chill out a little before the concert began.

Vans were delivering food early for the kitchen staff to prepare and the gardeners were placing tables and chairs in the courtyard, plus umbrellas to shield the guests from the sun.

Yannish wanted to spend a little time with the students as a few of them would be leaving straight after the concert. Others, like Daisy and her friends, would go the following day.

The evening would begin at 6.30pm and end later that evening with a firework display. It would be a magnificent finish to a great day. Reporters and photographers would be there and even a television crew would film them during the orchestra's morning practice. The academy had attracted so much attention it was on national news.

Daisy met Massoud as he went into the Concert Hall. He looked a different boy. Gone was the cringing, fearful servant used by Oleander. In his place was a laughing, happy soul, freed from tyranny and emotional blackmail.

Of course it would take time to rid himself of the years spent under Oleander's domination, but now there was hope. The next important step was to confess his part to the students and ask for their forgiveness. Daisy hugged him, telling him to tell them simply about his dilemma. They would understand. Massoud nodded his head with a wishful smile on his face.

'My mum is coming,' he said to her. 'Shakita arranged it.'

'That is fantastic, Massoud.' Daisy was thrilled for him.

'You were right, Daisy. The forces of Light are greater than those of destruction.'

***

The television crew busily set up their cameras. The chairs of the auditorium that had been arranged for the audience had been repositioned again. They were quick and efficient, used to slotting in between programmes.

The students were shy at first, not sure how to respond. Some played the parts of celebrities, smiling at the crew. Others slunk in, not looking at the cameras. For most, a brief smile and then a quick walk to their individual chair where they re-tuned their instruments, was enough.

Yannish came in with a flourish and an appreciative nod to the director of the film crew. He thanked Jovan for standing in for him.

'I understand you did very well.'

Jovan blushed. 'It was a great experience,' he said truthfully. 'I learnt to be of service to others.'

Yannish looked at him deeply. He knew how much it had cost him to humble himself in front of his peers.

'Well done,' he said. 'Now we will begin.'

The camera crew made themselves as inconspicuous as possible, so as not to disturb the delicate balance of the musicians. Afterwards they chatted to some of them. The students talked about the music and their relationships between each other. No mention was made of the extraordinary happenings which had occurred within the academy. That belonged to them.

Carlos and Yannish had talked about this last night together with Frank, Ronnie, Francesca and Hamish and they all agreed that it was a private matter. Many of the students had talked about their experience at the academy and how they had changed. The music and Yannish had opened their minds to the beauty of sound. This had helped them to relate to people from other countries much more. When the problems started, it had bound them to the academy and the dream Professor Sanandez held dear to his heart, especially when he'd risked his life for theirs.

They also talked about their experiences with Frank and Ronnie, how movement and dancing had brought such fun into their lives and, lastly, the expression of art and the mural. The cruel act of destroying their work had made them think again of what was important and what was not. All of the students wanted to repro-duce the painting, not so much for themselves, but for Francesca and Hamish, whom they liked immensely. It was while they'd spent time clearing the wall and beginning all over again that the new mural had become alive and vibrant

It was time for the concert. The students were already seated in the Concert Hall. Daisy waved to her brother and Marc. Marc was feeling distinctly nervous. He felt the solemnity of the occasion and prayed he wouldn't let Yannish down. Hiromi nudged Winna and winked to Daisy. Aloysius beamed at his friends, his eyes shining. Lastly, Daisy smiled at Dan. His bright blue eyes twinkled back at her.

This was always an anxious moment, before the audience came in. The students had dealt with the camera crew filming as they played. Now the crew had gone and the auditorium had been put back ready for the streams of visitors. The students made their last minute adjustments, tuning up their instruments, giggling and joking to each other, feeling stage fright.

The audience drifted in, helped to their seats by ushers. The auditorium began to fill. The students pretended not to look, preferring to check their music, but couldn't resist an occasional peek.

Chelsea kept an ongoing chat with Daisy behind her music stand about how wonderful Jovan was and that she was definitely going to ask him to come to America to meet her dad.

'My dad will help him get into the best orchestra,' she announced. 'Jovan is, like, so talented. He will be a famous soloist or conductor.'

Daisy almost felt sorry for the arrogant Jovan. Had he met his match? But on reflection, it would give him the opportunities he longed for.

At last the final person found their seat with apologies as he pushed his way past a row of seated people.

A few minutes later, when everyone had settled themselves, Professor Sanandez came in. He walked straight up to the rostrum and then turned to face the audience. He explained the philosophy of La Reunion and of its dream to bring nations of conflict together through music and creativity.

As he spoke he noticed that some parents of the Middle Eastern students were obviously having difficulty sitting with their neighbours. So far, though, they hadn't erupted or demanded to be moved. Carlos smiled to himself. His students were more grown up than their parents, but the seed was sown and the older people were here to listen and learn. When he finished, applause broke out in the auditorium. This was the perfect way to begin the concert. The students were poised to begin, the audience waiting with expectation, with now, perhaps, a more open mind.

Yannish strolled in. The men shook hands and Carlos went to his seat.

Yannish smiled at his students to give them confidence. Each one in turn was precious to him. He looked at their trusting faces.

They were clear and bright with hope and determination for the future. He raised his baton and began.

***

Calidus and Shakita at the University of Light heard the sounds as they floated up into the hemispheres. Many people believed Mozart's music was touched by the Divine. Each note mirrored a harmonic sound in the cosmos. As it did so, it touched every atom within the earth - the streams, the cells of bodies both human and animal, leaves, flowers, mountains, oceans and more. As he listened, Calidus saw an uplifting of the human souls of the students and those who listened to them. He watched the spiral of pure energy rise in a collective spirit, like a beautiful ballet.

He saw the concentration and joy of the students as they played as one, in total unity. Only the music mattered. There was perfect dialogue between the musicians and the open response of the audience. Yannish was the medium who brought them together. Calidus smiled contentedly at Shakita. He was looking forward to seeing his young friends again.

As the symphony came to an end, Yannish mouthed 'Well done' to the orchestra. They relaxed, breathing a huge sigh of relief as they changed their music for Star Wars. Daisy caught Jonathan's eye and winked.

Waiting for the audience to settle down, Yannish once again held up his baton. The change from classical to popular music delighted the listeners. It was fun and magical. The students forgot any inhibitions and simply enjoyed the experience.

When the last note was played, there was a moment's silence and then thunderous applause. The audience rose as one, clapping and whistling their appreciation. Yannish bowed low and then acknowledge all the musicians as he raised his hand for them to receive the applause. It was a wonderful moment.

Standing up, they waited as the warm reception continued. Finally, Yannish and his students bowed for the last time and he walked off.

Whilst the visitors strolled to the reception and dining area for the buffet, the students frantically arranged the space in the concert hall for the Jazz interlude. Chairs and music stands were hurriedly packed and stored and a piano was rolled in. Aloysius mopped his brow, checking everything was in place.

'It's fine, Al.' Dan reassured him. 'It's going to be a buzz.'

They placed four chairs next to the piano, one for Al on the saxophone, the next for Louis on his trombone, one for Jonathan on his trumpet, and one for Eli Beke with his bassoon. Marc and his drums stood behind them and Winna would accompany them on the piano. The six of them looked at each other nervously, eyes wide, pulses throbbing with the excitement of what was to come.

It was time. Winna sat at the piano, dressed in a frock with off-the-shoulder sleeves. The fabric background was orange with a design of little flowers in yellow, purple and pink. She had an orange ribbon in her hair and sandals to match. The boys wore different coloured shirts over denim jeans. Daisy laughed when she saw them. Apart from Eli, who wore a red shirt, the others were predictably wearing the colours they represented.

Al half hoped Yannish might say something to the audience, but he sat down with the others with a twinkle in his eye. Al looked at him expectantly. Yannish went up to him and spoke softly.

'What are you waiting for? Just play!' he said, smiling. These were the exact words Tatanka had said to him in the Red Ray. 'Don't talk - just play.'

Al beamed at him, understanding the order and the significance it had for him. Turning to his friends, he nodded, then picking up his saxophone, he began to play.

As he played, Eli joined in with Jonathan with Louis mirroring the harmonic theme, then Winna came into the action as naturally as though she'd been born to play jazz. Marc kept the steady beat, holding the others together as each began to expand their music.

The audience sat entranced, whistling and shouting, some even caterwauling their approval when a solo performance finished. For Aloysius, he was in his element. He played his saxophone like a master. When Jonathan played Daisy watched him, fascinated, as his adrenalin flowed. She wondered who was playing through him. He let rip, confidence bursting as the improvised notes hit the ceiling. Each one had their space to show what they could do and then together they continued, with the theme coming to its conclusion.

There was rapturous applause at the end with whistles and shouts of 'Bravo!' again and again. Al and his team bowed, flushed with excitement and triumph. He thanked the audience for their appreciation and withdrew.

Daisy and Hiromi congratulated them behind the scenes as the

The Colour Code

next students changed for dancing.

'That was unbelievable,' Daisy said. 'You had the whole place rocking.'

Another student added 'That was totally volvo.' His eyes rolled with awe.

'What's volvo?' Daisy asked Hiromi.

'Volcanic, I think.'

'Come on, you guys,' Ronnie said. 'Brilliant, Al, but we need to get going now. Raps and Hip Hoppers move. Street Dancers line up!'

Rap music started as each student lined up to do their dance. First Jovan, then Chelsea and the other Rappers flew onto the stage dancing, ducking and diving. As they finished, others came on with different themes. They twisted and turned, did complicated steps which brought roars from the crowd. They somersaulted backwards, landing on their feet. Some rolled on their heads, twisting in impossible situations.

The crowd started clapping as each student came on and finished. It was an exhibition of skill and total joy. They were irrepressible and loving every moment of it. As the last one finished, Frank congratulated them on their performance.

Next, the Street Dancers performed their rehearsed routine to the delight of the audience and Ronnie.

Lastly, Hiromi and Yoshi, Hannah and Felippe appeared, dancing a beautiful routine to a Latin dance joined by four other couples. Ronnie had choreographed a Spanish extravaganza taken from Tango, Salsa and a little Flamenco.

The steps were intricate as each dancer circled their partner. The girls' coloured dresses were tight over the bodice, their skirt flaring out as they moved around their partners. The boys wore the conventional Spanish high-waisted black trousers and loose sleeved shirts. They wore their hair sleeked back. The girls wore camellias in their hair.

The dance was fiery and electric. Jonathan and Marc sniggered with embarrassment, watching as the figures danced closely, melting into each other's bodies. Part of them thought the dance was fantastic, but the boy part of them was still pubescent and feeling awkward about relationships with girls. Aloysius laughed at them.

'You're only jealous, Jonno. Secretly you wish you could dance with Chelsea, right?'

Jonathan blushed scarlet. 'I do not,' he growled. 'I don't want to dance with any stupid girl.'

'Nor me.' Marc sniffed, pushing his glasses back with emphasis.

Daisy looked at Dan, thinking she wouldn't mind trying to dance with him. Winna, as usual, was quick to pick up any information and grinned at her.

'Well, get you,' she whispered in her ear.

'What are you on about, Winna?' Daisy pushed her away.

'Don't you just wish you and the lovely Irish Dan could do a little Salsa together?' Winna smiled wickedly.

Daisy looked her straight in the eyes. 'About as much as you would with Al,' she replied, smiling politely back.

Winna backed off and then walked away. Daisy turned around to see Dan looking at her with a curious look on his face. Turning back, she felt both furious and intrigued at the same time.

The visitors were enthralled with all the dancing. Ronnie and Frank came out with their students to receive congratulations. It had been worth the hard work and they were thrilled with the reception.

Finally, Francesca and Hamish led the way into the Art Room to unveil the mural. It was an emotional moment for them, especially after the earlier damage had been done. Massoud had confessed he was to blame and how Collette had threatened his family. He had been forgiven. The tutors still could hardly believe that the pretty little French Collette, who had been their friend, could have fooled them so completely and for so long.

As the ribbon was cut, the veil dropped to show an extraordinary journey, rather like a picture from Geoffrey Chaucer's Canterbury Tales. This was written in the fourteenth century about a group of pilgrims who walked from London to Canterbury to pay their respects to Saint Thomas Becket's tomb in Canterbury Cathedral. Many of the pilgrims told their story about their journey, and it was this that Hamish was reminded of as each student painted his or her experience in the mural.

Some had painted their story of coming from countries of conflict. Others painted scenes from their countries and their musical journey to the academy. Most of them described their journey from hardship, especially those from the Balkans, Poland, Russia, the Middle East and North Africa. They painted their homeland, the people who had helped them and they had painted their relationships at the academy which were hostile at first, but as the music moved them, their relationships had changed to harmony. Each individual story was told simply through the painting.

Those from Europe and America recorded how their eyes had been opened to others' problems, perhaps for the first time. They were the lucky ones who had grown up in comfort and without fear for their lives. They painted their story of how playing with people from difficult backgrounds gave them a new understanding both musically and as human beings. Before they'd come to the academy, they'd been ignorant and untouched emotionally and spiritually. Now they felt a strong sense of union because of what they had shared.

As each visitor filed past the mural, they were surprised and moved by the many stories depicted by these students. Some viewed it silently, some with obvious distain and others with great admiration. They recognised these young people were the ambassadors of the future. It was a hopeful sign.

The concert came to its close. There was an air of exultation and relief that every part of it had gone well. Professor Sanandez thanked each visitor in turn for coming. He could have asked for contributions and support for the academy but he kept silent. His only concern was to help change the consciousness of those who'd attended. It was enough if he had prompted questions in their minds. It was like sowing a seed. With steady nurturing, the seed would flourish.

They finished with an exciting display of fireworks bursting out into a blaze of sparkling colours as they lit the sky, each starburst more exciting than the last. For the visitors, it was a fitting end to a memorable evening.

For the academy, it signified a deep achievement in which each one had played their part to accomplish a new sense of purpose for the future. It symbolised a change of attitude, from distrust to a positive willingness to communicate.

The remaining students spent time together, going over the evening with shrieks and laughter. It was their way of letting go. They wanted to extend their friendships for as long as possible. There was talk of a Youth Orchestra. Yannish would send them information. He had planted a seed of co-operation and goodwill to inspire governments in all countries. This was a new beginning.

Daisy wondered what their role might be. After all, they weren't genuine musicians. Aloysius was and could easily join, but the rest of them couldn't. She felt a little sad about not being a permanent part of the orchestra, but there would be other work for them to do.

They would have to let this go and wish their friends well.

She sighed deeply. Maybe this was how Time Travellers felt. They had to learn to be detached from everyone they met, except each other.

The Colour Code Gang left the students and went back into the girls' room. None of them could believe that tomorrow they would leave. They felt tearful and stunned. To arrive at this point of success and triumph was both thrilling and exhausting. In some ways they felt like pawns in a game between good and evil, not knowing who they were dealing with. They knew the why, but not how or who until the last moment. This had made their lives more difficult and yet it had brought them much closer together. Daisy smiled to herself as the others talked animatedly.

The whole experience had been about La Reunion - coming together on all levels.

 *Chapter 40*

Job Done

There was a different feel to the day. A sense of winding down and clearing up after the concert's activities. There was sadness too. Most of the staff would miss the students. The academy would feel derelict, at least for some weeks, until a new programme began. The tutors would either take up another assignment elsewhere or design a new project at the academy. Francesca and Hamish decided to travel around the country and then return later in the year. Ronnie and Frank were going back to America, but promised to come back the following year.

Yannish and Carlos would concentrate on the work they had begun. Out of this experience of bringing together young musicians, they wanted to build on its success and create a Youth Orchestra to play in all the major cities of the world, to show what could be done. It was a daring plan but, judging from the remarks and support after the concert, they felt inspired to continue. This would be their life's work. At the same time, they would continue giving musical workshops to encourage other young people to go beyond their own boundaries of limitation. Of course, they knew there could be objections and opposition, but they knew, too, they were not the first to work in this way and wouldn't be the last.

Isobel, the receptionist, lived on site. She would never leave the academy. Sylvie, the Canadian nurse, came to say goodbye to the students. She was off to Montreal. She smiled at Jonathan, advising him to avoid all insects in the future. Whatever she may have discovered about the strange goings on, it would be forgotten. She touched her lips as though to tell them it would remain a secret.

To make matters complete, Shakita appeared before them as Josefina to say goodbye to the students. She had made herself part of the institution and they would all miss her.

Waving to the students as they left by car, she grinned mischievously at Daisy. 'I will see you later,' she whispered.

With their bags packed, the Colour Code Gang waited at Reception. Carlos Sanandez and Yannish came to say goodbye. Carlos shook the boys' hands and kissed the girls.

'I thank you for all you have done,' he said. 'You have been an inspiration to all of us and we will always be in your debt. Please feel free to come anytime. You will be so welcome.'

Daisy thanked him warmly. 'We are so happy your wonderful dream worked after all, Professor. It was touch and go there for a while, wasn't it?'

He smiled at them. 'As you say, it was touch and go. Yannish has told me of the wonderful support you gave him, and us.' He bowed and saluted them, the emotion clearly showing on his face as he walked away.

Yannish spoke quietly to them. There was nothing more to say except his Master Calidus had chosen well in sending such brave young people to help them.

He laughed when they mentioned how scared they were at having to play musical instruments. Two of them had never even picked an instrument up before and the rest, except Aloysius, only played at school. He told them that the look on Jonathan's face said it all when he told him the instruments had arrived.

'I nearly gave the game away.' He grinned at Jonathan. 'I hope our paths cross again, my friends.' He hugged them all in turn, then beckoned to Al to come with him to his room.

Aloysius excused himself, saying he'd be back in a minute. He followed Yannish, wondering what he would say to him. Yannish opened his door, inviting him in.

'I can't go without thanking you for all you have done for me,' Al burst out.

'You are a fine musician, Al, and I would love you to join the Youth Orchestra.'

Al gasped, pleasure spreading all over his face.

'Gee, Yannish, that's the best gift anyone could have given me.'

'I will contact your school and make it official that you have received the opportunity, but no one will know we have met before.'

'Thanks, Yannish!' Al clasped his hand, tears flowing down his face. 'This is a chance I'll never forget.'

'You gave me a gift once, my young friend, which you made yourself.'

Al stared at him, puzzled. Then he remembered the flute Yannish had played to harmonise the distorted sounds in the dining room. It was the same flute he had made for him as Tatanka. Yannish drew the wooden flute from his pocket. He held it lightly in his fingers, turning it over with great love. He looked deeply into Aloysius's eyes.

'This will be with me always, my young friend.'

Al sobbed. His heart was so full of emotion he was unable to speak. The love and respect he felt for this man was beyond anything he'd experienced before.

Yannish was Tatanka. He had helped him to reach a higher level of music that he knew lay within the boy. Al's potential was great and he, as a fine musician, had recognised it.

'Now you must go.' Yannish told him briskly. 'You will hear from me later.'

Al stumbled out of the room, making his way back to his friends.

'Hey, Al, seen a ghost?' Winna said. 'You look sort of pale, man.'

He told them the story in a rush of emotion.

'I knew it!' he kept on say. 'I knew he was Tatanka.'

Dan congratulated him, wishing he might be invited too. On the other hand, he didn't want to spend his life as a musician like Al. None of them did. They all had other interests and plans for the future.

'Come on, Dais,' he said, and grabbed her bag. 'Let's start walking.'

'Get you!' Winna sniggered to Daisy. 'Didn't I tell you?'

'Belt up, Winna.' Daisy smiled politely. 'Go play with Al.'

'Got yer.' Winna laughed, linking her arm through Al's. 'Come on, maestro, let's sing about going home.'

They made their way down the dusty road with their bags slung over their backs. This time they looked at the fields and terraces with more appreciation, waving at the peasants as they walked by. Some of them came to say farewell, giving them gifts of bread, cheese and olives for their journey. Pedro's mum touched Daisy's sleeve.

'Es hierba?' she asked.

Daisy nodded her head. 'Si.'

The old woman looked interested and surprised. 'Uno, dos?'

Daisy looked at Al. He held up two fingers.

'Dos,' she said, smiling.

Al pretended Daisy was going to take the herbs back to England for her study. Pedro's mum was pleased she had been of help.

'Gracias, mama,' Daisy said, kissing her on the cheek.

The old woman shrugged her shoulders, as if it was nothing, but a smile spread across her weathered face. She waved them goodbye, saying they must come back again.

'Thanks, Al. That was the best thing to say. I wonder if she believed you?'

'It doesn't matter now, anyway.' He grinned at her.

'No, I suppose not, but these old peasants aren't stupid. They must have known something odd was going on, what with the explosion and all.'

'They'll keep it to themselves,' Hiromi said. 'The locals have a strong bond with the Professor, so I guess it will remain a secret.'

They followed the winding path close to the river. Both Jonathan and Marc looked at each other, remembering the woods beyond and Massoud and how Marc had plunged into the water to escape. It seemed an age ago now. Jonathan slapped his friend on the back.

'Not long now.'

Dan nodded to them. 'We'll soon see the spaceship.'

'Isn't it odd? I'm not sure if I want to go back,' Winna said. 'I feel kind of nervous, don't you?'

'Yes, it is strange.' Hiromi sighed. 'Last time I was ready to leave but this time, in spite of that awful woman or monster, I really loved it here.'

'You were great, Hiromi,' said Winna. 'What with your oboe and dancing. And how about the lovely Yoshi? Are you going to keep in touch with him?'

Daisy looked at her. Winna was always the one to ask questions about relationships. She was so nosy. Winna looked at Daisy with a question in her eyes as if to say 'What have I said?'

Hiromi laughed. 'It's okay. Yes, we're going to keep in touch. He's a doll.'

'Did anyone say goodbye to Chelsea?' Jonathan asked suddenly. 'I completely forgot.'

'I said goodbye for you.' Daisy reassured her brother. 'She was in such a rush last night with her father and mum being there that she almost forgot herself. She wanted to introduce her beloved Jovan, so hugged me and was gone, saying we must visit her.'

Jonathan sighed, thinking of the gorgeous Chelsea. 'She was all right.'

'Yeah, she was.' Daisy agreed, linking her arm through her brother's.

As they approached the bend, they saw the spaceship waiting for them. Volarus and Kassan stood smiling as they walked towards them.

'Welcome. You are right on time.'

'Are we?' Dan grinned. 'We didn't know what time we should be here.'

'We knew when you would arrive,' Volarus smiled, shaking his hand. 'Come, we must go.' He waved them aboard.

Marc giggled, telling Jonathan this was like having their own private jet.

Kassan came behind them, pulling up the ladder and securing it inside with a lever.

They arranged themselves as before, strapping themselves in securely for their flight, although they were hardly conscious of any movement. The spaceship just lifted effortlessly into the air and within seconds was rushing through space itself.

With so much going on in their lives and then the long walk, the Colour Code Gang drifted into sleep. Daisy still clutched the cheese, bread and olives in her lap. It had been her intention to share it with her friends on the trip but, within moments of taking off, her eyes closed.

The next thing they knew was the familiar slowing down as the spaceship approached the landing stage of the University of Light. They sat up, rubbing their eyes and shifting their bodies as the ship passed through the great coloured window.

'That was quick,' said Jonathan, nudging Marc. 'We're home.'

Daisy leaned forward in her seat looking for Lo. Sure enough, there was the distinctive figure waving at them as the ship came to a halt. As soon as the door lifted, the youngsters rushed down the steps.

They encircled him, speaking at the same time, the girls hugging him and the boys shaking his hands. He beamed with pleasure, allowing himself to be smothered by their attention.

'Welcome, my young friends. We are so happy you are here.'

Armed with their bags, they walked beside him, all still speaking at the same time. He laughed with delight. Daisy thrust the food into his hands, saying that one of the local peasants had given it to them for their journey but, as they hadn't eaten it, perhaps Lo would like it. Lo took the cheese and bread, smiling his thanks.

'It is kind of you, Daisy, but it is not the food we eat. I will serve it for you when you have your refreshment.'

Daisy clapped her hand to her mouth, apologising.

'Sorry, Lo, that was dumb!' She looked at Hiromi, her eyes rolling upwards.

'It was a kind thought, Daisy.' Lo squeezed her hand. 'Now my friends, your rooms are prepared. When you are ready, come to the Golden Room for some refreshments.' As they turned around he was gone.

'He's the invisible man.' Dan laughed. 'See you in a bit. I'm going to dump my bag and head for food.' He grinned, smacking his lips.

'Gotcha.' Jonathan joined in with Marc.

The girls were in no rush. They wanted to spend time in their bedrooms again.

Daisy checked her bathroom to see her blue and pink towels warming on the rails. And there was her violet tracksuit hanging up, ready for use. Warm water began to fill the bath, although she hadn't turned the taps on. But it didn't seem strange to her.

She smelt the new bath essences with delight and then quickly whipped off her clothes and stepped into the bath, sinking into the delicious, sweet-smelling warm water.

'This is the best,' she murmured to herself. Food could wait.

The water was healing, easing away any sense of doubt or loneliness she'd suffered after the events at La Reunion. She hadn't told the others how she'd felt, not even Dan, though she wondered if he'd guessed because he'd been more attentive than usual. Winna had remarked on it. This was something she had to let go within herself, and the University of Light was the only place where she could transform the effects and impressions she hadn't had the time or space to release at the academy.

She let her thoughts wander as her body relaxed and it was if the traces of anxiety, fear and tension just lifted from her and evaporated into the air. She was conscious only of the warmth and comfort as it enveloped her, and a deep seed of recognition inside her, something she had always known, yet not known or understood, until this moment.

It was like an acceptance, an affirmation, an unquestioning belief that flowed into her mind, her body, her whole being. How strange, she thought. How wonderful.

When she arrived at the Golden Room her friends were in excited discussion about how they wanted to continue playing music.

'I don't think I could bear it if I couldn't play drums,' Marc said, looking grief stricken. 'This is my life now, not academia or mathematics. It's okay for Al, 'cos he's a genius, but for the rest of us...'

'Look, Marco, don't worry about it,' said Al. 'We'll still play together. Nothing need change that.'

'What about you two?' Winna asked Daisy and Jonathan.

'I think I'm okay as I am.' Jonathan answered thoughtfully. 'It's not such an important part of my life. What we did was great and I loved it, but it's not as important as it is for you two.'

'Nor me,' said Daisy. 'Art is more important for me. And you, Dan?' She looked at him with interest.

'I play with my dad and I've joined a local band, which is fine for me until I go to University. Then, I guess, I'll join the Uni band.'

Lo appeared satisfied the youngsters seemed relaxed after their journey. He asked questions about their adventure in Spain and listened to their stories, watching their faces as they told him all the grisly bits and the wonderful parts.

'Now, my friends,' he said at last. 'Calidus is waiting for you, if you are ready.'

Immediately they went into the Halls of Learning and took their usual seats around the table, as always a little nervously.

Daisy saw his aura radiating into the room before he entered. The whole room became illuminated by his presence, the Lord of Light, followed by Shakita, Lady of the Orange Ray.

He sat down opposite them. She sat by his side. He held out his hands to them in welcome. They gazed back in awe, as they did every time they saw him.

He thanked them in a simple manner for all they'd achieved. This seemed strange, coming from one of such august stature and authority. They felt so small sitting there before him.

'You have all surpassed yourselves with courage and ingenuity in very demanding and dangerous conditions.' He looked at them each in turn.

They remained silent. It wasn't their time to speak. Shakita spoke next, her glowing orange colours radiating with warmth and peace.

'Although I was always there in disguise, it wasn't necessary for me to show myself until the last moment. It was through your ability to cope with the day-to-day situations that left me free to do what was needed. You used your initiative.' She turned to Daisy. 'You intuitively felt the need to find medicinal herbs so you were ready when Yannish was poisoned. You acted immediately on both accounts. If you hadn't, he would have died. The Oleander plant is very toxic and lethal. Together with Hiromi and Dan, you saved his life.'

Daisy looked down into her lap, peeking at Dan under her lashes. His face was red. Hiromi smiled slightly through politeness, not knowing what else to do. Calidus nodded his head.

Shakita continued, bringing in the whole group.

'You all did your part beautifully, without being told what to do. You met each day to link into the Light and the Orange Ray.'

'Daisy suggested that. She's impossible if crossed,' Jonathan said dryly.

They all broke into giggles, the tension lessening.

'I can imagine.' Calidus's eyes twinkled. 'And what about the daring investigations that you and Marc pulled off?'

'That was Marc's idea. He's brilliant at detective work but nearly got caught.'

Marc blushed and his glasses began to steam up. He took them off and hurriedly wiped them to hide his embarrassment.

'You found out important information. No professional could have done more,' Calidus said. He thought for a moment then spoke directly to Jonathan, holding his eyes gently. 'You were very brave over the spider incident.'

Jonathan shrugged, his face twitching a little as he remembered.

'Shakita helped me. It's okay now.'

'How did you find Yannish?' Calidus asked.

'He was aaaaamaaaazing!' Aloysius shifted in his chair, his dark eyes shining.

Daisy nodded her head. All of them had tried to keep their thoughts to themselves.

'Did you know he was Tatanka from the Cheyenne?' asked Al. 'I didn't think that that was possible.'

'Why not?' Calidus answered. 'You went back in time in the Red Ray. Why can't anyone come forward too?'

'It never occurred to me, but I recognised him as soon as he began to talk about how we listen. There was something familiar about him which excited me. He's just awesome!'.

'He's thinks you are very talented, Aloysius. Now I would like to hear how this experience was for you.' He addressed them all.

Winna told him of the joy she'd felt when playing the piano. The flute was good, she added quickly, not wanting to offend him, but playing Jazz was the best part. She finished with a rush.

'You have discovered a natural talent, Winna. If you take lessons, you will find you will learn quickly. Now tell me if you learnt anything else?'

She thought for a moment, still excited about learning the piano.

'I found, for the first time, I was part of the team. I began to feel responsible for the others, especially Al because he trusted that horrid Collette woman and couldn't see how creepy she was.'

'Well done, Winna. You watched over him.'

Winna pulled a rude face at Al, who just beamed back.

Al began to describe his feelings of playing with students from all over the world. None of them knew how good they were until they came to the academy. Yannish inspired all of them to be better than they ever thought they'd be.

Dan joined in with this, saying the experience had changed their lives and their attitude towards each other. He added he had personally learnt how important and satisfying it was for their team to work together to support Professor Sanandez and Yannish.

'You were the rock, Dan,' Calidus said. 'You gave strength to everyone around you.'

Dan mumbled his thanks.

Hiromi looked at Daisy before she began.

'It was wonderful and frightening,' she said to him. 'I don't think we could have got through without each other and Yannish. We weren't certain what role to play, whether to show support to the students or to stand back, so we tried both. I was frightened when Massoud singled out Daisy to dance with him, because we knew Collette meant her harm, and when Yannish was attacked we didn't really know what we were doing - at least Dan and I didn't. I think Daisy did, so we just followed her.'

She finished, uncertain what to say next.

Calidus patted her hand. 'As always, you bring beauty and harmony to any situation, Hiromi. Daisy couldn't have done her work without your sense of balance and loving support.'

Daisy nodded her head in agreement. 'I wouldn't have had the strength to hold Yannish's life without you and Dan,' she said quietly.

'I felt Tai wa wa working through me, but I was just as frightened as you were. As for the rest, it was just as you said - none of us were prepared for the troubles that happened.'

She turned to face Calidus and Shakita. 'I didn't really know what fear was until I saw Collette change into that awful monster.' She shuddered as she remembered. 'The spider thing with Jonathan was horrible, too, and sudden, but we all worked together with the students to kill them. We weren't there for the explosion, though many of our friends were hurt. The worst part for me was suddenly recognising that Collette was Oleander. She knew that I knew, and from that point I didn't dare tell the others in case she picked up our thought forms.'

Calidus nodded in sympathy. It must have been hard for a young girl to keep silent.

'What did you learn about the Orange Ray?' he asked.

'That was the best part for me.' She smiled, relieved to be talking about the beauty of the Ray. 'I don't think any of us thought about how to use the energy of the colour orange until things started going wrong. Then we remembered what you'd said about the destructive forces trying to stop Yannish, so we began to meet early in the morning and sort of meditated, using orange. It was brilliant, and then Yannish gave us the gemrays and I learnt how to change the energy in the music room by turning them from the darker colour to the lighter. It just blew my mind.'

Her friends laughed, remembering how it was.

'Then we used them against the flying monsters and that was terrifying.' Daisy continued. 'We had no idea how powerful the colour orange was and how it could actually transform matter. It was awesome. We'll never forget it.' The others nodded vigorously in agreement.

'The best bit, but also the worst part,' said Jonathan grimacing. 'Was when Yannish and Carlos appeared and Collette created that awful noise from the depths of the earth. I'd never realised sound could hurt so much. We were nearly done for and then Yannish played his flute and the noise disappeared. It was weird.' He giggled nervously.

'You're right,' said Marc, interrupting. 'If it wasn't for Yannish, we'd all be dead. I see now he had to use sound to combat her sound, and that the Orange Ray is the biggest stunt of all time, except for Shakita.' He grinned at Jonathan. 'You should have seen Shakita get rid of Collette. It was unbelievable. Absolutely unreal. She just disappeared!'

'Collette could not hold her destructive elements against the light, nor could her creatures,' Shakita said quietly. 'Without your help I couldn't have done it.'

'We wanted you to experience the qualities of colour but also that of sound and how both these elements can uplift and transform negative energies,' Calidus said to them. 'Yannish was instrumental in this as he first showed how the beauty of music could uplift the soul and change attitudes of those living in conflict. It is important for all of you to be more aware of what happens in the world as well as your own country.'

They all nodded in silence, appreciating what he said.

'You were then subjected to the effect of discordant sounds.' Calidus continued. 'That was painful, wasn't it?' He smiled. 'Then Yannish demonstrated how harmonic music could raise its vibration, bringing discordance back into the whole. Finally, Shakita showed you how dark forces could be transformed back into light.'

'Is darkness negative?' Marc asked.

'Light and darkness are the Primordial Creators. They form the great cosmic unity from which all of creation originated. Darkness was the first. Light came out of darkness. We need the experience of both polarities, for this is the way the soul learns. The negative forces we have been facing - and will face throughout all time - are more to do with the negative thought forms of man and how these manipulate human behaviour. You know these things and how they can attract the same energy with disturbing effects.'

'Is this what you meant, Shakita, when you told Collette her purpose was done and she must return to the light?' asked Daisy.

'Yes, sometimes a great soul may take on a negative role in life in order to help others see the light or reach a deeper understanding. It is hard for you to accept, especially as you have been through so much.'

'That's a hard one,' Daisy replied, still feeling raw about Collette. 'Maybe, when I am older, I will understand and accept her part.'

'I think, in a way, it was probably better we didn't know what was going to happen,' Hiromi said quietly. 'Would we have learnt so much or acted differently?'

'You are all quick to learn,' Calidus said to her. 'But if we know before the event, we don't learn or appreciate anything new.'

Dan stretched his arms. Winna yawned and Marc fiddled with his glasses. Daisy and Jonathan looked at each other, sensing they were coming to the end of their discussion and to their time at the University of Light.

'What happens now?' Jonathan asked Calidus.

'Now, my young friends, is the time for you to go home.'

There was always this sense of loss when he told them. Daisy felt a lurch inside. Part of her was longing to see her parents, but another part yearned to stay here and learn everything about energy and colour.

Calidus smiled at her. 'You will be back soon enough. Next time, Jonathan will be the Yellow Ray. Your colour, I think.'

Jonathan brightened up considerably. 'Yeah. Yellow is my colour. I can't wait!'

Lo appeared beside him. 'All of your bags are on the spaceship.'

The moment had come. It was hard to separate, not only from these wonderful Beings, but from each other. The friendships they had formed were soul connections, deep and ever binding.

'Just think of each other.' Lo told them, sensing their feeling of separation.

'Farewell, my dear young friends,' said Calidus as he and Shakita hugged each one in turn. 'May the Light be with you, always.'

He turned with Shakita to walk away. The teenagers watched them until they could see them no more.

'Come.' Lo led them to the spaceship where their loyal pilots, Volarus and Kassan, waited for them.

They climbed aboard, saying goodbye to Lo with tears in their eyes. He kissed each one and watched as the spaceship slowly taxied onto the lift-off platform.

There was no noise, no wind. The spaceship gently lifted up and flew out into space.

The End

Find out what happens when 'The Colour Code' gang is contacted again.

This time it is all about the power of 'The Yellow Ray'

Read On...

Next in 'The Colour Code' series...

The Yellow Ray...

Once again the Colour Code Gang are summoned to the University of Light to experience the qualities of the Yellow Ray .

Calidus the Lord of the Light explains how this energy also represents the Solar Plexus , the nervous centre of power and intuitive knowing within the body.

He introduces them to Charalambos the Lord of the Yellow Ray who tells them that they will learn how to use their intelligence, how to judge wisely and how to use their intuition but the Solar Plexus is also very sensitive, emotional and can be re-active.

They are sent to Greece, the land of the greatest thinkers and philosophers of all time on a quest to find the lost Secret Scrolls of Aristotle from the 4th 5th century BC. Seton the Incinerator or Torcher who kills people with his eyes is after them, to steal what they find.

They go through many terrifying and exciting adventures meeting legends from the past. This is a powerful quest unlike anything else that they have experienced before.

About the Author

Pamela Blake Wilson

Pamela has been a teacher and Colour Therapist for many years and has enjoyed meeting people in many countries. She has loved her life and felt that she wanted to give something back into society. Pamela said "we don't always get the chance so the idea of writing books appealed to me".

Pamela did not want to write instructional work on Colour for other therapists since she believed there were enough already. However, the idea of writing books for young people appealed to her immensely. Pamela commented that "few people really understand the concept of Light and Colour energy, in fact most of us take it for granted as the sun shines by day and the moon and stars come out at night. The fact is, we live in a world of energy and everything we do or say has an energetic effect. Colours of the spectrum have differing frequencies of vibration which affect everything on every level of consciousness. If we can begin to understand how each colour works, we can begin to apply it more in our lives".

Visit Pamela at www.thecolourcodeworld.com for the latest in all things about 'The Colour Code' series.

Acknowledgements

I would like to thank White Lodge, 'The Centre of New Directions' for the experience in working with Colour and inspiring me to create these books.

To Simenon Honore for his brilliant help in guiding and altogether formidable instruction in pulling out the best in me.

To Peter Goldman our Director, for his love and support and to the Pick-a-WooWoo team for their encouragement.

CPSIA information can be obtained at www.ICGtesting.com
Printed in the USA
267241BV00012B/41/P